THE ACE OF SPADES

A car is stolen—routine stuff, this is L.A., after all . . . but who would want a clapped out old jalopy that can barely make it round the block? Predictably, the car doesn't go far and is soon returned to its rightful owner. 'Schoolkids,' grumbles the traffic cop. 'Happens all the time.' None of this should be any concern of Lieutenant Luis Mendoza—he's Homicide, not Traffic— but this is his girl-friend's car, and it soon transpires that whoever stole it left something on the back seat . . . Something they'll go to any lengths to retrieve.

THE ACE OF SPADES

Dell Shannon

ATLANTIC LARGE PRINT
Chivers Press, Bath, England.
Curley   Publishing,   Inc.,
South Yarmouth, Mass., USA.

Library of Congress Cataloging-in-Publication Data

Shannon, Dell, 1921–
  The ace of spades / Dell Shannon.
    p. cm.—(Atlantic large print)
  ISBN 0–7927–1151–3 (pbk. : lg. print)
  1. Large type books. I. Title.
[PS3562.I515A65 1992]
813'.54—dc20   91–39889
                                                                CIP

British Library Cataloguing in Publication Data available

This Large Print edition is published by Chivers Press, England, and
Curley Publishing, Inc, U.S.A. 1992

Published in the British Commonwealth by arrangement with Victor
Gollancz Ltd and in the U.S.A. with Dominick Abel Literary Group

U.K. Hardback ISBN 0 7451 8385 9
U.K. Softback ISBN 0 7451 8397 2
U.S.A. Softback ISBN 0 7927 1151 3

Photoset, printed and bound in Great Britain by
REDWOOD PRESS LIMITED, Melksham, Wiltshire

For the love of money is the root of all evil.

—I Timothy 6:10

THE ACE OF SPADES

CHAPTER ONE

'Oh, damn,' said Alison Weir. '*Was* it the next block? I could have sworn—'

'You left the car right here,' said Patricia Moore firmly. 'I remember noticing that particular bed of begonias. Especially fine ones.' Pat's British raising, as it affected gardens and the King's English at least, was incorrigibly untranslated to citizenship.

'*I'm* not sure. All these little streets look so much alike. Damn. I don't know why I wore these shoes, my feet are killing me. *¡Qué incomodidad!—¡es el colmo! I thought* it was along here—'

'I notice you revert to Spanish a bit oftener these days,' remarked Pat, sitting down placidly on the low brick wall flanking the sidewalk and fanning herself with the programme of the exhibit they'd been looking at. 'The car's been stolen, obviously.'

'Don't be ridiculous,' said Alison crossly. 'Who on earth would want it?' She sat down beside Pat and lit a cigarette. 'It's Luis' fault,' she added. 'After Dad died and I came back north, I didn't have much reason to use Spanish, you know, except for an occasional girl coming in to school—But there *is* one thing about it, it does give vent to one's feelings better than English sometimes ... It

1

must have been the next block.'

'You and your policeman. It was here. I remember distinctly. It's been stolen. Did you leave the keys in it?'

'If you think,' said Alison, 'that I attained the age of thirty without acquiring a little sense—of course I didn't. And really I must say I should think I could visit a respectable place like the County Museum in broad daylight without having my car stolen. If we'd been in a bar down on Skid Row it'd be different.'

'Wickedness flourishes everywhere,' said Miss Moore philosophically.

'And I can't really say the exhibition was worth it. Personally I think Renoir was overrated.'

'That's your photographic eye. You're inclined to be over-realistic yourself. Too much detail. And such *strong* colour—of course I suppose it's only to be expected from a red-haired Scots-Irishwoman.'

'I refuse,' said Alison, 'to discuss painting techniques sitting on bricks with the thermometer at a hundred. It's ridiculous. I want to go home and take off my clothes and have a large cold drink. *Can* it have been stolen?'

'It happens every day,' said Miss Moore. 'You'd better call the police. You've got an in with them, they'll probably produce it for you in no time.'

2

'Luis isn't Traffic, he's Homicide. I suppose I had. Oh, damn!' said Alison. 'And I don't suppose there's a public phone nearer than the central building. No rest for the wicked. And I cannot imagine why anybody should take the thing—of course they might not have got far, that's one comfort, if you don't know just how to manipulate that hand-choke, it dies on you every fifty feet ... I wonder if I'd look *very* odd if I took off my shoes? You see teen-agers going barefoot—'

'Really, Alison!' Miss Moore, who was dumpy, dowdy, and without an iota of personal vanity, but with strong notions of respectability, regarded her severely. 'I'll walk back with you, and you shouldn't delay reporting it.'

'I suppose not.' Alison got up with a grimace, and they started back to the building they'd just left. The one public phone, of course, was at the very end of a long marble hall, and when they got there neither of them had a dime. Under Pat's disapproving eye, Alison accosted a passer-by and got change, and eventually was put through to Traffic.

'Yes, ma'am,' said an efficient, reassuring voice there. 'The exact location, please ... If you'll just remain on the spot, there'll be an officer there directly to take particulars.'

Alison thanked the voice gloomily. 'And now we have to walk all the way back there again, and after they've taken down all the

3

details they'll drive away in their nice new patrol car, and we'll have to come back here to call a cab.'

'A *cab*?' said Miss Moore. 'Sheer extravagance! There's a bus goes right down Exposition Boulevard—'

'Yes, I know, you can take it if you like,' said Alison. They went back and sat on the wall. In about five minutes a black and white patrol car came along and a uniformed officer got out of it and projected courteous efficiency at them. Description of car, please—when was it parked here, when was the loss discovered?

'It was about two-thirty, wasn't it, when we got here? And if you can tell me why anybody should deliberately—I remember there was a brand-new Buick right ahead. It's a Ford, almost thirteen years old, light grey, a two-door sedan. I've got the licence number on a thing on my key chain.'

'Oh, that's very helpful, ma'am. You didn't leave the keys in it, then?'

'Certainly not, I don't know why you always automatically assume women drivers are all fools—'

'Now don't take it out on the officer,' said Pat.

'Don't they have ways of starting it going somehow without a key—I've read—'

'That's so,' said the patrolman, who'd taken another look at Alison and doubled his

4

gallantry. 'And some of these kids, you know, the hot-rodders, they *want* old stuff like that, to strip down and rebuild.'

'That makes me believe the stories about the younger generation having no sense,' said Alison.

He laughed, handing back her key ring. 'Chances are we'll pick it up within a few days, Miss Weir. You'll be notified, of course. Damn inconvenient, but there it is—it happens every day to a lot of people. Don't worry, it'll go on the hot list right away.'

'Thanks very much ... And now back to the phone to call a cab, what did I tell you? I've heard there *are* some people in L.A. who don't own cars. How do you suppose they exist?'

'The lesser breeds without the law. We manage to get about on the two feet Providence provided,' said Miss Moore. 'Much healthier. Also better for the figure, although—' She compared her dumpiness to Alison's excellent distribution of poundage, and laughed.

★   ★   ★

The Los Angeles Police Department is a large one, and not all the men in it are acquainted with one another. In the ordinary way, Sergeant Edward Rhodes of Traffic would not

5

have had any contact with the Homicide division, but as it happened one of his personal friends was Sergeant Landers of that office. Through Landers, Rhodes had heard this and that about Landers' superior, Lieutenant Luis Rodolfo Vicente Mendoza, and over a period of time he had caught some of Landers' hero worship for this personage. Both of them were young unmarried men, and over their coffee breaks and shared dinners in cheap restaurants, they talked shop.

Rhodes, in fact, cherished a secret ambition towards some day getting into Homicide himself, and Mendoza had not only a professional reputation any man might envy, but other kinds. Mendoza was, by all accounts, quite the hell of a fellow in three ways—at his job, at a poker table, and with the girls—and thereby hung a number of tales, which Landers had passed on at length.

So Rhodes, from a distance as it were, had set Mendoza up as a model. Not that he could ever hope to attain some of Mendoza's attributes: for one thing, there was all the money. Mendoza had come into a sizable fortune from a miserly grandfather and didn't stint himself enjoying it. Landers guessed that he didn't pay a dime less than two hundred bucks for any of his suits; he dressed to the nines, dapper and elegant, never a hair out of place, the precise line of black moustache always trimmed even and neat, the long narrow hands manicured—but nothing flashy, everything quiet, good taste. And he'd just taken delivery of a new car, which both of them had admired in the lot—it had cost the equivalent of Rhodes' salary for three years. It was a long, low, custom-built gunmetal-coloured Facel-Vega, a two-door hardtop sports coupé, and Landers reported with awe that it was said to be capable of acceleration from a stand to a hundred m.p.h. in eighteen seconds, only Lieutenant Mendoza never drove that way, he was real careful with a car and had never got a moving-violation ticket at all, ever.

It wasn't to be supposed either that Sergeant Rhodes could ever attain the talent—as per Mendoza's reputation—for uncanny hunches and brilliant deductions. But he could admire—from a distance—and that he did.

As it further happened, Landers had casually heard from Sergeant Lake, who was desk man in Mendoza's office and now and then had to track him down out of hours, the name of Mendoza's current girl-friend, or at least one of them. Landers had met her once, when he was relaying some urgent information to Mendoza, and reported her to be evidence of Mendoza's excellent taste—a real redhead, and quite something, he said. Funny sort of a name, for a girl, Alison: but

7

for that reason it had stayed in Rhodes' mind.

Which was why he noticed it on the list of hot cars, and read the meagre information with interest. A thirteen-year-old Ford: he thought instantly, respectfully, a nice girl, not a gold-digger, taking Mendoza for his money. Of course, *that* kind Mendoza wouldn't be such a fool to take up with in the first place. Landers said she ran one of these charm schools, and painted pictures on the side—kind of an artist. Couldn't have much money, driving a car like this ... His chivalrous instincts were aroused, and also he had a vague vision of Mendoza dropping into Traffic—say some time when Captain Edgely was around to hear—and thanking him for such an efficient, excellent performance of his job in the matter.

He exerted himself, therefore, with dispatch, to find Alison Weir's car for her; he sent out a special bulletin about it, and each morning eagerly scanned the list of stolen cars located.

But it wasn't until Thursday—it had been stolen on Sunday afternoon—that it turned up, on a routine check of overparked cars. Out in a rather lonely section of Compton, left along a new residential street.

It was brought in and Rhodes looked it over. Awful old piece of junk, he thought. These kids!—no discipline, no principles at all these days. Anything sitting around loose, if they wanted it for half an hour—

That was about half past four on Thursday afternoon, and he succumbed to temptation, called Miss Weir, reported the finding of the car, and said it wasn't any trouble at all, he'd deliver it himself, bring her the formal papers to sign acknowledging its recovery.

Not exactly according to Hoyle, but he went down to the garage and got one of the boys to start the Ford for him and trail him in a patrol car to bring him back, and drove up to Hollywood to Miss Weir's apartment.

'We'll have to ask you to look it over, Miss Weir—you know, say what damage's been done, if any.' Landers had been quite right: nothing cheap, a plain sort of tan summer dress, not too much jewellery, but a looker, in a ladylike way: you didn't often see real red hair that wasn't carroty, and she had the complexion to go with it, milk-white, and hazel-green eyes.

'Oh, certainly,' said Alison, 'but I don't suppose there's much they could have done to it. It's seen quite a lot of life already.' She came downstairs with him obligingly. 'It's never really got used to the good roads up here—you see, it was the last car my father bought, he was a construction engineer and worked a good deal in Mexico, it passed its adolescence mostly down in Coahuila, negotiating burro trails, and I really think it's suspicious of anything else ... Well, I can't

9

see that it looks any different.' She opened the door and peered in. 'The seat covers have had that rip for months, and that dent in the dashboard, that was Ferdinando Gomez the time he got the D.T.s and Dad drove him down to the missionary hospital. No, it's all just the way it was. Nothing missing from the glove compartment as far as I can tell—heavens, what a lot of junk one does accumulate.'

'You want to be sure, Miss Weir, before you sign the receipt—on account of the insurance, you know. If you put in a claim—'

'Oh, lord, I'm just thankful to have it back, and still running—I don't see any need to do that. There doesn't seem to be anything wrong mechanically?'

'Well—er—' said Rhodes.

'I mean, it *is* running?'

'Oh, it *runs*, sure. I just drove it up, of course.'

'Well, then, that's all right. I still can't imagine why they took it. Where'd you find it?'

He told her, handing over the receipt and a pen. 'Just kids, probably, out for a joy ride. It'd been sitting there quite a while, they didn't keep it long.'

'Well, thank you *very* much,' said Alison with a nice smile, handing back the receipt and pen. 'I *am* glad to have it back.'

'No trouble at all,' said Rhodes gallantly.

Possibly, he thought, she'd say something to Mendoza: such a nice efficient officer who brought it back; but in any case he'd been interested in meeting her. Of course, he reflected further on the ride back to headquarters, she'd actually have been better off if they'd wrecked that piece of junk and she could put in the full insurance claim.

*   *   *

The car had come back on Thursday, and Alison drove it to her school next morning and back again that afternoon, and found it just the same as usual. On Saturday she drove it down to the beach, up past Malibu, where she spent most of the day working on what turned out to be a rather unsatisfactory seascape. Unloading her painting gear when she got home, she reflected that the poor thing was badly in need of a bath—a job she loathed—but it was later than she'd thought, and she had barely an hour to get dressed before Luis came to take her out to dinner. Tomorrow, she'd clean the car. The better the day the better the deed.

So late Sunday afternoon found her in the cramped apartment garage, equipped with a stiff brush, several rags, and a pail of water. She started by brushing out the inside—seats and floor. The front seat had accumulated quite a surprising amount of sand from her jaunt to the beach, and she brushed vigorously, getting well down into the crack between the back and the seat, kneeling on the seat to press it down.

Sand, dust, anonymous fluff, dirt—and of all things, a long dried twig with a couple of mummified leaves clinging to it, probably blew in the window and got crushed down—she ran two fingers down the crack to be sure of getting it all out, and suddenly felt something else there, and delved farther. Damn, when she pulled the opening wider the thing just slipped down—but eventually, at the expense of a torn nail and several muttered curses, she persuaded it out, and looked at it.

'¿Y qué es esto?' she said to herself absently, turning the thing over in her palm. 'What on earth is it and where did it come from? How very odd...'

CHAPTER TWO

The body turned up that Monday morning, halfway down a narrow alley opening on Carson Street not far from Main. Unlike a lot of alleys down there, this one wasn't used for anything much, and as the corpse was beyond the entrance, it hadn't been discovered at once; some kids had finally stumbled over it, running through. Sergeant Arthur Hackett went down with a crew of men to look at it, and was not enlightened. Or, if the truth were told, much interested.

It wasn't that he expected the kind of corpses and mysteries found in the paperback novels at drugstores, every time he got a call to a new case; that sort of thing just didn't happen; at least in his nine years' experience of being a cop he'd never run across it. But some corpses were just naturally more interesting than others, and this one was, in a word, routine.

'Just another piece of flotsam,' he said to Mendoza when he came back. 'On the big H and finally took too much of a jolt and didn't come out of it. God knows who he was—probably nobody cares any more.'

'Really,' said Mendoza. 'Nothing on him to say?'

'*Nada*. Maybe he'll get identified by somebody while he's on file, but maybe not, too. You know how they drift. Not very important either way, I'd say.' Hackett brought out a manila envelope. 'Here's all he had on him. Damnedest thing how they set out to commit suicide—what it amounts to. He was a good-looker, and I'd say not over thirty.'

'A lot of answers on that one,' said Mendoza, 'and maybe as many answers as there are users.' Business had been a little

13

slack lately, and he was unoccupied for the moment; idly he up-ended the envelope on his desk and looked at what it disgorged.

A clean folded handkerchief, plain white, cheap cotton, dime store variety. A flat longish box bearing the name of a chain drugstore and containing a much-used and dirty hypodermic syringe and several needles. A cheap pocket-knife. Forty-eight cents in change. A crumpled package of cigarettes with three left in it. A scrap of paper, irregularly torn across one edge, about four inches wide at the broadest part and narrowing down to a point. Torn off a corner of something.

'What's this?'

'Piece torn off a letter or something, I suppose. I wouldn't have seen it at all, but the staple bit my finger when I was going through his pockets. You can see the holes—there were a couple of pages, or more, stapled together. I just stuck it in, thought there might be something on it to say who he was, but—'

'Yes,' said Mendoza, 'and an odd sort of letter it seems to have been. Nymphs and dolphins. *¡Comó, oyé!* I'd heard that heroin gives some people hallucinations, but what superior hallucinations!'

'What? Let's see, I didn't—'

Mendoza passed it over. Automatically he began to tidy the desk, setting the deceased's

14

possessions in a neat little pile at one side, brushing off tobacco crumbs, lining up the ashtray with the blotter and desk-box. That was Mendoza: the orderly mind, place-for-everything-everything-in-its-place. Probably one of the reasons he had acquired a little reputation as an investigative officer: ragged edges worried him, the thing left all untidy, patternless. He might be and often was irritable at the frustration of continually being presented with another box of jigsaw pieces to put together, but he was constitutionally unable to leave them alone until every last little piece had been fitted in where it belonged.

He glanced up at Hackett, and got out a cigarette: a slim dark man, the black hairline moustache, the sharp arch of heavy brows, the widow's peak, punctuation marks to a long nose and a long jaw: impassive, an unremarkable if regular-featured face, but it could flash into sudden charm when a smile touched the dark eyes. 'Nymphs,' he said. '*¡Caray, qué hombre!*'

Hackett looked at the two lines of typing on the scrap of paper. It had been torn off the right hand top edge of the page, and the typing was double-spaced; there was such a wide margin, however, that only four words were included on the scrap. The top line said, *verse, nymph* and the end of the line below it said, *small dolphin.* 'That *is* a damn funny

15

one,' he agreed.

'A *small* dolphin,' said Mendoza, leaning back with closed eyes, smoking lazily. 'Somehow that makes it sound so much more—mmh—individual, doesn't it? Only a small dolphin. I wonder what it was all about. *Nothing* else on him? Well, well. You know, that dolphin—to say nothing of the nymph—intrigues me. I think I'll go down and take a look at him.'

'As you please,' said Hackett, 'but it's just another dope case, obviously. Or are you going to have one of your hunches about it and say he's the heir to a Bulgarian millionaire assassinated by the Communists?'

'Once in a while,' said Mendoza, getting up and going to get his hat, 'I read a detective novel—and once in a while I wish I was in one. Everything made so easy for those boys, such complicated problems that inevitably there are only a couple of possible answers. I don't think there are any Bulgarian millionaires left. But I haven't much else to do at the moment, for once, and I may as well take a look.'

He went down to the morgue and looked at the dead man. There were aspects of the dead man which mildly interested him further. Hackett had said, good-looking—that was an understatement. Even several days dead, it was a handsome face: a purity of line like a cameo profile. A young man, twenty-eight to

16

thirty, and his indulgence in heroin hadn't left any apparent marks of dissipation on him. A tallish, well-set-up young man, he'd have been.

Mendoza went back to his office and sent down word that he'd like the autopsy report expedited. Not that there'd be much in it, but on the other hand—a *nymph* and a *dolphin*—it might be something a little more interesting than it looked at first glance.

★   ★   ★

The dolphin, in fact, stayed so persistently in his mind that he was somewhat absent-minded with Alison that evening, and when she complained he apologized by telling her about it.

'A *dolphin*,' said Alison, intrigued despite herself. 'It sounds exactly like the start of a detective story, doesn't it? That *is* odd.'

'A *small* one,' said Mendoza almost plaintively. He was relaxed on the end of his spine in her largest armchair, minus jacket and tie; the temperature still stood at ninety.

'It reminds me of something—what? ... Did you have any English literature in high school?'

'That's a long time back,' said Mendoza. 'Probably some was inflicted on me ... *Por Dios*, twenty-two years ago, and the school's been torn down—that old Macy Street school—when they built the new Union Station. I had to cross through Chinatown to get there.' He laughed. 'Then we moved, because Johnny Li-Chong taught me to shoot Chinese craps, and my grandmother was horrified. Gambling's still one of the major sins to her. I was supposed to be selling papers after school, and I never told her when I quit—I found I could earn twice as much running a Spanish Monte bank in the back room of Johnny's father's restaurant over on Main. *Caray*, she was pleased, the old lady, when I started to bring her five dollars on Saturdays so quick! You know something, I never did tell her. She'd have raised the roof—another good-for-nothing going the same way as the old man, gamble his last copper—or hers. That five dollars on Saturdays, it came in useful. And the old man sitting on nearly three million bucks then, in a dozen banks, and swearing about a four-dollar gas bill. Damn it, you encourage me to maunder...'

'*Earn* twice as much?' Alison took him up. 'I don't know but what your grandmother's right—'

'I said Spanish Monte, *chica*, not three-card. Perfectly legitimate deal. I was never as crazy a gambler as the old man—'

'¡*A otro perro con ese hueso!*—give that bone to another dog!' Alison laughed. 'You'd gamble the gold in your teeth if you had any.'

'Well, not,' said Mendoza, 'without asking about the odds. And very young I found out what a lot of gamblers never seem to—the odds always run in favour of the bank. It's simple mathematics. Even at seventeen, I never just sat in at Monte—that way, as somebody's said, madness lies. I saved my money, industrious young fellow that I was, and set up as a banker. But what was it you asked me? There was a poor devil of an English teacher, Mr.—Mr.—Mr. Keyes. The only thing I remember about high school English is that Mr. Keyes had a passion for Chaucer, and it wasn't until he made me read some of *The Canterbury Tales* and I came across the Miller's Tale that it dawned on me there might be something interesting— pornographically speaking—in these musty old classics.'

'Really. Maybe I missed something, not finishing high school.'

'Women don't get a kick out of pornography, or so the psychiatrists say.'

'Psychiatrists, hah. Since when do they know what they're talking about? What I was going to say—your small dolphin somehow reminds me of something in—*can* it be Dickens, or was it Trollope?—there was a housemaid who had an illegitimate baby, and when they criticized her she said, Please, ma'am, it was only a little one.'

He laughed. 'And very logical too. Damn

it, what *could* it mean? Unless it's some new pro slang I haven't caught up with yet. *Nymph* would be easy enough in that connection—if a little fancy—but the dolphin eludes me.'

'Which reminds me further,' said Alison. 'I have a mystery for you too.' She got up and opened the top desk drawer. 'I told you some idiot borrowed my car. Well, when it came back I got round to cleaning it and I found this in the crack down between the seat and the back.'

Mendoza took the thing and looked at it. 'Foreign coin of some kind.'

'Holmes, this is wonderful—how do you do it? That I can see. But no engraving or whatever it's called, to say what country or anything.'

'No. I'll tell you something else, it's old—maybe damned old. Not milled, and not a true circle.' It was not very big; and it was a silver coin, or had some silver in its alloy, though darkened. On one side of it was a design vaguely resembling that on some early U.S. coins, an eagle with outspread wings, but head down; it seemed to be holding something in its talons. The other side bore a design he couldn't puzzle out; a thing which might be a stylized flame growing out of a vase, or a bell with curlicues on the top of it, or two roundish triangles point to point. 'Somebody's pocket-piece,' he suggested. 'A man's, probably, because owing to the curious fact that tailors still put side pockets in our trousers at an acute angle, things do tend to fall out when we're sitting down. Of course, it might also have got pulled out of a woman's purse when she reached in for a handkerchief or something. Are you sure the thing wasn't in the car when it was stolen?'

'No, of course not. Which is exactly what that sergeant said. It occurred to me that it might be some sort of clue to whoever'd taken the car, and I thought I ought to tell them about it, you know—so I called, and got hold of the man who brought it back. A very nice obliging young man named Rhodes. And he asked, was I sure one of my friends hadn't lost it in the car beforehand—which I'm not. Anyway, he said, it probably wouldn't be much of a clue, and I might as well keep it or throw it away. I do want to ask around, see if someone who'd ridden with me might have lost it. I suppose it might have been someone's lucky talisman, something like that—but you'd think whoever'd lost it would have said something, in that case—asked me if I'd found it—if it was someone I know.'

'*De veras*,' agreed Mendoza absently, still looking at it. 'It feels old, somehow. I wonder if it's valuable at all. Curious. You might take it to an expert and ask.'

'Well, surely nobody'd have lost anything worth much and not tried to follow it up,

21

everywhere they might have—though if it *was* whoever took the car—Oh, well, I'll keep it awhile and ask everyone, just in case.' She dropped it back in the drawer.

Presently Mendoza put on his tie and jacket and went home, and as he cut up fresh liver for the dignified Abyssinian feline who lived with him, the sleek brown green-eyed Bast, and let her out and let her in, and undressed and had a bath and went to bed—and eventually to sleep, after Bast had walked her seven mystic times around a circle and chosen exactly the proper place to curl up beside him—he did not ruminate at all on Alison's little find, but on his own puzzling small dolphin.

*　　　*　　　*

The autopsy report was waiting for him on his desk next morning, and he read it with interest. The deceased, said Dr. Bainbridge, had died of a massive injection of heroin. Probably not long prior to death he had received a blow on the head, a blow severe enough to have rendered him unconcious—a blow to the parietal area on the left side. He had been dead between five and seven days—impossible to pin it down further; say between last Monday and last Wednesday. He had been six feet one inch tall, around a hundred and seventy pounds, and between

22

twenty-six and thirty years of age. He had a medium-fair complexion, black hair, and brown eyes; not much dental work, an excellent set of teeth—no scars or birthmarks—blood type O. His fingerprints were being checked in their own records and in Washington, to try to identify him.

But all that was the least interesting of what Bainbridge had to say.

'The body,' so the report went on, 'bore at least two dozen puncture marks in the areas which a drug addict most commonly uses for injections—both arms and thighs. However, when I came to examine these areas in detail, it was evident that none of these had in fact penetrated an artery, or much below the first layers of the epidermis.'

'Well, well,' said Mendoza. He called Hackett in and got Dr. Bainbridge on the inside phone. 'This corpse. The one with the puncture marks. What did you think about that?'

'Did you haul me away from work just to ask that? I should've thought even a lieutenant of detectives could reason from here to there. The obvious deduction is that he was not an addict. Maybe somebody wanted to make it look as if he was, or maybe it was him, I wouldn't know—people do damned funny things. Maybe he committed suicide and those marks are relics of where he kept trying to get up his nerve. You get that kind of thing, of course.'

'Yes, but heroin's not a very usual method. And why and where would he get hold of any if he wasn't an addict? And why and where did he get that knock on the head?'

'That's your business,' said Bainbridge.

'Well, you examined the body pretty thoroughly—'

'I did. I'll tell you this, Luis. In the ordinary way, an autopsy wouldn't have uncovered that about those puncture marks. No reason to—er—go into such detail. But I happened to notice that not one seemed to have left any cyanosis—he was very well preserved, of course the clothes had helped, and he was on his back, so all the natural death-cyanosis had settled there—and you'd ordinarily expect to find local cyanosis, black-and-blue spots to you, around the most recent of the punctures. And a few others which had faded some, being older. You know, what always shows up on any user. A real mainliner, he's giving himself a jolt two or three times a day, and pretty damn clumsy too—even if he uses a hypo instead of the teaspoon method, he leaves bruise marks. Well, I noticed that, and I investigated, and I think all those marks were made about the same time, and after he was dead, or just before.'

'Now isn't that interesting!' said Mendoza. 'I presume the body's still in the morgue—'

24

'Did you think I'd take it out to Forest Lawn and bury it myself?'

'What I meant was,' said Mendoza patiently, 'you're done with it, you're not doing any further research? It's on file, ready to be looked at by anybody who might know it?'

'Complete with replaced organs and roughly sewn together, yes. Don't tell me you want a complete analysis of everything.'

'But I do, I do, *amigo*. Please. If possible, what he had for his last meal, any chronic diseases, any foreign bodies or inflammations, any suspicious differences from other bodies, etcetera. Look at everything.'

Bainbridge uttered a howl of protest. 'But, my God, there's no *reason*! We know he died of heroin, and after all this time there won't be much else—'

'You go and look. What kind of injection was it, by the way? Could it have been a normal dose?'

'You know as well as I do how that varies—it *could* have been. A pretty big one to be called that, but the kind of jolt a lot of users take.'

'Mmh. Well, you go and look.' Mendoza put down the phone and grinned at Hackett. 'I knew that dolphin had something to say to us, Art. This corpse is a bit more mysterious than you thought.'

'So it seems,' said Hackett, still reading the
25

autopsy report. 'I'll be damned. But it can still be an ordinary business, Luis. His first shot maybe, and he overdoes it or has an idiosyncrasy for it—like they say.' Hackett found the role of the big dumb cop useful, and sometimes forgot to lay it aside in private; as he also looked the part, it came as a little surprise to most people that he was, in fact, a university graduate. 'And he was nervous about the shot and made a lot of tries at it.'

'Could be,' conceded Mendoza. 'Could still be . . . Cigarettes but no matches. Handkerchief but no billfold—where most of us carry some identification.'

'You've done time down on Skid Row like most of us—you know how they live, hand to mouth. I've picked 'em up, dead, drunk, and sober, without so much as a handkerchief on 'em.'

'Sure,' said Mendoza, 'and once in a while with a few hundred-dollar bills in a back pocket.' He picked up the inside phone again and called the crime lab, and got Dr. Erwin himself. 'Over at the morgue is a body, and I presume they still have its clothes. The body of a handsome young man who died of a shot of heroin. I'd like the clothes gone over thoroughly, if you'll be so good.' He added the last as a sop to Dr. Erwin's reputation; you didn't give arbitrary orders to a criminological scientist who had several times been consulted by Scotland Yard's C.I.D.

'What for?'

'Anything. If I knew specifically I'd have told you.'

'Really, Luis,' said Dr. Erwin, annoyed, 'must you be so difficult? We do like to have some idea, you know.'

'Me, I'm not a chemist,' said Mendoza. 'I read in the papers that criminological scientists make miracles these days—peer at the microscope and tell the cop on the case just who and what to look for. Science, it's wonderful, *¿no es verdad?* You just take a general look and see what turns up.'

'Really,' said Erwin. 'Oh, well, we'll do our best.'

'I wonder—' Hackett was beginning, when Sergeant Lake looked in the door and said Lieutenant Carey would like to see whoever had that Carson Street homicide. Carey of Missing Persons.

'Ah,' said Mendoza happily, 'the next instalment of this thrilling mystery, maybe. Bring him in, Jimmy.'

CHAPTER THREE

Carey was a big stocky man with a pugnacious jaw. He'd been a lieutenant only for a few months; neither Hackett nor

Mendoza knew him well. He came in on the sergeant's heels and nodded at them. 'I had a memo from Sergeant Hackett—about this latest unidentified corpse you've got. It might be somebody we're looking for.'

'Sit down and let's hear the details. Have you looked at the corpse yet?'

'Just got back from the morgue. I didn't have a photo, but I think it's him all right. Stevan Domokous, working as a clerk. Greek but had his first papers.'

'My God,' said Hackett, 'I must have caught it from you, Luis—hunches—that's close enough to Bulgaria, isn't it? Was he a millionaire's son, Carey?'

'I don't know,' said Carey, looking a little surprised. 'But he's been missing about the right time, and the description matches. Fellow came in to report it last Wednesday—head of a local import and export firm, an Andreas Skyros—I'd lay a bet on that one being a millionaire, all right. Dressed to the nines, diamond ring, gold tooth, custom-made suit, the works. He's a citizen, but came from the old country—you can cut his accent with a knife.'

'I take it this Domokous hadn't any family here, if it was this fellow came in. Friend, or *is* he a relative?'

'Employer. Domokous was working for him. Skyros said he felt kind of responsible, the guy was lonely, didn't speak English so

28

well yet, you know. Which was how come, when Domokous didn't show up for work last Tuesday, he went round to see him, see if he was sick—or maybe sent one of the other fellows, I don't know. Domokous had a cheap room in a hotel on Second Street, we went over it. Not much there, a few odds and ends of clothes—no cash—album of family pictures from the old country—stuff like that. He paid by the week and it was almost up, they wanted the room—they'd seen him last on Monday—so seeing there wasn't much and it looked as if he hadn't taken off voluntarily—I mean, Skyros said probably he wouldn't have had much else but what was there—we impounded it, cleared out the room. Skyros says, and of course he's got something, that a stranger here, he's apt to get in trouble easy—wander into the wrong part of town, run into a mugger, something like that—'

'Which happens to a lot of people who've lived here all their lives,' said Hackett ruefully.

'And Skyros said too that he maybe felt a little worried sooner than he would have about anyone else because the guy wasn't the kind to take up with any cheap skirt all of a sudden, or go off on a bender. Anyway, when Domokous didn't show up on Wednesday, he comes in.'

'So we'd better have Mr. Skyros take a look

29

at the corpse,' said Mendoza. 'But even if it is Domokous—very nice to know, but it doesn't explain much besides. Where do we find Skyros?'

★   ★   ★

'Oh, this is very sad,' said Mr. Andreas Skyros. He sat down on the bench along the corridor and brought out a handkerchief to polish his bald head and his glasses. 'I don't pretend, gentlemen, I had any great—you know?—emotion about the young man, this way, that way—' he shrugged massively. 'He was such a one to feel sorry for, you know what I mean? But a very good, honest, hard-working young man.' As Carey had said, Mr. Skyros had a thick accent, but he also had a good command of English; for the rest, he was large, round, genial, and obviously prosperous. 'Tell me, how does he die?'

'He had an overdose of heroin,' said Mendoza. He stood in front of Skyros, hands in pockets, watching him.

'Oh, God help us, so? I was sorry he has no family here, but perhaps it is better, none to know this sad thing. You know? I—Gentlemen, perhaps we go somewhere else to talk? I don't like dead people all around.'

'Certainly,' said Mendoza cheerfully, 'we can go back to my office, if you like.'

'I would be so pleased to buy you

gentlemen a drink,' said Skyros wistfully.

'Now, now, you mustn't corrupt our morals, Mr Skyros! Not at all necessary.'

'Oh, my, no, you mustn't think such a thing,' protested Skyros. In Mendoza's office he polished his pink skull again. 'But such weather, a foretaste of hell, isn't it? I go out in it as little as possible—my office nice and air-conditioned, like this.' He glanced around approvingly. 'I didn't know they're so kind to you policemen now. Since the new building is up, isn't it, I suppose?'

'That's right. The labourer worthy of his hire, you know,' said Mendoza, beaming at him. 'So you do positively identify the body as that of Stevan Domokous. We're very glad to know who he is. Have you any more information about him we ought to know?'

'I am afraid I have, gentlemen. A terrible thing. I know the law says those who take drugs, dope you say, are guilty of offence too, but so many of them,'—he spread his fat hands—'only victims of those who sell! Domokous, as I have said to Mr.— Lieutenant?—Carey, he's been in this country only less than a year. I don't think any family back home, all dead in the wars maybe, you know?—and he's lonely. Me, I know him only, let's see, three months—it was the last June he comes to work for me. He's been in New York, but somebody tells him—he says to me—that California, it's like

31

Greece a little, down south, the climate you know, and vineyards—olive trees, isn't it? He thinks he likes it better. But he's a very shy, what's a good word, diffident young man—he doesn't make friends easy—and for the girls, oh, God help us!—a pretty girl looks at him, he runs!' Skyros rumbled a laugh.

'You surprise me,' said Mendoza. 'A handsome young fellow like that?'

'Oh, well, people, queer. Another one without his looks, the girls crazy for him because he's got the charm. Domokous maybe he never knew he was good-looking, isn't it, and it don't mean so much without the, as we say personality.'

'How true,' said Mendoza. 'That's very well put. He was lonely. No hobbies, not many acquaintances.'

'Like I say. Of course, I don't know him except as one of the fellows works for me—he helps unpack things sometimes, keeps the record books in the stockroom—but you gentlemen know, you make a success in business, you got to keep a personal eye on it, isn't it? So I'm out there in back, coming and going, I see the fellows there, talk to them, try to be a little friendly—you know. Don't know what to do with himself out of working hours, he tells me. And I must tell you, gentlemen, I've been suspicious maybe he's been up to something like this, the last month it is. At first I think he's maybe drinking too

32

much, he's not quick at his work and so on, a couple of times I'm there I see him—you know—stumble against things, like he's as we say tight. But now it seems it was this dope. Now I know, I say to Lieutenant Carey, he's not the kind to go off getting drunk somewhere, that's why I wonder when he goes off sudden, like this, say nothing about quitting. But a little difference, you see—way he's been, that I see, it's not that he's bad drunk, to fall down—just unsteady, you know?—like he's drinking a little all the time. I've read in the paper, isn't it, how these men selling this dope, they act friendly, talk you into trying it once only, to make more customers? Gentlemen, I see it could happen so with Domokous—anybody acted friendly with him—you know? He'd want to keep new friends.'

'I see,' said Mendoza interestedly. 'Yes, that's very plausible. Tell me, Mr. Skyros, did you ever—mmh—remonstrate with him, over not doing his work properly—ask him about the reason? Did he ever say anything to you about such a hypothetical new friend?'

'That's what I come to,' said Skyros, leaning forward earnestly. 'And I don't know does it help you at all, gentlemen. But these terrible men, this terrible business—and so many unhappy young people they get, I read, like Domokous—anything we can do to help, we must. Yes, I have spoken to Domokous, I ask if he's maybe taking a little too much wine, and he says—now I see, he knew better than to confess the truth—he says maybe so, he's got acquainted with a couple of nice jolly fellows who like to drink more than he's used, and just to be friendly, you know, he goes along. But he says he knows it isn't good, and don't mean to go on. He says, like to himself, you know, "I just tell Bratty, I can't afford it no ways!"'

'Bratty,' said Mendoza. 'When was this, Mr. Skyros?'

'I got to think. It'd be about three weeks back.'

'Ah. Now, of course, when there's no family to claim the body, the city'll take care of the burial—but perhaps you'd like to arrange for a little something extra? The morgue authorities—'

'I been thinking,' said Skyros, nodding. 'It's a sad thing. And a long while since I come from the old country, but he came from there too—young man, try to do better for himself—ambitious. Sad to end so. If it's O.K. with the law, gentlemen, I claim the body and see there's a little kind of service, nice and respectful, you know.'

'That's very good of you, sir,' said Lieutenant Carey.

'Well, we got to be charitable sometimes. Thank you very much, gentlemen, and I hope I help you a little.'

Carey got up on Skyros' departure, 'Well, I guess that's that. My part of the job cleared up anyway, and I suppose you'll be turning this over to Callaghan in Narcotics.'

Mendoza leaned back and shut his eyes, and Hackett looked at him in wary exasperation as Carey went out. 'Whenever you're that genial and polished, I suspect you. If that amiable Greek knew you better he'd suspect you too, like hell. What didn't you like about him?'

'*Un cuestión insensato.* He tells us Domokous had been wearing a monkey on his shoulder for some time. We know—or are pretty sure—he hadn't.'

'We don't know he hadn't been drinking. The kind that ends up on foolish powder is the kind ripe for other sorts of what the head-doctors call escape methods too. Liquor as well as other dope. Nine times out of ten they've tried 'em all before they get to the bottom.'

'*Es verdad.* Granted.'

'Well? What's in your mind?'

'I wonder,' said Mendoza dreamily, 'how much Mr. Skyros will report on his income tax that this charitable funeral cost him—and how much he'll actually lay out ... Go and brief somebody to pick him up, will you—home or office—we'll run a tail on him awhile.'

'And why, for God's sake?'

35

'¡*Yo he hablado*—I have spoken!'

'O.K., O.K.,' said Hackett, and went to dispatch the tail.

When he came back Mendoza said, 'You've forgotten the nymph and the dolphin. Sure, look at it once, it might be just the run-of-the-mill thing. Domokous inveigled into trying a jolt just for kicks, he gives himself too big a one—after being so nervous about it he makes a couple of dozen tries at getting the needle in—and passes out. The dirty hypo, obviously used—maybe the pusher sold that to him too. But look at it twice. How does that kind of thing usually go? You don't need to be told, the pusher either superintends the first jolt, to see the mark gets just the right kick to make him want another, or he hands out precise instructions. Even if it was his first shot, Domokous ought to have known better than to give himself such a dose. And he had a room. He must have known a little something about the effect to expect—that he'd probably be incapable for a while—and he wouldn't want to get picked up on the street full of heroin. Why go down that alley, like any vagrant drifter, instead of home? A mainliner, sure—you get that—when they've just bought a deck, they can't wait for a pick-up, they'll hit the nearest semi-private spot. But apparently it *was* his first experiment. Much more natural for him to have secluded himself

36

in his hotel room.'

'Why do you suppose he didn't?'

'I don't know, but it could be because he never intended to experiment with heroin at all. And because even a cheap hotel on Second Street is an awkward place to smuggle a body into.' Mendoza took up the phone again and asked for Lieutenant Callaghan in Narcotics . . . 'Patrick, *mi amigo bueno*, does the name Bratty ring any bells in your head?'

'Bratti,' said Callaghan. 'Mr. Giuseppi Bratti. It does indeed. Like a whole cathedral full of bells, all playing tunes. And I'm committing slander to say it, because we've got no evidence at all. You know how that goes—damn legal red tape—you got to have a bookful of witnessed statements to make a charge, and how the hell d'you get a user to tell all when he knows damn well it means a charge on him too?—or another kind of witness when he knows some loyal friend in the pusher's gang'll see he gets beaten up but good some night? Bratti runs a stable of pushers. Probably about a dozen. One of six or seven fairly big-time boys—local, that is—operating wholesale hereabouts. He'll do his own wholesale buying from some syndicate agent, but who and which I couldn't say. Eventually we hope to be able to. Probably the same agent who supplies other local runners. Naturally we have an eye on Bratti, but nothing yet to take to court.'

'Difficult, I know. And an eye on all the others?'

'Those we think we've spotted. Kind of like batting at mosquitoes, of course—you get one, there's another one right there to carry on.'

'Would you know whether Bratti has offended anybody lately?'

'It's very damn likely,' said Callaghan. 'He offends me every time I think about him. But I wouldn't know, specifically ... Oh, quite the respectable merchant on the surface—he owns three restaurants—lives in an apartment over by Silver Lake. And now, why?'

'I couldn't say, right now. It's this new corpse, the one full of heroin—'

'I noticed it, Hackett sent me a memo as maybe an interested party. Bratti cropped up behind it, I hope?'

'Away out in left field. I'll let you know if anything more definite comes up, *un millón de gracias* ...' Mendoza relayed that to Hackett. 'Now. Just file this in our minds, and let's get back to the corpse. I want to see all his possessions, but I don't suppose there's much interesting there—'

'If you're not just making up fairy tales,' agreed Hackett, 'it'd be a lot easier to ransack a hotel room than bring a body back to it.'

'—In fact, I think the only thing of real interest we've got is this little scrap of paper. I think it may have been the one thing they

38

missed, down in the bottom of his pocket—such a little thing. Just take another look at it. Torn off the right top corner of the page—doesn't that say a little something to us? Stapled: you find people who work in offices, businesslike people, writing personal letters on the typewriter and stapling the sheets together—but at the *left* top corner. Since this was stapled at the right, I'm inclined to think it was also stapled at the left, and who does that to a letter—and a letter, or anything, of only a few sheets? I don't think that scrap came from a letter. I think it came from a list of some kind, a list containing a good many pages stapled like that across the top. A *nymph* and a *dolphin*, it says. So, I'm reaching for it maybe, but Skyros—who employed the corpse—is an import-export dealer. And among the various items imported from abroad these days are, as usual, a lot of bric-à-brac—ornaments for the gracious home—porcelain and alabaster and bronze figurines, vases, and so on. The kind of thing you might reasonably expect to find decorated with nymphs and dolphins.'

'Yes, I see what you're driving at. It's a nebulous sort of connection, but could be. How do you read it, maybe he found out something funny about Skyros' business and got taken off to prevent his talking? But how and why heroin?'

'I'm not reading it any way yet,' said

39

Mendoza. 'I want to know a lot more about everything first. About Skyros, most of all. Business, private life, the works.'

'And as usual I'm the office boy to do all the finding out,' said Hackett. 'O.K., I'll get busy and we'll see what turns up.'

CHAPTER FOUR

Alison got home as usual about half past four that afternoon; classes at her school were over at four, and she hadn't any errands to do. She was feeling irritable and out of sorts—principally the weather, she reflected, stripping off her clothes and heading for the shower—why on earth she'd ever settled in this climate! Scarcely from ignorance, either, after having been mostly brought up in Mexico, which could be even worse. Doubtless from an unconscious love of martyrdom, she told herself savagely, emerging from the shower shuddering: and not only the climate. So, if she hadn't settled down in L.A. and opened this damned charm school, she wouldn't be saddled with these little morons who paid her to tell them to take a bath occasionally and not pluck out all their eyebrows or wear lace to a picnic. Also, of course, she wouldn't have met Lieutenant Luis Mendoza, which might have been another good thing.

She sat at her dressing table and was annoyed at its clutter, result of a series of mornings of hasty dressing: she tidied it automatically, and of course that reminded her of him all over again—Luis rearranging things all neat on the coffee table, the desk, anywhere in reach of him, and apologizing—'My grandmother says I'd get up off my deathbed to straighten a picture on the wall.' Way he was built: one of those tidy-minded people. Luis. Just as well she was somewhat the same way, because, if—

She bent forward, brushing her hair vigorously, angrily. And that was woolgathering with a vengeance, all right! Anybody as smart as Alison Weir—or as smart as Alison Weir *ought* to be, at least—with one abortive short-lived marriage behind her and thirty years of varied living, should know Luis Mendoza for what he was at one look. Luis—like one of his beloved cats, fastidious, independent, aloof. Not for any one woman, maybe ever.

Luis ... She laid down the hairbrush; and the phone rang. 'Oh, hello, Pat,' she said, putting false cheerfulness in her tone.

'I just called to say that Cheryl Bradley dropped in this morning, and I asked her about that thing you found—you'd said she'd ridden home with you from that dreary party at the Mawsons'. It's not hers, she says.'

41

'Oh, well, thanks. That really about covers everybody I know who might've lost it in the car. I think it *must* have been whoever took it. You know, the more I look at it the more I feel it is awfully old and might be valuable. Luis said so ... D'you suppose I ought to advertise it? I mean if anyone showed up to claim it I could tell that Sergeant Rhodes—'

'Nobody would dare,' said Miss Moore.

'But if I said something like, found in the Exposition Park area? They might not realize it'd dropped out in the car—'

'Finders keepers,' said Miss Moore. '*I* don't suppose it's anything but a worthless so-called lucky piece, but just to be on the safe side, I'd advise you to take it to an expert and see if it *is* worth anything. And in the unlikely event that it is, take the profit and return thanks to Providence.'

'Yes,' said Alison, 'but—Oh, well, I suppose it is the sensible thing to do. Thanks anyway. Are you going to the Vasperian exhibition on Friday? Then I'll pick you up, about one o'clock? O.K., thanks, Pat.' As she put the phone down and went back to the bedroom to finish applying lipstick, the door-buzzer sounded, and she said to herself, 'Damn,' snatched up her dressing gown and struggled into it on the way to the door.

The woman standing in the hall didn't look quite like the ordinary house-to-house salesperson: nor did she act like one. She

42

surveyed Alison head to foot and said, 'But I did not expect such a one! You look to be, how is it said, a cut above!'

'I beg your pardon,' said Alison. The woman was dark, elegant, exquisitely dressed: middle height, slim but rounded, waxen-white complexion, dark eyes cleverly elongated, polished dark hair in the latest fashionable cut, cameo-pure features. Over thirty, but not much, and not looking it. And dressed in what Alison instantly recognized as not only the latest fashion and exactly the right thing for her, but the latest original fashion, for which a very respectable sum of money must have been paid out. That subtly-cut powder-blue silk-faille afternoon gown, the elbow-length gloves to match, the small bit of blue frivolity with a veil meant for a hat, the sapphire (-coloured?) earrings and bracelets, the big diamond on the ungloved hand, the cobweb stockings, the spike-heeled black patent pumps, the black faille bag with a big rhine-stone initial—an ornate L—all of them, probably, would have cost as much as Alison earned in six months. And the cloud of musky, heavy scent wafting out from her, as much again per application, very likely.

'It is not you with cause to beg the pardon,' said the apparition, 'but *him*! Is he here?' Her gaze swept over Alison's printed rayon dressing gown. 'You are in the centre of dressing—undressing? If he is here—I come

43

in, I wish to speak with him!'

'You *don't* come in,' said Alison, angry and bewildered. 'What is it you want? You must have mistaken the apartment—'

'No, no, I memorize the address! Miss Alison Weir, it is? You have very nice hair, my dear, if one does not mind the colour. I come in!' And she brushed by Alison regally, to the middle of the living room. 'But what a pity to live in such a little squalid flat! Can you do no better?'

'Look *here!*' said Alison, furiously conscious that the dressing gown had only cost nine dollars new and that she was in her bare feet and hadn't any lipstick on, 'this is *my* apartment and I don't know you—if you don't leave at once—'

'Naturally you do not know me. You have a temper—so indeed have I. Is he here?' She swept into the bedroom, into the bath, back across the living room to look into the kitchenette. 'Ah! He is *not* here! But you expect him, perhaps?'

'Are you implying,' said Alison, drawing herself up to her full sixty-four inches, 'that I—'

'Imply, what is this? You need not put on the good face for me, miss! I beg you, be calm, I have no quarrel with you at this moment! It is that women, we should be sisters together, not so, and help one another? That is why I have come. I reason, there it is

44

probably I find him alone—except for you, of course—and it is much better to make the direct talk. I promise myself, I will restrain my temper, I will be dignified—however difficult, considering the dishonour he uses with me! But I see he is not here.'

'I must ask you to leave,' said Alison in her iciest tone.

'I will go, because he is not here and it is of no use to stay. A pity, for I had in my mind all the things I wish to say to him, and you know how, when one loses one's temper, the words go out of the head and one can only stutter! But you will tell him, miss, I am not so stupid and innocent as he think! You will tell him, he does not give Lydia the—the *stall*, the *run-about*, forever!—you see I know even your American slang, I am not what he would say the easy mark! You tell him this—that I deal direct with him, one chance more I give him to be honourable with me—in two days, he take it or he leave it—and he will be very wise to take it! He knows where I am to be found.' She gave Alison a significant, queenly nod and sailed out of the door.

For thirty seconds Alison was too possessed by rage to move. Then she whirled for the phone at the desk, had to look up the number, dialled it wrong twice, finally got police headquarters and demanded the Homicide office, got Sergeant Lake. 'I want to speak to the lieutenant ... Oh, yes, I'll hang on! With pleasure! ... This is the lieutenant speaking? Lieutenant Luis Rodolfo Vicente Mendoza, the well-known great lover? *Well*, Lieutenant, I have several things to say to you—' and she took a deep breath and commenced to say them, beginning with the announcement that if he thought it amusing to hand out her name and address to his other girl-friends, she did not, and in any case she didn't feel at all flattered to be one of a company which included this Lydia—

'What, who? What have I done?' protested Mendoza. 'It's a lie! *¿Como dice? Tómelo con calma, chica*—'

'—Lydia,' said Alison distinctly. 'If you search your memory, or maybe you keep a neat little list of them all, you'll remember her, I'm sure! A black-eyed hussy in spike heels and a Jacques Fath original—with a phoney-sounding accent—and about half a pint of Chypre. *Surely* you haven't forgotten Lydia? You really should keep a list! Yes, *¡villano, tú canalla, tú calamidad!*—I *am* annoyed, *¡estoy muy molestada!*—*¡no lo niego!*—looking at me as if I was a peasant or something, and smelling like a high-class brothel—very nice if one likes the colour, she says, this—this *¡perra negra!*—*¡nunca abbía visto tamaño descaro*, such impudence *¡Es demasiado*, too much!'

'Wait a minute, *chica, calm* down, what the

46

hell is this all about? *¡Eso no es cierto*—I'm absolutely innocent, I don't know any Lydia! I never—'

'Oh, you liar—*¡tú mentiroso!*—*¡no tengamos la de siempte*, the same old story! And, damn it, I hadn't even any lipstick on—looking at me as if I was—and—'

'*¡Vaya despacia, no hay tal!* I swear to you—what the devil is all this? I'm innocent as day, *querida* . . . All right, all right, hold everything, I'm coming round. I want to hear about this! *¡Por Dios!*—ruining my reputation, calling here through the switchboard—*¡no mentan tanta bulla*, not so much noise!'

'I couldn't care less, and besides they must all know what you're like by now—I wouldn't doubt having a good laugh over it—Men! A—a—a poor man's Gabor, looking down her nose at me—'

'I'm coming, I'm coming!—*¡ni qué niño muerto!*—nonsense!' The phone clicked firmly in her ear.

Alison went on talking to herself, kicking the hassock in passing and groping after some of her father's favourite swear-words, for about five minutes. Then she went to the kitchen and got down the bottle of rye, and eyeing it began to laugh. So all right, how senseless could you get. She didn't like rye, but he never drank anything else.

'Is it safe to come in?' asked Mendoza

when she opened the door. '*Querida mia*, what have I done to deserve this? One female at a time is enough to keep any man occupied!'

'Have you placed Lydia?' asked Alison grimly.

'I have not. I never knew one. I don't know one now. I don't want to know one. *Mi novia, mi hermosa*, why would I want a Lydia—'

'Now you just keep your distance!' said Alison. 'Oh, yes, try to pass it off and make me forget it! Walking in cool as you please, this *hussy*, and calling it a squalid little flat!—it's a wonder I didn't kill her—'

'No, really now, no joke—no little games, *chica!*' He pulled her down beside him on the couch. 'What happened?' She told him, more or less coherent by then. 'I will be damned,' said Mendoza. '*Honestamente*, I don't know her—don't know anything about it. What the hell could have brought her here? She knew your name, you said? Me, for better or worse I was raised halfway a gentleman—you don't bandy females' names around! I'm surprised at you, thinking such a thing of me.'

'Well!' said Alison, relaxing slightly. 'I was mad. *With* reason. And she said—'

'Yes, let's hear it all, as clear as you remember . . . That's a very funny little story. Where could she have got your name? And a couple of things she said—all that about dealing direct—it doesn't exactly sound like any romantic affair, does it? More like a business deal of some kind, maybe? ... And who is "he"? I wonder ... *¡un momento!*—the car! Now I do wonder—whoever took the car—maybe she'd had a ride in it, and noticed the registration slip, and thought you were the girl-friend of the chief. It could be.'

'I suppose so,' said Alison doubtfully. 'It seems sort of far-fetched ... Luis? You're not just making it into a mystery to take my mind off it, are you?'

He laughed and kissed her. 'You're too suspicious. I don't know one thing about it—it's just a funny little story. Go and get dressed—that amber thing—I'll take you to dinner. *Más primero, acérquese*—come nearer ... O.K., *querida*?'

'Well, O.K.,' said Alison, with a sign. She drew away and looked at him, head cocked. 'Of course, I might feel a little more satisfied if I didn't happen to know you're an awfully good poker-player ... D'you want a drink while I'm getting dressed?'

★   ★   ★

It was after midnight when Mendoza got home, to the rather old-fashioned apartment building on a quiet dead-end street, and put the car away in the garage, let himself into his apartment. The sleek brown Bast greeted him with pleased soft cries. Various visitors had left five notes in a row propped on the mantel; he read them from left to right as he took off his coat and tie. That autocratic old lady Señora Teresa Maria Sancia Mendoza, who at eighty-six was enjoying life far more than she had in her youth, living in a Wilshire Boulevard apartment and telling everyone grandiloquent lies about her impeccable Castilian ancestry, informed him in a black scrawl that he should be more careful about what persons he gave access to his quarters; she would not put it beyond this Carter woman to pry into one's drawers, having found her on the premises when she called. And it was nearly two weeks since he had come to see her and she trusted he would not forget her birthday next week. When he acquired a wife, which was devoutly to be hoped for, as he was not getting any younger, these affairs would be better arranged for him—always supposing he had the sense, which she frequently doubted, to choose a sensible and satisfactory wife. She much desired that he should make time to visit her soon, as there were some pleasant new neighbours she would like him to meet.

Mendoza grinned at the scrawl: the old lady had been trying for fifteen years to get him married to a comfortable, modest, practical wife—of her own choice—preferably one who could coax him back to the priests. Probably had a new candidate to trot out.

Mrs. Carter from across the hall informed him that Bast had had her wheat germ in fresh liver at four o'clock and he was *not* to give her any more until Thursday.

Mrs. Bryson from upstairs, front, informed him that she had let Bast out for a little run at nine o'clock.

Bertha, the eminently satisfactory maid-of-all work who managed the domestic lives of the whole apartment population, informed him that he was out of half-and-half and that there was a sale on that coffee he liked this week at a local market.

Mr. Elgin from upstairs, rear, expressed himself as uneasy concerning Bast and that smart-aleck young Siamese tom of his; it was, he thought, quite possible that he and Mendoza might find themselves joint owners of some crossbred kittens presently.

Mendoza looked at Bast. 'What, have you grown up finally and discovered sex? Misbehaving yourself, *gatita*—he's a good year younger than you! Well, time will tell,' and he wandered into the bedroom unbuttoning his shirt.

But he sat up another half hour, ruminating not only on his latest corpse, but now on Alison's visitor—and a few other things.

CHAPTER FIVE

When Hackett got to the office on Wednesday morning, early for once, there was someone waiting to see Mendoza—Sergeant Lake passed over the business card noncommittally under the visitor's eye. *Charles Driscoll*, and the name of a national insurance firm.

Hackett looked Driscoll over. About forty, tallish and broadish, sandy, and by the coolly insolent stare he gave in return, a brash one. Flashy pencil-striped suit off the rack, a garish tie. 'Yes, Mr. Driscoll, if you'd like to come into the office?'

'You wouldn't be Lieutenant Mendoza,' said Driscoll, standing up, 'don't tell me.'

'Sergeant Hackett. Just come in, the lieutenant'll be here soon.' Hackett exchanged a look with Lake, left the office door open, saw Driscoll settled in the armchair beside the desk facing the door, and offered him a cigarette.

'Thanks very much. Quite a setup you've got here—compared to most police H.Q.s.' Driscoll ignored Hackett's proffered lighter, produced an ornate black-and-gold one of his own.

'We find it satisfactory,' said Hackett.

'But kind of stultifying all the same, you know—' Driscoll gestured with his cigarette.

52

'I always feel sorry for you guys—having to stay inside so many rules and regulations. Must be damn annoying. Bein' in the private-eye line myself, I know all the ropes, if you get me. Though *I* get the hell of a lot more interesting cases than you poor bastards, acourse ... That your lieutenant?' He dropped his tone only a little, looking out to the anteroom where Mendoza had stopped to have a word with Sergeant Lake. 'My, my, what the best-dressed man will wear—quite the gigolo, isn't he? Protégé of the Chief's, to be sittin' at a lieutenant's desk? Doesn't look much like a cop.'

Mendoza came in and said good morning to Driscoll. 'Some odds and ends on Domokous, Art—go out and see Dwyer, will you, he's just checked in ... Now, what was it you wanted to see me about, Mr. Driscoll?'

Hackett went out regretfully. He wasn't equipped by nature to reach the Driscolls with any kind of back talk that really got to them: they just made him mad, and that only pleased them, naturally. About thirty seconds from now, when Mendoza had sized him up, Driscoll was due to be snubbed more subtly than he'd ever been in his life, and it would have been gratifying to see. Mendoza was so good at that kind of thing when he wanted to be—the polished aristocrat condescending to the bumptious peasant. He could get more insult into one polite phrase than any other

53

man Hackett knew, and all smooth as silk on the surface.

What Dwyer had to say was that Domokous' wallet had turned up. Empty of cash, whether or not it had held any, but everything else probably intact, and not much: I.D. card laboriously filled out in English, Social Security card, L.A. Public Library card, and that was all, except for a snapshot of a girl, a rather fuzzy close-up of a not-very-pretty dark girl smiling into the camera. The wallet had been turned in to a Main Street precinct station by a housewife who'd found it near the corner of San Rafael and Main; she said it had contained no cash when she picked it up.

And that tied in to a run-of-the-mill business, sure. Somebody coming across Domokous in that alley, either dead or unconscious, and taking the only thing of value on him—a few bucks, maybe, in the billfold—taking the cash, dropping the billfold on the street. Kind of thing that happened every day, this way or that way.

Hackett thought himself that Luis was building this thing up into more complexity than the facts indicated: so, all right, say that scrap of paper was part of a list of some kind, to do with Skyros' business. Domokous had been a clerk there, no reason he shouldn't have it in his pocket, was there? You wanted to be intricate about it, say it'd got torn off accidentally and he'd felt guilty, stuck the torn piece in his pocket instead of throwing it away.

Domokous still looked quite straight-forward to Hackett. He didn't like Mr. Skyros much, any more than Mendoza did—a very canny customer and out for profit for Mr. Skyros every time, but what was that? A lot of people like that. Most people. Domokous was just another victim of a pusher, probably one of those employed by this Bratti.

But, run-of-the-mill or not, there was still routine to be done on it. Hackett went down to Carey's office, signed the necessary forms, and received the contents of Domokous' hotel room. Not much: he went through it desultorily. A suit, probably his Sunday one, fairly new if cheap: a few shirts, socks, a little underwear, a modest pile of dime store handkerchiefs: odds and ends of personal possessions otherwise—an ancient cardboard-covered album of family snapshots, all obviously dating from years back in the old country—a little box containing an old-fashioned tie pin with a red glass stone in it, a tarnished silver ring, an old pocket watch—a couple of letters in some language Hackett took to be Greek, funny looking sort of stuff, both recently postmarked *Athens*.

He'd gone through collections like that often enough before, the relics left of a life:

55

they always secretly saddened him a little. All there was to show—whatever sort of life it had been, good, bad, or indifferent; and so immediately losing any importance, what had had value in someone's mind . . . *No pockets in a shroud*, he thought vaguely, putting the album back in the cardboard carton where Carey had stashed the smaller articles.

Dwyer, Higgins, and Reade were on Skyros; Dwyer had reported in, and so far as Hackett could see there wasn't much there either. All looked on the level, perfectly ordinary. Andreas Skyros, Inc., had been operating for seventeen years, dealt mostly in European imports from a number of countries; Skyros had never been in trouble with the law, privately or businesswise. He was married, but had no family: owned a house in a good residential district of west Hollywood, and ran an almost new Buick; his wife had a new Chevvy convertible. He was doing all right, especially in the last six or seven years, but all above-board. So? Skyros was exactly what he looked like. The whole thing was a mare's nest.

He left Domokous' possessions with Sergeant Lake for Mendoza, and drove down to Skyros' offices on Figueroa. Skyros wasn't in, which was just as well; Hackett introduced himself to the clerk in the front office, and interviewed all the personnel who'd worked with the dead man—four other stockroom clerks and the bookkeeper, a pretty brunette. He didn't get much more than they already had, or anything to contradict Skyros except a nuance or two.

Sure, Domokous had been kind of lonely, they all said: couldn't seem to settle down, like. Quiet sort, and not talking English so good he couldn't join in, if the sergeant saw what they meant—didn't get jokes and so on. They'd all liked him well enough, but what with his being quiet anyway and not talking the language much he was hard to get to know, and he hadn't been here long. He liked to read, used to go to the public library and get books in his own lingo. But he had a girl, all right—he'd said a little something about her, and he had her picture in his wallet. The girl bookkeeper spoke up then, pertly, and said maybe he had but if she was any judge and she figured she was, he wouldn't have let that hamper him—way he eyed her every time she came out back. Awfully good-looking he'd been, and it was terrible, have anything like that happen—she'd never have thought he was the kind to go for dope. Which the others confirmed: reserved, you might say, but not nuts, or queer any way.

None of them remembered Domokous ever mentioning anyone named Bratti. And none of them could say what his girl's name was or where she lived. And it didn't matter much, because probably the news story would bring her in—unless, of course, she'd been mixed up in his death somehow, which didn't seem likely.

*   *   *

The news story about Domokous' identification had, in fact, already brought her in; she was sitting on the edge of a chair in Mendoza's office, looking less grieved than sullen. She was about twenty-five, dark and thin, no striking beauty but not ugly either. She sat with head bent over her clasped hands, and looked at Mendoza through a tangle of black hair fallen across her cheek.

The other woman said nervously, 'He was a good young man, sir. Never would he do such a thing as that you say. He save his money to marry Katya, like we tell, in the spring they are to marry, all is arranged.' She was in black like the girl, a spare old woman, patience and tragedy in her big dark eyes. The grandmother. Slav, from this place or that, and definitely Old Country: but the girl born here, probably—little accent. 'Someone tells lies about him, fixes up a lie, to make you think this. Stevan, not even much wine he drinks—he's careful with money.'

'It's that man, where he worked!' burst out the girl.

'And what makes you say that, Miss Roslev?' asked Mendoza.

'When he did not come, on the Thursday, for Katya's birthday, we knew something bad happen—the man at the hotel, he knows nothing, and we did not like to go to his place of work—Katya said—And all the time, lying out so, dead, none to care for him, pray for him—Oh, it is bad to think! And he is so full of hopes, the long journey here and the better chance to make success—'

'Always you're so scared!' said the girl contemptuously. 'Thinks this looks bad, that don't look right—had my way, I'd have gone and asked, all right! I knew there was something funny going on—Stevan, he was worried—'

'Katya, you talk too much, you get us in trouble,' whispered the old woman. 'We don't know nothing at all, it's only in your head—only we know Stevan was a good boy—'

'He was too good!' said the girl. '*I* said—oh, well, never mind that ... You scared even come to the police, they don't eat you, here.'

'Katya, so rude to the officer, please take care.'

'But Miss Roslev's quite right, we don't bite,' smiled Mendoza at her. 'Why do you think his death is connected with Mr. Skyros?'

'I'll tell you why, what I came to say, see? Stevan, he told me about it—told *us*—last

59

time he was there, it was. He'd found out something about this Mr. Skyros—something bad, he thought—See, he'd had to work late one night, there was a big shipment some kind come in—and he went up to Mr. Skyros' office, ask him something, and heard him and somebody else talking—and he said it sounded like it was about something bad, crooked you know—he said. I wouldn't put it past Mr. Skyros, be mixed up in something like that, only—'

'Something crooked. What kind of something, what did he overhear exactly?'

'I don't know,' she said, sullen again. 'Just, it was about a lot of money, he said. Worth an awful lot. He didn't say exact—but I thought—maybe since, he found out more, and they killed him so's he couldn't tell, see? Because he said then—police ought to know about crooks, if they was—'

'Katya, you shouldn't say, we don't know for sure—Mr. Skyros, a lot of money he'll have, he see you get in jail, to say—'

'I guess not! I'm not afraid o' him, nor the cops neither! You go and ask *him* what he knows, see?'

'But you haven't given me anything very definite to go on, Miss Roslev. If you could remember a more specific phrase, a word?'

She was silent awhile, looking at him; and then she said, 'I s'pose you got to have more, like you say. Can't do nothing if you don't

60

know ... Well, I told you anyhow. I guess—all I could tell you, mister—and maybe—'

'Katya—' The old woman was still nervous of Mendoza, of Authority; and the girl let herself be urged out ... Mendoza was still ruminating on them when Hackett came in, and they exchanged news.

'It's nothing at all, of course. No, I wouldn't be surprised if Skyros sails a little close to the wind in business, but so what? Even if Domokous had somehow got hold of proof, I don't see Skyros doing murder over it, do you? More likely to buy him off. And that kind of murder—a very pro business ... Of course, there's such a thing as cover. And maybe he's running more businesses than one. Like Mr. Bratti. Yes, a couple of little points in what these other clerks said. I have an idea that Mr. Skyros, shrewd a businessman as he may be, underrates us just a little, you know. He didn't think we'd check up far on what he said about Domokous—and evidently he didn't know about Katya Roslev and her grandmother. But nothing much to get hold of in all that.'

Hacket agreed. 'By the way, what did that obnoxious insurance fellow want? I was sorry to miss the snubbing you'd hand him.'

Mendoza grinned. 'Why, Art, you know we're trained these days to be as polite as can

61

be to civilians. I never said a cross word to him.'

'I'll bet,' said Hackett. 'I gathered he's an insurance investigator.'

Mendoza regarded his lighter meditatively. 'If the head-doctors are right in some of their theories—which I frequently doubt—our Mr. Driscoll must have a king-size inferiority complex. Overcompensating, as they say, like mad. He's read all the paperback mysteries about the smart-as-paint private eyes—quite a fad lately for making them insurance detectives, you know—and he knows just how he ought to act. I'll bet you fifty to one he religiously wears a shoulder holster and drinks five Martinis before dinner whether he likes them or not, or could hit the side of a barn with a shotgun. And addresses every female under forty as Beautiful—and, *Dios*, how he'd like to have everyone think they all fall for him in rows and he's never slept alone for the last twenty-five years, since he was a precocious teenager.'

Hackett laughed. 'I read him the first look too. What was he after?'

Mendoza snapped the lighter and lit his cigarette. 'I'm damned if I know. And also damned curious. What he wanted to know was why Skyros had been here yesterday. And when I told him and asked why he was interested, he came with a couple of smart-aleck unfunny wisecracks, said it was private firm business and I wouldn't be

interested anyway, and swaggered out.
Private eyes, you know, they always act that
way with these solid stupid regular cops.'

'You don't say—interested in Skyros? So
maybe it's an insurance racket—this piece of
crookedness that's going to be worth a lot of
money? I wonder if Skyros ever had a
warehouse burn down or something like that,
and the insurance company's a little leery of
him, looking into his private life?'

'Which bright thought crossed my mind
too. I've got Landers looking into it. I also
attached a tail to our Mr. Driscoll. After all,
he asked for it . . . No, nothing in Domokous'
stuff, I didn't think there would be. Maybe
there never was, or maybe somebody got
there first. One thing, I want those two letters
translated *pronto*. And—' Mendoza sat up and
called Sergeant Lake. 'Has Higgins called in
on Skyros? Where is he now?'

'Just a little bit ago. From the
Beverly-Hilton—looks like Skyros is fixing to
have a lunch there with some dame.'

'Well, well. Could this also be the same
dreary old tale, tired middle-aged
businessman cheating on his wife? I think I'll
go and take a look—you can hold down the
regular table at Federico's, Art.'

Higgins was propping the wall just outside
the main dining room of the hotel, looking a
little seedy in comparison with most of the
guests and visitors in this haunt of

sophisticates. When he saw Mendoza he stepped out to meet him.

'It's O.K., Lieutenant, he can't see us from where they're sitting, and there's only one entrance—I looked. The dame kept him waiting quite a while, and I grabbed a sandwich at the bar where I could keep an eye on him. Six bits for a cheese sandwich!'

'Well, it goes on your expense account,' said Mendoza.

'It's the principle of the thing. Highway robbery. This looks kind of N.G. to me—he's just been ordinary places, home and work—and if he's stepping out on his wife, it's not exactly illegal, you can't arrest him for that. Me, I never can figure out why they bother. Go to all that trouble, thinking up lies to tell the wife and so on. I don't say there isn't any female worth it, but I do say they'd be the hell of a lot smarter to get rid of one before they take on another.'

'But then you're a very moral fellow,' said Mendoza.

'It's not my morals, it's my blood pressure,' said Higgins. 'I like a quiet life myself. You quitting the tail on him?'

'No, you carry on.' Mendoza went into the dining room, glanced around casually for Skyros, was trapped by an obsequious headwaiter, just as he spotted him, and ensconced at a small table where all he could see of Skyros' companion was her hat. It was

64

a large hat, with a transparent stiff brim of black lace, and sat nearly on the back of her head, effectively screening her profile when she turned, and a good deal of Skyros across the table. Visible below it were round white shoulders only partially covered by a black-and-white printed gown, low-cut back and (probably) front, and one round white arm bearing a wide gold bracelet, a scarlet-nailed hand extravagant in gesture.

'Something to drink before lunch, sir?'

'No, thanks,' said Mendoza, whose vices did not include alcohol as one of his life's necessities. He ordered at random, an unobtrusive eye on Skyros. He would not be displeased if Skyros happened to notice him: this whole thing was up in the air, nothing to get hold of, and if Skyros was mixed up in it in any way, it could be useful to give him the idea that they knew a bit more than they did. Frequently that prompted a suspect to do something silly and revealing.

Skyros, however, wasn't doing much looking around; he seemed entirely occupied with the girl-friend. At the same time, he didn't look quite like a man entertaining the extracurricular sex interest. He wiped a perspiring brow frequently in spite of the air-conditioning; he fidgeted with the cutlery, and his expression was now unhappy, now falsely genial. The girl-friend was doing most of the talking; he tried to interrupt several times and shrugged at failure.

Mendoza ate an anonymous lunch absently, watching and thinking. They had almost finished when he came in; they sat over drinks of some kind—brandy, by the glasses—and as the waiter whisked Mendoza's plate away, offered more coffee, Skyros got up. The woman was more leisurely, sliding gracefully out of her chair, smoothing her skirt—revealing a pair of eye-catching legs ending in slim spike heels. Skyros put a gallant hand on her elbow as they turned for the door.

And she was something to be gallant about, all right: a very handsome piece of goods indeed, in exotic style. Black hair in a smooth fashionable coiffure, dead-white complexion, sharply arched brows, dark red lipstick, flashing stones at her ears and throat.

They had to pass within a few feet of his table to reach the door, and Mendoza watched them steadily, willing Skyros to look and see him: but Skyros was oblivious, wiping his brow again, looking agitated. And she was scarcely, by her expression, bent on exuding glamour; she looked very angry. They came past, the woman still talking in an undertone over her shoulder, and he caught a phrase or two—not English: Greek, Russian? He also caught a waft of powerful musky scent. And then they were out the door and gone—transferred to Higgins.

'Will that be all, sir? A little cognac perhaps?'

'No, that's all ... *¡qué disparate!*' said Mendoza to himself, reaching for his wallet. '*¡Bastante!* This is making up fairy tales with a vengeance.' Alison's black-eyed hussy in spike heels, smelling like a high-class brothel ... 'Impossible. Ridiculous. This is *not* one of Mr. Driscoll's paperback thrillers!'

CHAPTER SIX

'But you must be sensible, dear madame!' said Mr. Skyros. 'These wild ideas—' He wiped his brow agitatedly.

'I am surprised,' said Madame Bouvardier, 'that a businessman should be so impractical. But two thoughts I have about this also, and *n'importe* the second one. I find you irritating in the extreme, Mr. Skyros.'

'My dear lady, there is a saying, one cannot have one's cake and also eat it. This insurance money, it is obviously impossible to claim it when—'

'It is not impossible at all, and I see nothing whatever criminal in doing so! I will most certainly not do as you suggest, to give it back to them and tell this elaborate lie of how I recover the collection! The company, it has insured the Lexourion collection, has it not?

The, what is the word, premium, it is paid—all is good faith both sides—very well—the collection is stolen, it is gone, so the company must pay. Why do they not pay me? That is their business. Anything else to do with the collection, it is my business. It belonged to my father, I am his only child, naturally it now belongs to me. There is nothing difficult to grasp here.'

'But, my dear lady—you do not suppose the insurance firm will pay, or allow you to keep the money, without investigation—when they find you again have the collection—'

'Naturally they investigate. There is a man comes to see me only yesterday, a very unpleasant ill-bred man named Driscoll, who does not know how to behave with a lady. But then he is of course an American. I must say, I find it uncouth of these insurance people that they should at once suspect there is wrong-doing—but I am very gracious to him, I tell him he is welcome to search, he can see I have not got it, they know from the police it is truly stolen, and it has not been sold to anyone by the thieves—the police watch, I daresay, the insurance men also, and it is still vanished. Very well, then they must pay. I am not a fool, Mr. Skyros, and I do *not* let it be at all obvious that I have got the collection back! In Europe, there are men of honour who will pay me privately to have the privilege to house it. But also, I do not allow

68

myself to be held up by gangsters! This—this Irishman, this Donovan, he is not an honourable man and he is also much too greedy. In the nature of things, a thief sells his plunder in secret, he is lucky to receive a fifth of its value—this is well known. The bargain you say you made with Donovan, for ten thousand of your dollars. And now he tries to withdraw, he says it is not enough, he will have twenty. I think I was a fool to trust you to make the bargain.'

'Dear madame, you surely don't suspect that I would be dishonest with you? I protest—it's only a favour on my part, I'm earning no profit—'

'Me, I am Greek too,' she reminded him darkly, 'if I do live in France most of my life—we know each other! Better do deal with this gangster directly. I am not afraid of gangsters, I have seen them on the films. They are like little children playing with wooden guns, behaving very *tough* as you say, but stupid men without cunning. Well, there is another saying, two can play at one game. He will keep the bargain he has made or he will be sorry.'

'I assure you, *not* children,' said Skyros. 'I would not dream of allowing you to deal with such men—they can be very dangerous—you know they have already killed this poor clerk of mine, because he overheard some talk—'

'Yes, but they would not offer harm to *me*,

69

for in that case they get no money at all! I will see that he keeps the bargain, and after the insurance money is paid, all is accomplished, and I take the collection home.'

'All is *not* accomplished. You can't have it both ways, we shall all be in trouble if you persist. It will be known you have the collection again, the insurance people will call you a thief—'

'That is very stupid and bad faith, they are liable to pay when it is stolen, anything afterward is my own affair. And besides—'

'But you can never smuggle it out of the country—'

'Oh, that is easiest of all! But there is no need to discuss that at the moment.' Suddenly she produced a gracious smile, reached to pat his hand. 'You have done your best, Mr. Skyros, to help me in this matter, and be sure I appreciate it. It is only, perhaps, that I am one of those people, I never feel a thing is properly done unless I do it myself! Do not worry about me, my friend—I know my own business.'

'But I do beg you to take care,' he said earnestly. 'Do not be foolhardy, dear lady.'

'That I never am, Mr. Skyros.'

*   *   *

Women! thought Mr. Skyros exasperatedly. Especially these strong-minded ones. The

70

deal had been set up—in a bit of a hurry, admittedly, but a perfectly straightforward deal—before he had met the woman, and he had never expected her to be so difficult. And worst of all, he had a vague feeling that she no longer trusted him as the innocent middleman.

He drove back to town, shut himself into his office, and called Donovan. 'She is obstinate, very obstinate. She refuses to pay more, and my friend, I think we'd better leave it there, isn't it? The profit's not so bad—and she has some crazy ideas in her head, you know, get us all in trouble—'

'Listen, I'm not born yesterday, I know what it's worth now and when I know it's insured for two hundred thousand smackers, listen, Skyros, I don't go along with no piddling deal like ten G's! Particularly when I got to cut it with you. You set it up with my kid brother, so O.K., but I'm handling both our affairs now just like it allus was, and you're dealin' with me now. She's got no choice—she wants the stuff, she pays.'

'But, my friend, she is the only customer!'

'That don't necessarily mean she can set the price. She takes it or leaves it. You say she wants it damn bad. O.K., then she pays.' The phone slammed down at the other end.

Mr. Skyros cast his eyes to heaven and swore several oaths in two languages. He was a fool ever to have got mixed up in this

71

business. And it had looked so easy, so casual, to start with—money dropping from heaven! All, you might say, for a few kind words spoken. Nothing to it at all. This crazy female—this crazy idea about the insurance. A thousand devils, she'd get them all in jail with her if she tried that! And try to talk to her! Sure, sure, the ordinary thing, the diamond necklace, the bearer bonds, it's just another little deal, you keep the insurance easy—company can't prove anything. But a deal like this, just not good sense. The customs—Two hundred thousand—

For that matter, try to talk to Donovan, who was just as crazy. These low-class robbers, no understanding of finesse, not the most rudimentary cunning. It was a simple matter of supply and demand, couldn't he see that? Here was a thing almost impossible for a fence to dispose of in the underworld market: no fence would take it off his hands, much less give him ten thousand for it. And here was a buyer willing to pay that. One could not be too greedy: it never paid in the end. One had to sell goods for what one could get. And now, because Donovan got this crazy idea in his head—

Mr. Skyros swore again. He had the dreadful feeling that this thing, which had looked so little, so easy, was putting him in personal danger. He had always been so careful (like Bratti, and one thousand curses

72

on him too) to keep clear of the business on the surface, stay looking respectable. If any of this came out at all ... And Domokous had come very close to connecting him. Inevitable that he'd had to appear in that business, and it had been a brilliant inspiration, to try for two birds with one stone, involve Bratti in the death—but had it come off? He hadn't dared say more. He was confident in any case that Domokous was written off safely.

But he felt as if he was walking a tightrope between Donovan and this crazy woman. Just because both of them were so greedy. The love of money, reflected Mr. Skyros unhappily, is the root of all evil. Indeed.

And about that time his bookkeeper came in to tell him that the police had been there asking questions about Domokous, and gave him something else to worry about.

★   ★   ★

'Listen, I don't like it, Jackie,' said Denny Donovan anxiously to his brother. 'Ask me, the quicker we're out from under this one the better. Why, hell, it's all gravy anyways—only luck I got the stuff first place—'

'I ain't no flat wheel,' said Jackie Donovan obstinately. 'Who was it had sense enough find out how much it *is* worth, 'stead o' taking this Skyros' word for it? Anybody crazy, pay two hundred G's for *that*, but that's what the guy said, I told you. So O.K., we don't let go for less 'n twenty.'

''S bad luck,' said a dreamy voice from the other side of the room. 'Allus, bad luck, anythin' to do with an ace o' spades—bad luck. Don't want mess with it, Jackie. Get shut o' the hot stuff, an' shut o' the ace o' spades.'

'What the *hell*!' said Jackie. 'So what if she's an ace o' spades? I ain't so damn superstitious. You guys lost any sense you had since I got sent across, ain't been here keep an eye out, fix deals for you. Angelo never did have much, but look at him now—out on a sleigh ride half the time—'

'I quit any time I want, Jackie,' said Angelo in the same dreamy voice, 'any time. Don't matter. Smarter'n some guys, before *or* after a fix, me—never got inside on a taxi, I didn't.'

'You just shut up! And you just as bad, Denny—lost your nerve, gone to pieces! Don't tell me ain't all your fault the kid brother got it—if you'd held things together like, kept it steady 'n quiet like I allus did, Frank wouldn't never've got onto *that* lay, my God—sure there's money in it, but you got to draw a line somewheres! So Angie thinks it's bad luck get mixed up with an ace o' spades, so O.K., me, I think it's bad luck get mixed up with pushers! But here's the deal thrown

74

into our laps, and only sense to get what the traffic'll stand!'

'I tell you, Jack, you kinda lost track o' things while you been in.' Denny was nervous, criticizing. 'It just ain't so easy no more, making a living. Don't pay near so good, account o' the cops are different, sort of, even worse 'n just fifteen years back. You can't blame Frank—just the breaks, it was—besides, Jack, like I said I don't figure it was damn safe, go out to that museum place like you did—I mean, hell *they* ain't got nothing to lose, they mighta called the cops right off—'

'My God, you ain't seen no sign of it, have you? So O.K., they didn't bite on buyin' the stuff under the counter like I maybe thought, it was just a try, anybody's crooked give 'em the chance not get caught, even professors or—So it didn't come off, but that guy told me what it's really worth, didn't he? Insured for two hundred G's, he said—Oh, the hell with it! You just gone soft in the head, Denny. Listen, you remember just how it used to be, see, just let ol' Jackie do the brainwork for you, boyo. Don't worry about nothing, just do how I say, and everything'll be O.K., see?' Jackie Donovan banged him on the shoulder and made for the door.

'Where you going?'

'None o' your business where—you hear what I just say? Way it used to be,

Denny—ol' Jack's the brains o' the outfit, you just leave it to him and don't ask no questions, see?'

Denny watched him out uneasily. 'I still don't like it,' he said half to himself. 'Ask me, something fishy about the whole deal, anybody pay so much as a sawbuck for that stuff. Lot o' dirty old stuff you couldn't even—'

'Ask no questions, you get tol' no lies,' said Angelo. He rolled over on the sagging old couch in the corner of the shabby room and smiled sleepily at Denny. 'Jackie, he get some older inside, don't he? Maybe forget a li'l bit, how things go. Maybe not the same ol' Jackie, fifteen years back, you guess?'

'I—well, kinda, I guess,' said Denny unwillingly. He fidgeted around the room. 'Sure, I guess—only natural, for a little while—you know, Angie, away *that* long—only natural. He get back on an even keel, O.K., couple of months maybe.'

'Sure. Maybe. Look a lot older, Jackie.'

'Well—fifteen years,' said Denny. 'I—you know something crazy, what really bothers me—that damn car! Crazy fool thing. This perfeckly good almost brand new Caddy I get for him, a *present*, an' he says he can't handle it—goes off like that an' stalls her, an' that place too—comes back with this piece of old junk, my God, pickin' up a thing like—stickin' me with a hot short to get rid
76

of! Says he can't get the hang o' these new models, dashboard like a airplane or something—Jackie! Don't make sense. Well, fifteen years ... So O.K., maybe he's got something, get all we *can*, but I don't like the setup. That Greek—well, I got no grudge on him for bein' Frank's boss, he acted real sorry, he allus treated Frank O.K., I guess, but—'

'Not Skyros watch out for. The ace o' spades. Bad luck.'

'Oh, damn it to hell!' said Denny. 'I wish to God I'd never picked that damn place to knock over!'

★   ★   ★

'He quotes proverbs at me,' said Madame Bouvardier, 'so I too remember one, Berthe. When in Rome one behaves like a Roman.'

'Yes, madame,' said the maid stolidly.

'So—so!' Madame Bouvardier could not think in silence; indeed, she seldom did anything in silence; and she kept her excellent Berthe, though she was not *chic* or very intelligent, because Berthe was utterly loyal and it did not matter what one said before her. 'Since I have no longer a husband to arrange these affairs, I am pleased enough that this Skyros offers himself, as a compatriot and a sympathizer, to help me come in touch with these robbers. But no, I am not a fool, and I have now thought twice. Since when should a Skyros be so obliging for no profit? I think perhaps he gets a little piece of that money, and when I agree at once to the price, they think I am so anxious I will pay anything! Well, they must think again. Berthe, I will have another glass of wine.'

'Yes, madame.'

'It is true I am anxious to have it—in his dotage, my father was, heaven rest him—to think of selling it in America! Sacrilege! These precious relics of our nation's past—of course it is also true that for the moment it would perhaps be unsafe that the collection remain in Athens, so close to these never-enough-to-be-cursed Russians, who knows what enormity they conceive next? But it should *not* be in America, for these uncouth strangers to own! We shall see that it is taken out safely, Berthe. I say *we*, for you are the seamstress, and I have thought of an excellent way to carry it. It shall be all sewn in the hems of my clothes—piece by piece—*well* wrapped, of course, and only a few in each, lest the weight make the customs officers suspicious. But this is for the future. Before, there is this Donovan.' She sipped wine reflectively. 'Skyros need not think I am so ignorant. I have seen on the films how it is here, with the gangsters. Quite like the war, Berthe. This little gang and that little gang, and bitter rivalries between. And the police

78

are not at all like the police in Paris, intelligent and honourable men—they are quite as bad as the gangsters, everyone knows that. They would not interfere if they were paid—but only if it is necessary, I do not want to pauperize myself in this affair. We shall see, about that. For the rest, well! This red-haired woman of Donovan's—this Alison Weir—has told him my message by now, he has one more day to take the offered price. If he does not—' She got up and paced back and forth to the window, to the little wine-table, sipping again. 'Ah, let him try to give me the *stall*—I know a trick for that too! These gangsters, one may hire them. One goes to them and says, such a one I wish shot, and the bargain is made. *Voilà!* And I even know one, or at least the name, I remember one small thing Skyros says—it is as if to himself, but I hear the name. Italian—all gangsters are Italians. Except a few like this Donovan who are Irishmen. I have not made up my mind whether I have him shoot Donovan or this red-haired woman—Answer the door, Berthe.'

When the maid came clumping back into the suite she bore a card. 'It's the man who was here before, madame. Monsieur Driscoll.'

'Ah, how annoying! But I must be very polite to them, until they have paid me the money. Very well, let him come in.'

CHAPTER SEVEN

Jackie Donovan sat on a bench in Pershing Square, watching the pigeons, and smoked cigarettes nervously. Pigeons! he thought, savage at himself. Him, Donovan, two weeks out and he sat watching pigeons in the park. The hell of a lot of things he'd kept thinking about, wanting, promising himself for when he got out, and what the hell was wrong with him, he couldn't just go and—

All *different*, somehow. He felt he couldn't get a hold on anything.

Like the car. Damn good of Denny, have it all ready and waiting like that. Handling cars since he was a kid, God, the first job he'd got dropped on for was hopping shorts—but it was *different*. Kept reaching for the clutch, just habit; my God, he'd driven a couple of those first automatics that come out, couple years before he was sent across this time, he ought to catch on quicker. And tell the truth, these freeways, they scared the bejesus out of him. They had different kinds of signals too, those little green arrows, first off he couldn't figure them out. Oh, hell, give him a little time, things bound to be kind of strange at first. That was the longest stretch he'd done, after all. Fifteen years.

The women looked different too. Wearing

skirts short again, well, *that* was O.K., but most of them, it looked like, with these funny short haircuts too—crazy—straight, like a man's, left just anyhow, not curled.

But things like that he'd kind of expected. Bound to be changes. Have to get used to things outside again.

What he hadn't expected, what made him feel funny inside, was this—this not being *sure*. Him, Donovan! Always the brains—ask Jackie, Jackie'll know just how—and God, he didn't, no more. Things in the business changed too, all kinds of the business, names he didn't know, all the old fences gone, new fellows all over. He felt kind of still out of everything.

And some things he'd pulled—Jesus, a ten year-old kid swiping stuff off dime store counters'd know better—Him, Donovan. Been on the list of Ten Most Wanted, once, he had. A big-timer.

He kept thinking about that short— goddamned crazy thing, it didn't *matter*. He'd felt nervous with the Caddy, and when she stalled out there, that day, it'd been kind of like an excuse he was waiting for. That short he'd picked up—you could've fixed her up a little, a real nice piece to handle—you knew where you *were* with her. Always liked a hand choke, and these new things, you never—She didn't ride so good maybe, but—

He'd like to've kept her.

The damn hot short—

It was a hot feeling in his chest, the little panic. Hadn't told Denny, hadn't told anybody how he'd lost that little bit. God, like a kid couldn't be trusted out with a dime—Him!

It must've been in the car. All he could figure: he hadn't a hole in his pocket, and he'd looked good. Damn fool to carry it loose. Must've come out in that car, somehow.

Well, all right, so it could be fixed up O.K. No call to get in a sweat about it. It was just damn lucky he knew how to find the car, on account—damn it, the kind of short he was *used* to—he'd had a kind of crazy idea of keeping it, all on the up-and-up, so's not to mess around with new plates. Denny said you'd pay the hell of a lot for safe plates now. Thought about making up some story, about seeing it parked, wanting it just for transportation like they said—after the guy had it back, go and offer him a hundred bucks for it. So he'd remembered the name on the registration. Funny name for a guy.

Just a little piddling job. Ten to one the thing down in the seat somewhere, nobody knowing it was there. Just had to look up the address, that he didn't remember, find the garage, get in easy—tonight—and go over the car. Why the hell all this sweat about it? Nothing to it. And nobody'd ever know he'd done such a damn fool thing.

All *right*, he thought vaguely, angrily.

Go look up the address, public phone someplace, now. And maybe have a little drink on the way. O.K.

They nicked you six bits for Scotch mostly now. Hell of a thing. Except joints where it was baptized stuff, or made under the counter and like to send you to the General.

And that was another thing. This deal better go through pretty damn quick. Nice of Denny to have a little stake for him, coming out—pull off that job special, celebrate his getting out—but it hadn't been so much as he'd figured, Denny said, account half of it turning out to be this crazy stuff no fence'd look at.

All the more reason, get as much as they could.

He walked out of the park slowly and started down Sixth Street towards Main. He felt more at home down on Main. As much as he did anywhere.

If just things—ordinary things—didn't look so *different*.

He was forty-three years old this year, and he'd spent almost twenty-two of them behind bars.

*   *   *

What the hell, thought Driscoll, and drank out of the bottle, shuddered. He had never consciously admitted to himself that he didn't really like the taste of whisky. It was just one of the things you did, any kind of a fellow at all.

The whisky settled sickly in his stomach and he groaned involuntarily, slumped down on the hotel bed. Damn hot weather. Damn miserly company wouldn't allow enough expenses for a decent hotel, air-conditioned. Damn Howard, supercilious—suspicious— Not *quite up to par lately, Driscoll, and—er—complaints about your offensive manner—I'm afraid—*

Hell with Howard. With his record, let Howard fire him—always find another job. Damn old-fashioned company was all, obsolete ideas about things. You had to keep up a front, play it smart. People took you at face value. So all right, maybe he had been pouring it down kind of heavy, my God, *everybody* did—any fellow who *was* any kind of fellow—Set your brain working better, gave you bright ideas sometimes—and besides—

Damn cops. That Mex, sneering at him—so damn polite, looking down his nose—Looked like a damn gigolo. That suit, Italian silk: and the cufflinks the real thing too—money—a cop: sure, sure, so they said, rare exception these days find a crooked cop!—higher standards, higher quality of men—Probably just as many as there always

84

were, anybody could be bought—

Dirty Mex cop, looking down his nose. Damned if he'd tell him anything. Sure, hell of a lot easier, ask for help on it—their records—fellow who handled the case—way you were supposed to do it. But he could handle it alone, and make Howard sit up and take notice—Say to Howard, damn regular cops no help at all, didn't bother with 'em—

Something going on, all right. Something fishy. That foreign skirt, snotty bitch the way she looked at him, she owned the stuff, or would when the estate was transferred, she had an interest—a racket, sure, shouldn't be hard to get evidence on it, *that* stuff.

Crack it but good, and say to Howard (act real tough, people took you for what you looked like), say, There, boy, who's not doing so hot these days, who's slipping, hah?

He sat up unsteadily and reached for the bottle again. Say to Howard—

★   ★   ★

'Ekaterina Nikolayevna Rosleva,' said the old woman softly, 'speak the truth to me now.'

The girl knew she was in earnest, by the formal address—the old-country form. Anything to do with the old ways and ideas she hated, reminder of how people looked down on her for the foreign name—she'd been born here, she was a citizen, wasn't

85

she?—it wasn't fair. She hated living with the old woman, her slow old-fashioned ways, her needless stories about old days and people all dead now: she resented having to share the money she earned, for this hole-in-the-corner place and food and all it took to live, two people. If it wasn't for the old woman, she could escape.

'Ekaterina—'

'All right, all right, I heard you!' she said, ladling out soup carelessly into the bowls on the table. 'What you think I haven't told you?'

'There is something in your mind, I know.'

'So there's something in my mind. Usually is. Work I got to do tomorrow, clothes I got to mend, bills I got to pay.' She sat down opposite and picked up her spoon.

'You forget, we ask the blessing first.'

Escape—how she'd planned it! She resented the old woman, but one did not leave relatives to public charity, it was a duty. Secretly and often she thought of the old woman dying—then she would be free. She'd go right away from this place, didn't matter where so long as it was a long way off; she'd just leave everything, and start to be somebody else. Somebody new. Not Katya Roslev, but Katharine Ross, good American name, and a better job too, in a high-class shop where ladies came, to watch and listen

86

to for how they acted. All her money her own.

'Somehow I do not feel it is a good thing in your mind,' said the old woman. 'You should be thinking of Stevan. Praying for his soul.'

'I am thinking of Stevan,' said Katya submissively. It was no lie: she was. For perhaps the first time with any real feeling—gratitude.

Catch her marrying a Stevan Domokous! He had been the old woman's idea: *old-fashioned*. These days!—fixing it up all like they did in the old country a hundred years back, *thousand* years back—the bishop and all—a good steady hard-working young man of good family, if all alone in this country. Bah! And to him that's how it had been too—way a man took a wife—picked for her dowry and family and character—not interested in *her*, he'd been, in herself. And a slow one, anyway: a plodder. Honest: too honest.

She'd have found some way out of *that* before spring, that was sure. Katharine Ross, secure in another life, was going to marry somebody with another nice American name and a better job than a clerk's, and that was for sure too. It was a pity Stevan had to die, but at least it did get her rid of him; she was sorry for him, but there it was, it had happened. And maybe it was good luck for her another way, an exciting way too. Escape.

Money, always money, there had to be.

Oh, he had been a slow one! That night, when he'd said about Mr. Skyros talking: she'd said to him, after, when they were on the way to the movies, maybe if he let Mr. Skyros think he heard more, knew all about it, he'd get some pay to promise not to tell. He'd been shocked—or scared, she thought contemptuously—he said, not honest: anything bad the police ought to know!

Well, she wasn't one to split hairs like that. If there was some easy money to be had, she'd take any chance at it. And she'd take care to be smarter than Stevan too—protect herself. She could say she'd written it all out, what he'd told her—about the money—and the writing was—it was in the bank, in one of those boxes rich people kept where nobody could get at it but her—they'd never dare harm her then.

She'd been a fool to come out with it to that policeman, but she hadn't thought about it clear then—seen the chance it offered.

Money. It might be a lot of money. Could she ask for a thousand dollars? Even five thousand? Escape: because that would be the duty money, to leave behind for the old woman—the old woman off her mind then—she could manage on the little she'd saved from her salary—go away with a clear conscience then, the old woman provided for—and start her new life, a long way off.

'You are very silent, Katya,' said the old woman.

'I am thinking of Stevan, as you say I should,' said the girl, and held back a smile.

CHAPTER EIGHT

The two letters from Athens proved to be from casual friends, apparently; there was nothing in them of any significance— references to other friends, to politics, to a church festival of some kind, the weather, questions about Domokous' new life in America.

Nothing else interesting turned up from the more complete examination of the body, or from Dr. Edwin's patient scrutiny of the clothes.

'I suppose I'm a fool to say it,' said Hackett, 'because a lot of times when I say you're barking up a tree with no cat in it, all of a sudden something shows up to prove your crystal ball gave you the right message. And don't complain about mixed metaphors, I'm just a plain cop. But I think it's a dead end. Everything doesn't always dovetail so nice and neat as a detective story, you know.'

'Unfortunately, no,' said Mendoza. 'Ragged edges. No hunch, Arturo—or not much of one. Just—' he swivelled around and looked thoughtfully out of the window of his office, 'just the little funny feeling you get, on discard and draw—better hold onto this worthless-looking low card, next time round it might be worth something ... Damn. I wish I had four times as many men as I had, to keep an eye on everybody. What it comes down to, I don't know much of anything about it at all, I just have the definite conviction there's something *to* know. I'm not really justified in keeping so many on it, but—Damn.' He got up abruptly. 'I'll be up in Callaghan's office if anybody wants me.'

And that was on Thursday morning; he missed Alison's call by five minutes.

He found Callaghan in a temper. Having gone to some trouble to secure enough evidence to charge a certain pusher, Callaghan had wasted yesterday in court only to hear the bench dismiss it as inadmissible by the letter of the law. 'So, my God in heaven, there's got to be law—but what the hell do they expect of us when they tie one hand behind our backs and give us a toy cap pistol and say, Now, boys, you go out and protect the public from the big bad men! Jesus and Mary, next thing they'll be saying to us, Boys, it isn't legal evidence unless you collect it on the northeast corner of a one-way street during an eclipse of the moon! They—'

'Very annoying,' agreed Mendoza, sitting down in the desk chair to be out of Callaghan's way as he paced. Callaghan was even bigger than Hackett, which was saying something, and it was not a large office.

'You can talk!' said Callaghan bitterly. 'All you got to think about is dead people! Who was there, who wanted them dead? Clear as day—evidence all according to the book! Nobody says to you—'

'Oh, we run into it too, occasionally. Now calm down and talk to me about Bratti.'

'I don't want even to think about Bratti,' said Callaghan. 'I'm goin' to quit the force and take up some nice peaceful occupation like farming. Why should I knock myself out protecting the public? They don't give a damn about me. They call *me* an officious cop, persecutin' innocent bystanders—'

'You'll wear out the carpet, Patrick.'

'And I'll tell you something else! One thing like this—and the good God knows it's not the first or the last—and every single pro in this town, he has a good laugh at the cops, and he gets twice as cocky as he was before, because he knows damn well we can beat our brains out and never get him inside—'

'You'll give yourself ulcers. Bratti.'

'Get out of my chair,' said Callaghan, and flung himself into it and drove a hand through his carrot-red hair. 'What about Bratti?'

'He'll be in competition with some others in business on his level. Middlemen, who run strings of pushers.'

91

'Oh, all very businesslike these days. Sure. Same position, almost exactly, as the fellow owns a lot of slum tenements. Fellow who says, hell, you always get some people who like to live like that, why should I go to the expense of cleaning up the place, make it a little fancier for 'em? In six months it's just as bad. I don't cut my profits for any such damn foolishness. But he doesn't live there himself, oh, no, he's got a nice clean new house out in Bel-Air. He hires an agent to collect the rent so he needn't mingle with the *hoi polloi* and listen to complaints. *If* you get me. Gimme a cigarette, I'm out ... There's Bratti. And in this burg, call it about a dozen like him. Sure, 'way up at the top there's a hook-up with the syndicate—with the real big boys, and we know where *they* are these days. Sitting happy as clams in some country where they can't be extradited—even if, God help us, we had any admissible evidence to charge 'em with—'

'Pray a moment's silence,' said Mendoza sardonically, 'while we return thanks to the Bureau of Internal Revenue for small mercies.'

'Very damn small,' said Callaghan gloomily. 'Sure, sure, about the only legal charge on some of those boys. Only some of them. I'm not worrying about 'em—I can't, who can?—like worrying about the bomb. I don't know the answer to the syndicates, except it's a little bit like killing fleas on a

92

dog—you've got to get after the little ones so they can't grow up to be big ones—and you can't stop a minute because they breed like, well, fleas. The ones here and now I got to worry about are the syndicate agents and the boys like Bratti and the boys they hire. The port authorities can worry about the stuff coming in, and isn't it God's truth, they could do with ten times more men like all of us. It gets in. This way, that way. And it gets to the agents. And they get it to the Brattis. And the Brattis—wearin' kid gloves and takin' great care of their respectable surfaces—they see it gets to the pushers. Everybody making the hell of a profit every time it changes hands—strictly cash basis, no credit—because it gets cut so much on the way. A little deck of H worth a hundred bucks raw, coming in, by the time it gets to Bratti to distribute, it's twenty times bigger and worth a thousand times the cash.'

'This isn't news to me, friend. I've been on the force just as long as you. All about Bratti, *por favor.*'

'I could write a book,' said Callaghan, 'and what good would it do me? I don't know what kind of background he came from, but I'd guess he's had a fair education, he uses pretty good English. Let that go. I don't know where he got his capital. For the legitimate business, that is—about *that* I know, it's out in the open for anybody to see—ambitious

93

young man makes good: starts with one small hole-in-the-wall joint and builds it up. Once in a while it does make you think—he's doing all right on the right side of the law, you know. A lot of people saying the pros, it's because they get branded—nobody'll give 'em a job, nobody'll teach 'em a useful trade, so they stay pros—that's not the answer, as any cop could tell them. They've just got a king somewhere. I don't know how long Bratti's been in the other business. That kind, they spring up overnight like toadstools. And when he drops dead of a heart attack—*or* when we get the goods on him—and the position's open, somebody else'll be right there to take over. Just as he took over—or maybe built up *that* business for himself. No, my God, that's not the syndicate thing—why should the big boys worry about organizing that low?—it's standard business procedure. And how do I know about Bratti? I'll tell you, though God help me if I ever said it to a judge! About eighteen months ago we picked up a pusher by the name of Fred Ring—we thought we had some nice solid evidence on him—but at the last minute the witness reneged and jumped bail on us, and he had a record so the judge looked down his nose and said the mere signed statement wasn't worth a whoop in hell, and threw it out. But while we had Ring, we ran a tape on some of his interviews with visitors, all underhand as hell—and of course since that Supreme Court decision *that's* inadmissible evidence too—but it gave us Bratti's name. We gathered Bratti was paying the lawyer. Which put Ring, ten to one, as the head pusher. Bratti and the boys like him, they don't want too many of these irresponsible underlings knowing their names and faces and addresses. For one thing, it's not very unusual for a pusher—the man on the street—to sample his own goods. There's a big turnover in pushers: the personnel, as a business report'd say, fluctuates. Some of 'em get to be customers, on the other side of the fence, and that kind—or any of 'em—could be dangerous to the next highest man on the totem pole. O.K. There'll be one, usually, heading the string, taking delivery of supplies and handing 'em out, the one who knows the middleman. We think Ring was it at the time. We kept a very close eye on him, but didn't get anything. We have also been keeping an eye on Bratti, with the same result. Ring didn't last long after that—'

'Fished out of the bay one foggy morning?'

'Why, you bloodthirsty Latin,' said Callaghan, 'you ought to know as well as me we're twenty, thirty years away from that kind of thing. Of course not—he got to liking his own wares too much and finally passed out in the General. They aren't gangsters any more, they're just syndicate men, and employees of syndicate men, and customers of the syndicates. Like the big corporations of other kinds, the syndicates deal with subsidiaries—and it's all very quiet and business-like. They know it doesn't pay, it's not only dangerous to their continued operation but cuts into net profits, if they go roaring around like I've heard tell they used to, pumping lead into anybody gets in their way. That just doesn't happen any more. The big boys are awful leery of the law these days, and the hell of a lot smarter—they've found out, for one thing, a smart shyster is less expensive in the long run than the old-fashioned canister man you just gave orders to go out and bump off So-and-So, and don't waste cartridges. Look at Bratti. Thirty years ago Bratti would have been a barely literate lout—standard type as per the Hollywood version—anybody'd know him for a gangster minute they laid eyes on him. Today, you can't tell him from any other man in a crowd, except maybe he's a little better dressed. He knows how to behave in polite society, he's married and has a couple of kids, he pays his bills on time, he's a respectable householder. Far as I know, never even got a traffic ticket. Most of 'em are like that these days, the boys with any authority—even the junior executives. One thing, they've got to have cover for the tax boys in Washington, and most of 'em are running legal business on the side. They've found out it's a lot nicer, quieter life havin' a permanent home and all, not being on the run half the time. Sure, human nature doesn't change, and there are still the feuds between gangs of this sort and that, the jealousy *and* the fear and the loose-mouths who'll tell what they know to anybody pays 'em, and the men who'll do the same thing to pay off a grudge. But why should Bratti or anybody else keep a hot cannon man at his elbow? Almost impossible to tattle to the cops on one man, you know—a threat on one is a threat on all, and all of 'em know that.'

'You're lecturing,' complained Mendoza. 'Now listen to me for a minute. I've got a very simple little problem, nothing so vast as yours by a long way. Here's a dead man, full of heroin. I don't *know* whether it was his first shot or whether he gave it to himself, on the evidence, but in my own mind I'm pretty sure it was, and he didn't. It looks, and it could be so, as if he went down an alley to take his little jolt, took too big a one and died there. A lot of holes in him where users stick their needles—arms and thighs—but all put in him, the surgeon *thinks*, after death. Can't swear positively it wasn't just before death, that it wasn't him, getting up nerve. If it was, that doesn't, of course, look like a habitual user. But it could have been his first, voluntary jolt. O.K. His employer was one

97

Andreas Skyros, importer, prosperous, looks very much according to Hoyle on the surface, ¿comprende? He's very shocked and sad over this unfortunate misguided young fellow led into bad ways by new acquaintances. And he says when he reprimanded the young man for being slow at his work, the young man mentioned the name Bratti as—by implication—one of the said acquaintances.'

'You don't say,' said Callaghan. 'Not much there. Bratti wouldn't be working the street himself, making up to potential customers, all pals together. Try a little of this for what ails you.'

'Exactly. I have the feeling that—as so often happens—we're being underrated. Nobody else who knew the corpse remembers him mentioning the name. So I just got to wondering about Mr. Skyros.'

'Never heard of him.'

'But there was heroin in the corpse—that's how it got to be a corpse. And—'

'Down on Carson Street,' nodded Callaghan. 'I got the memo somewhere. Whereabouts?'

'In an alley just down from Carson and Main.'

'You *don't* say,' said Callaghan. 'Bratti's first joint is on that corner—he still owns it. He branched out later in classier directions—has a place out on Ventura and another on La Cienega now.'

'*Vaya, vaya*,' said Mendoza, 'does he indeed? That makes me wonder even harder. Have you ever sat in a game, Pat, with a pro sharp?—where the cold deck was rung in, and cards forced on you?'

'Yes,' said Callaghan, 'or I got a strong suspicion I have, anyway. I've sat in some hands of draw with you, before you got to be a millionaire and can't be bothered to shuffle a pack for less than five hundred in the kitty. Mind you, I could never prove it, you're too damn smooth, but a couple of times I had the distinct feeling that you had another deck up your sleeve.'

'Slander,' grinned Mendoza. 'It's just that I have more courage and skill as a gambler—you've got no finesse, and you let the thought of the rent and the car payment intrude and back out too soon. Fatal. What I started to say was, I just had a little feeling that that casual throwing off of Bratti's name was—mmh—something like the dealer handing me a royal flush first time round, out of a deck of readers. And me, it's maybe evidence of a suspicious and ungrateful nature, but a long while ago I learned you don't get something for nothing. I wouldn't be surprised about the royal flush if that particular dealer owed me a little favour—*¿como no?*—but as it was, why should Mr. Skyros hand it to me on a silver platter?'

'You think he did?' Callaghan cocked his
99

head at him. 'I don't deny it, you get feelings about these things, I know. Our Luis, crystal ball in his back pocket.'

'I think he did,' said Mendoza. 'I think he knew what card he was dealing me. And so I wondered, you know, if maybe Mr. Skyros had some little grudge on Mr. Bratti. And if so, why.'

Callaghan got up and paced down the office. 'It's a piddling little thing ... And I might feel the hell of a lot more inclined to take you at face value if *I* didn't have a suspicious nature—knowing you—and get the unworthy idea maybe you just haven't got the men to spare to keep an eye on this Skyros.'

'You wrong me. I'm being scrupulous— keeping you briefed on what might be your business.'

'Andreas Skyros. Where?'

Mendoza told him home and office address. Callaghan wrote them down. 'You think *I've* got any more men to send out?' he asked. 'And on a homicide! That's your business. For a change, *I've* got a hunch. End of this thing'll be a homicide charge, nothing for me at all, and you'll be the one to get your name in the papers—arresting officer. Talk about cold decks. O.K., O.K., I'll have a look into it.'

'*Muchas gracias,*' said Mendoza meekly.

*　　*　　*

He came back to his office and among other things found the message about Alison's call. Quite a few other matters, besides this nebulous business of Stevan Domokous, under his jurisdiction; and in any case he was scrupulous about mixing business with outside concerns. Ten-forty: she'd probably be lecturing her current class on the proper use of mascara or something similar. He went over a few reports on other present cases, from Sergeants Galeano, Clock, and Schanke: cleared up some accumulated routine. It was eleven forty-five when he called her, at her office.

'I wouldn't have bothered you,' said Alison, 'it's none of your business—scarcely so melodramatic as homicide—but really it is maddening, how even these days so many men seem to have it firmly fixed in their minds that all females are scatterbrained and prone to hysterics. I grant you, some of it's our own fault—these women who make a fetish of being career girls, twice as efficient as any mere male. I mean, a lot of it's automatic self-defence on the part of the implied mere males, and I can't say I blame them. Shakespeare—you know—protesting too much. Better or worse, females *are* apt to be less objective about things, it's the way we're made. Which I suppose is my excuse, automatic seeking for sensible male advice.'

101

'Yes,' said Mendoza, 'I agree with you every time, what you mean is women jump to conclusions and call it intuition. What—'

'And there's the pot calling the kettle black,' said Alison. 'What else is one of your famous hunches? Well, never mind. The thing is, somebody broke into my garage last night and apparently went over the car. As if they were looking for something, anyway that's what it looked like to me. When I came to get it this morning, the front seat was all pulled out—teetering on the supports. So far as I can see nothing was taken, but—'

'I'll be damned,' said Mendoza. 'Look, meet me at Federico's for lunch, I want to hear about this.'

'Well, all right, but I can't take much time—it's a little drive. Half an hour?'

'Half an hour.'

He was waiting for her when she arrived. 'I've already ordered, save time. Now, go on from where you left off. What about the garage door? I don't know that I've ever noticed the garages—usual arrangement, couple of rows of them, single garage for each apartment?'

'That's right. And to anticipate, none of them have windows, and five other garages had their padlocks forced. Mr. Corder happened to come out just after me, and found his broken, and we looked, and found the others. I hadn't thought much about

102

mine, you see. It's an old one, the padlock, and rusted, and it does stick sometimes—I'll think it's closed and then find it's just stuck halfway. I suppose it's careless of me, but quite a few times I've put the car away after dark and next morning found the padlock wasn't closed properly. So I hadn't thought twice about finding it that way this morning. Not until I saw the car, with the driver's door open and the seat pulled out. Everything intact as far as I can see—there wasn't anything there to take, of course, except some maps and cleaning rags in the glove compartment.'

'The seat,' said Mendoza. 'That thing you found—'

'Yes, I thought of it right away. It doesn't seem to belong to anyone I know. And we have it dinned into us so much about co-operating with the police—I was just trying to be a dutiful citizen. I called that sergeant again and told him about it, but he obviously thought I was imagining things—just a nervous female. Well, I thought *somebody* ought to know—'

'He didn't send anyone up to look?'

'Oh, yes. At least *he* didn't, but he said to call the local precinct. Which Mr. Corder already had. And a couple of men came up and looked at everything. It was a nuisance, of course, made us both awfully late—but we left everything just as it was for them. And they looked in the other garages, and said it was probably kids.'

'Any other car touched?'

'No. And that was just it. It was only mine. So I told those men all about it, because it seemed rather open-and-shut to me. There being no windows, I mean—he didn't know which garage, and he had to try several garages before he found the right car. And they looked at me pityingly—these imaginative females!—and said all over again it was probably kids, just messing around.'

'Yes. You can't really blame them, on the face of it it sounds too vague and—apologies—the sort of thing a nervous female might dream up. But it *is* suggestive, isn't it? It might be—it could be—whoever dropped that thing. And on the other hand—all that trouble, hunting up the car and so on, just for—Has there been any vandalism of that sort, kids roaming around at night and getting into mischief, in the neighbourhood?'

'Not that I know of.'

'And nothing to get hold of on it, any more than on my little business ... And I might have known,' added Mendoza as Hackett drifted up to the table, 'that I couldn't have lunch in peace, not opposite a pretty female anyway, without you barging in.'

'It's not the redhead,' said Hackett, '—hello, Miss Weir, and apologies to tell the

104

truth—it's the chance of sticking you with the bill, Luis.'

'Neither of you'll be sitting opposite long,' said Alison. 'I've got to get back. I wondered if I ought to advertise it, you know—d'you think it'd do any good?'

'I do not. If he, she, or it knows for pretty certain it must have been lost in the car, they'd recognize an ad as a trap.'

'Oh!—of course, I didn't see that. But it's such a little thing—'

'Yes. One piece of advice I'll give you, knowing your casual habits, *chica*. Put the chain up on your door and keep those two windows near the fire escape locked.'

'My lord, you don't really think—? But I'd suffocate, those are the north windows where the only air comes in—You can't think, just for a little thing like that—?'

'Somebody went to a little trouble to look in the car. If it wasn't just kids' random mischief, and you're not imagining things. *No se sabe nunca*—one never knows ... You remember what I say now, *¿comprende? Y hasta muy pronto*,' as she rose to leave.

'Well, all right, I can't stop to argue now,' said Alison, and fled back to her class.

'And what was all that about, if it's any of my business?' asked Hackett.

'It's not, but they say two heads are better than one.' Mendoza told him.

'That's a funny one, all right. Maybe one of

105

these superstitious nuts, it's his best lucky talisman or something?'

'Could be. I don't know. I don't know anything about anything,' said Mendoza, regarding his coffee gloomily. 'And there's another funny little thing tied up to it that—Maybe I'm getting old, Art. Losing my grip.'

'All come out in the wash,' said Hackett. 'The trouble with you is, you've got what they call a tortuous mind. You build up little picayune things to worry about, that don't mean a damn. Like this Domokous thing. It's *un callejón sin salida*, boy—a dead-end street. Higgins checked in on Skyros just after you left. If he's playing games with the exotic brunette, they haven't even got to Post Office yet. He goes from home to office and vice versa, and that's all. The brunette—I borrowed one of Galeano's men to check on her—is staying at the Beverly-Hilton. She's one Madame Rafael Bouvardier, of Paris, and she's apparently loaded. Has her own maid with her, and a suite. No expense spared.'

'That was the picture,' agreed Mendoza. 'What's her first name and what's she doing here?'

'How should I know? She hasn't confided in the hotel people. Just a pleasure trip, probably. Though why pick L.A. in this season, God knows. She's been here about three weeks. Don't tell me you want her

106

tailed too. We just haven't got a man free.'

'But I can think of unpleasanter jobs,' said Mendoza. 'I might even take it on myself—keep my hand in, so to speak.'

'*¡No hay más*, that's all, brother!' said Hackett. 'Since when do you need practice chasing skirts? Just an excuse to take the afternoon off!'

CHAPTER NINE

Mendoza had said, no hunch; and he didn't have that unreasonably sure conviction that this or that was so. It was more on the order of that uneasy doubt as to whether one had left the gas turned on or the faucet running.

He had no further guilty feeling that he was wasting time, but he drove out to the Beverly-Hilton, and was waiting his turn at the desk clerk to frame some discreet questions about Madame Bouvardier, when he saw her descending the nearest stair into the lobby. No expense spared, that you could say again, he reflected: very Parisian, very exotic—again the wide lace-brimmed hat, another black-and-white printed silk gown, what at least looked like diamonds, long gloves, fragile high heels.

And well met: so, wasting time, but might as well be hanged for a sheep as a lamb. He abandoned the line at the desk and strolled after her, with a vague idea of picking her up somehow, all very gentlemanly and polite, and getting confidential over a drink—as confidential as she could be persuaded, and at that he flattered himself he was far more accomplished than any of his sergeants.

But she didn't establish herself conveniently in the lobby, the adjacent lounge, or the bar; she walked purposefully out the main door, and Mendoza drifted up in time to hear her ask the doorman for Madame Bouvardier's car.

'Yes, madame, the chauffeur's just gone out, he'll be here directly, madame.'

Hell, thought Mendoza, and turned back for the side door and sprinted for the Facel-Vega in the middle of the lot. Hired car and driver, the chauffeur calling from the lobby to announce arrival—he wouldn't be sixty seconds picking her up. He thrust coins at the attendant and switched on the engine almost in one motion.

But he was just in time, taking the wide curve out to Wilshire, to catch a glimpse of the lace hat through the rear window of a stately black middle-aged Chrysler. He was held up a couple of cars behind, but the Chrysler wasn't hard to keep in view along here; it went straight up Wilshire at a steady pace, heading back for Hollywood. Before they got into town, Mendoza managed to pass the cars ahead and fall in directly behind it.

A couple of blocks this side of La Brea, the Chrysler turned left and went round the block, and Mendoza dropped back a little, guessing at a stop. Middle of the block, and the chauffeur'd gone around to drop her on the right side; he hopped out smartly, illegally double-parked, and opened the door, and out she came, said a few words. Probably as to where and when to pick her up. Mendoza was legitimately caught in this lane by the halted Chrysler, an excuse for watching. The chauffeur touched his cap, grinned apology over his shoulder at Mendoza, and ran around to the driver's door again. And Madame Bouvardier vanished through the door of an elegant black-glass-marble-fronted shop labelled in discreet gold script, *Shanrahan and MacReady*.

'Well, well,' said Mendoza sadly to himself. 'A mare's nest. With a clutch of wild goose eggs in it.' But he turned the next corner, miraculously found a parking space, and strolled back to keep an eye on the black glass door.

In twenty minutes it opened and she came out and turned in his direction. He stayed where he was, propping the wall of the bank on the corner, and his flagging interest was slightly aroused by her expression as she passed him: she was biting her lower lip, looking thoughtful and annoyed. She carried no parcel, and her bag was too small to conceal even a little one.

She walked on half a block, stopping a few times to look in windows, and disappeared into the plush elegance of Chez Frédéric, Coiffures.

'Oh, hell,' said Mendoza to himself. She hadn't stopped at the counter in there, but with a white-robed attendant at her elbow passed on into the rear premises. Be there for hours, very likely.

What did he think he was doing, anyway? You couldn't expect a tailing job to turn up something interesting in the first hour. If he wanted to know more about the female, put a man on her, and preserve patience.

And no reason she shouldn't have gone where she did. A place any woman might go. But, as long as he was here—

He turned around and walked back to *Shanrahan and MacReady*.

* * *

Mr. Brian Shanrahan welcomed him into the chaste quietude of the shop with subdued cries of delight, or what passed for that with a dignified middle-aged professional man of repute.

'And what may I have the pleasure of showing you today? Perhaps at last something

110

in a wedding set? I have—'

'You and my grandmother,' said Mendoza.

'And how is the charming señora? Such an interesting old lady—'

'You find her interesting,' said Mendoza, 'because she's the cautious type who likes to put money into portable value she can look at instead of six per cent common stock, and is one of your best customers. It's not for want of telling she hasn't grasped that you figure a two hundred percent mark-up.'

'Now that's slander, Mendoza,' said Shanrahan aggrievedly. 'Seldom more than a hundred and fifty. And if it's something for her birthday, she was in and briefed me thoroughly. There's this bracelet she has her eye on, very fine stones, if you'd like to look—'

'No,' said Mendoza. 'It's ridiculous, and I refuse to be a party to it. I'd like to inherit something from her eventually besides stock for a secondhand jewellery shop. I didn't come in to buy anything, I want some information.'

Mr. Shanrahan sighed and asked what about.

'A few minutes ago a woman came in here—a very exotic, expensive-looking young woman—black and white ensemble, lace-brimmed hat, gloves—'

'And diamonds in some very old-fashioned mountings,' nodded the jeweller intelligently.

111

'Friend of yours?'

'Heaven forbid, not my type—'

'Didn't know you had one.'

'What did she want? Who waited on her?'

'As a matter of fact I did.'

'Of course, you took one look and she spelled Money, so you wouldn't trust her to an underling.'

'Or I tried to. She looked at a couple of things, but she wasn't really interested. If she hadn't—um—as you say, looked quite so expensive, I might have put her down as an amateur novelist looking for information. The first thing she came out with was, what enormous value all these beautiful things must represent, we must have to be very careful about thieves. Did we have a burglar alarm? Did we have a night watchman? Had we ever suffered a robbery? All in machine-gun style, and a *very* thick accent.'

'*¡Vaya por Dios!*' said Mendoza. 'I refuse to believe that she came in to, as the pros say, case the joint! Now what the devil—'

'Good God,' said Mr. Shanrahan. 'You don't think—'

'No, I don't, it's ridiculous, I just said so. A suite at the Beverly-Hilton, her own maid—and those clothes—Impossible.'

'Good *God*,' said Mr. Shanrahan again. 'Burglary. Don't even suggest it. Another one. We average three a year, and this is really too soon after the last—only three weeks. My heart won't take this sort of thing much longer—not to speak of the insurance company. Really, Mendoza!'

'Don't look at me, I'm not the mastermind plotting it—if there is a plot. Lose much in that one?'

'Oh, well, it could have been *worse*,' said Mr. Shanrahan discreetly. Mr. Shanrahan would always be discreet, even with an old customer who was by way of being a friend. He glanced sidewise at Mendoza, opened his mouth for further speech, decided against it, and whisked out his handkerchief to clean his glasses instead. 'It's the principle of the thing. And, as I say, the insurance.'

'Yes. Did this woman say anything else?'

'One has to be polite. I was—um—noncommittal, you know, and then she got onto insurance. We must have to carry a terrible amount of insurance, all these valuable things, and also, it was to be supposed, sometimes things which do not belong to us. Was it not a great financial burden? My God, Mendoza, you *don't* suppose—?'

'No, I don't. I don't know what she was after. *Insurance. ¡Media vuelta!*—right about face! I don't know anything, damn it. *¡Mil rayos!* So far as I know, she's simply a rich visiting foreigner, eminently respectable, and she didn't mean anything sinister at all—just talking off the top of her mind. And I am

113

wasting the afternoon. I shall now cease to do so and go back to legitimate work.'

'I hope to God you're right,' said Mr. Shanrahan nervously. 'Now just a moment, Mendoza, as long as you're here you might as well take a look at this bracelet—no *harm*—won't take a minute, just let me fetch it out for you—'

Mendoza looked at it, heard the price, said it was outrageous, and named another twenty per cent below. Shanrahan told him coldly that this was not a street-booth in a village market, where haggling was expected; there were prices set and that was that, take it or leave it. 'Don't give me that,' said Mendoza. 'What with taxes and inflation, luxury business isn't living so high it can pick and choose customers. How long have you had this in stock without a bite on it?' Shanrahan looked offended and after much persuasion named a price five per cent under the original. They insulted each other for another five minutes and came to a deadlock on the Federal tax, Mendoza refusing to be responsible for it. Shanrahan offered to split it with him.

'I'll think about it,' said Mendoza, picking up his hat.

Shanrahan looked at him wistfully. 'I live for the day when you get hooked by some predatory empty-headed blonde.'

114

'And you'll still be hoping when they nail down your coffin,' said Mendoza.

*   *   *

He went back to his office and ruminated. First causes, he thought: so, what about Domokous? Look at the facts available, build it up from there.

Hackett had collected a number of little facts by now. The Second Street hotel was largely tenanted by residents, not transients; there was supposed to be a desk clerk on duty most of the time, but actually it was a desultory job. The clerk remembered Domokous going out that Monday night about seven o'clock, but couldn't say whether he'd come in again: didn't recall seeing him go out on the Tuesday morning, but he might have—the clerk didn't always see residents in or out. And friends of residents, if they knew the room number, would walk right up; the clerk couldn't keep track of everybody.

It looked as if that Monday night might be the crucial time, because Domokous hadn't come to work on Tuesday.

The clerk said he'd certainly never seen Domokous the worse for drinks; ditto, the other clerks and the pretty bookkeeper at Skyros, Inc. The artistic little tale Mr. Skyros had told looked fishier in consequence.

But there could be—considering the nymph and the dolphin—a relatively innocent

115

explanation. If Skyros was sailing a bit near the wind in his business, say over some matter of customs duty, something like that—it needn't have one thing to do with Domokous' death—Skyros might easily be nervous, want the death passed off as smoothly as possible without investigation too close to home. So he'd just bolstered up the truth with enough imaginary detail to satisfy authority, get the cops off his neck.

Driscoll ... Yes, quite outside Domokous' death, the insurance firm with an eye on Skyros? And Domokous just what he looked like, victim of a pusher. Those puncture marks in him—But it could be. People, as Bainbridge sententiously said, did some damned funny things. That knock on the head: all right, heroin didn't kill instantaneously, and he might have got it when he fell in that alley, when the heroin got to him.

A couple of funny little points that Mendoza didn't much like, the business about Bratti, for instance. Was there any connection between Skyros and Bratti? But even that could be innocent. Skyros might have heard the name from Domokous, some time when no one else was around. It just could be.

He had got that far thinking about first causes when Sergeant Lake came in and said, 'There's the longest beard I've ever seen just

116

came in—you can see there's some sort of fellow behind it, but not much of him—and says he wants to see you. Claims he's a priest of some kind.'

'I've just gone out,' said Mendoza, in instant reaction to the word. And then he said, 'Wait a minute—a beard? A priest—a Greek? Possibly a Greek bearing gifts? Shoot him in, Jimmy!'

It was in truth a magnificent beard—pepper-and-salt, and curly; it cascaded from high on its owner's cheekbones to somewhere well below where his waist would have been if he'd had one. Mendoza eyed it with respect and ambiguous feelings. Having the tiresome sort himself which called for a second shave if he was to appear in public in the evening, he'd often thought how convenient it would have been to live in an era when beards were *de rigueur*; on the other hand, in this kind of weather it must be rather like carrying around a portable electric blanket. He stood up and took the proffered hand; above the beard a pair of gentle grey eyes blinked at him shortsightedly through old-fashioned round rimless glasses.

'I hope I don't disturb you inconveniently, Lieutenant. Er—Nikolas Papoulos, if I may introduce—'

'And you are a parish priest of a local Orthodox church. I think perhaps—sit down, won't you—you've come to tell me that you

117

knew Stevan Domokous?'

'Dear me, you really are a detective, then.' The eyes twinkled at him briefly. 'We hear these days how efficient our police force is—just yesterday my wife called my attention to a most interesting article in the *Times*—but I digress—however, this convinces me. Efficient indeed.' The eyes lost their twinkle. 'But it's a sad errand I come on, yes. And I should apologize not to have come before. But I've been ill, and also I hesitated—it really seemed a minor—It was only yesterday I learned of this dreadful thing. Er—Mr. Skyros, whom I do not know—he approached me about the service for poor Stevan. I understand the city morgue had only just released the body. I was much shocked, Lieutenant—and I may say grieved, for though I had not known Stevan long, he was a faithful attendant at church and seemed an eminently good young man. I could hardly believe it, in fact, I *can* hardly believe it.'

Mendoza said conventionally that of course it was always a little shock to friends and relatives. It was charitable of Domokous' employer to assume the cost of the funeral.

'Er—I daresay,' said the priest. He unwound the thin wire bows of his glasses from around his ears slowly and began to polish the lenses with his handkerchief. 'I daresay. But—perhaps it's uncharitable of me,' he said earnestly, and his myopic naked

118

eyes swam blindly in Mendoza's general direction, 'but much experience with human nature leads me to wonder about it.'

'The Greek, in fact, bearing gifts?'

'Dear me, yes, very appropriate, Lieutenant. Indeed. I—dear me, it *is* difficult—I debated long with myself about coming. You know, one doesn't like to encourage *slander*, and yet, perhaps, it would be just as well for you to hear about it. I can only trust'—he began to wind the wires back around his ears, and his eyes swam into focus again, looking anxious—'that you will not place more importance on it than is actually warranted.'

'Well, we're used to evaluating statements. What is it?'

The priest sighed. 'It may mean nothing at all, you see. It seems that Stevan's death was only an unfortunate accident, that he was the victim of one of these drug pedlars—by what appeared in the newspapers, at least. I'd have said that it was quite incredible that he would be persuaded into such a thing, but I know these dreadful things happen. And it seems even more incredible that what he told me could have led to—to a *deliberate* accomplishing of his death—no, no, I cannot accept that. However, the more I thought about it—especially after Mr. Skyros called me—that is, one doesn't like to feel suspicious of the motives for charity, does one, but all the same—Well, I thought perhaps the police should hear. Just in the event that it *is* important. And I trust I am not spreading slander to tell you! Here is the matter, Lieutenant. Stevan came to me—now let me get the date right, I must be accurate—yes, a week ago last Sunday it was, the Sunday evening. He wanted advice. Perhaps you've heard that he was not quite as familiar with English as he might have been. Well, now, it seems that on the previous evening he had worked later than usual, and had had occasion to ask his employer some question, and so gone to his office. He said it was not usual for Mr. Skyros to be there after hours, but perhaps it was something to do with this shipment of goods just arrived; at any rate, there he was. And there was someone with Mr. Skyros—another man. Stevan heard them speaking together before he knocked on the door—you must not think he eavesdropped deliberately, but he hesitated to intrude, you see, when he heard that Mr. Skyros had a visitor, and possibly there was a transom open or something like that, I could not say. He was most disturbed over what he had overheard. He said it sounded to be something to do with a crime, and yet he wasn't sure—you see they were speaking English. And he asked me what I thought he should do. He was such a very honest young man.' The priest sighed again.

'I'll tell you,' said Mendoza slowly, 'this isn't the first I've heard of that. His fiancée and her grandmother—the Roslevs—have been in. He mentioned it to them too.'

'Ah, yes—I see—of course. Poor girl, poor girl. Not that I will say I feel quite the sympathy for Katya that I do for the old woman ... But then you know—'

'They couldn't tell me much. Possibly he told you more in any case. Did he tell you exactly what he overheard?'

'Well, frankly, Lieutenant, I must admit that I couldn't make much of it myself. He did try to repeat it to me. He heard Mr. Skyros say, "It will be necessary to make up some story for the insurance people, madness to keep that money of course, they'll be keeping an eye on her afterwards and there's all the trouble of taking the stuff out of the country—but that's for later, her business, and nothing to do with you. I'll fix up something." And the other man, who sounded, Stevan said, very uneducated, uncouth, he said it was—er—"a hell of a lot of dough for *that* stuff." And Mr. Skyros said something about it being all how you looked at it, and Stevan said, to be—how shall I put it—falsely genial with this other. And the other man said then, if that was so, how did he know it wasn't worth more than Skyros said; and Skyros replied that a thing one had to sell under the counter was worth only what

121

a buyer was willing to pay, and ten thousand was a good profit. And then the second man said something about the County Museum.'

'The *County Museum?*'

'Well, the actual words Stevan quoted to me were, I think, "that museum place out Exposition", which I took to be—'

'Yes. Odd.'

'It was, you see, the phrase "under the counter" which worried Stevan. He asked me what he ought to do, he said Mr. Skyros had been kind to him, giving him a job when he was still slow at writing the English and so on, and he did not like to seem ungrateful, but that on the other hand he wanted to become a good citizen, and anything bad, perhaps criminal, the police should know. I advised him—rightly or wrongly—to do nothing unless he was sure of some wrongdoing. I said he had really nothing to take to the police.'

'Quite right,' said Mendoza. 'Nothing there at all actually. That's all he heard? ... Yes. Well, I'm glad to hear a little more about it than the Roslevs could tell me, but—'

'It doesn't seem to mean much? I am relieved to hear you say so, Lieutenant. I only wondered—as I say, uncharitable of me. But I thought it my duty to come and tell you, in case it should mean more to you than to myself.'

'Yes, very good of you to come in,' said

Mendoza absently.

'Er—businessmen—doubtless merely a little something to do with his business—and Stevan misunderstood—I feel I may have been leaping to melodramatic conclusions—'

'Well, one never knows.' And was there any reason to ask for a formal statement? Hearsay evidence. Not yet: perhaps never. He thanked the priest again, listened to a few more mild ramblings about Domokous, and saw him out politely.

Nada absolutamente, damn it. He refused to believe that Skyros or anybody else had committed murder—and a fairly elaborate murder, at that—to prevent that amiable, honest young man from repeating that vague little story. It didn't mean enough. The obvious conclusion, if you were determined to make it murder, was that if Domokous had been killed over that business, he'd found out more about it, enough to be dangerous. The priest had told him, do nothing unless you are sure of wrongdoing. Had Domokous, perhaps, gone looking for something more to say yes or no? And, to his misfortune, found it?

CHAPTER TEN

Mendoza let all that simmer gently in his mind overnight—not much else he could do. It looked very much as if this was going to be one of those cases where there'd never be the evidence to bring anyone to book, even if he found the answer to the problem. The kind of thing where you were pretty sure there'd been funny business of some sort, but couldn't prove it. Of course, there was some gain: *if* Domokous had died because he was a little too honest, he had managed to call attention to Skyros and (if she had anything to do with it at all) Madame Bouvardier, and Callaghan at least would be taking a look at Skyros.

Once in a while you got something like that—the kind of thing Pat ran into more—no legal evidence available. And sometimes, a while later something else happened and you could say, Ah, so that's what was behind it—but ten to one no evidence forthcoming then—just the satisfaction of knowing for sure.

Insurance, he reflected. Mixed up in it somehow?—by the bits and pieces he had. A *nymph* and a *dolphin*—¡oye, qué va!—some precious shipment of imports? And what had the County Museum to do with it?

However, something useful might be got

out of that fellow Driscoll. Citizens' duty to aid the police when requested.

He had no chance the next morning to do anything about that; he'd got to his office when his inside phone rang.

'Returning favours,' said Callaghan. 'Fair exchange.'

'What, have you got something already?'

'A kind of interesting little bit that might be more for you than me. My man took over Skyros from yours about four o'clock yesterday. De La Torres—very good man, nose like a bloodhound. Well, Skyros stayed late at his office, and along about seven o'clock he had a visitor. At the back door, and as it happened De La Torres was halfway down the delivery-entrance alley and it wasn't dark yet, daylight saving still being with us, and he had a look at him as the fellow went in. Door left unlocked for him, all very hospitable. And De La Torres recognized him, so he slipped up to the corner drugstore—taking a chance on losin' 'em both but sometimes you've got to take chances—and put in a call for somebody to take on the guy when he left, if possible.'

'And who was he and why did De La Torres know him?'

'Believe it or not his name's Prettyman. He isn't, very. We picked him up about three years ago for unlawful possession, that was before they put in the stiffer sentences, and

125

he only got sixty days. No other record on him. But as it happened, De La Torres was the man picked him up, you see. And to anticipate you, there's no more evidence on him now, for all I know he's reformed and maybe Skyros is an innocent personal friend he's met since and he goes to see him privately at his office to chat about chess problems or the weather. Off the record, thanks very much for Skyros—I really think you got something there. We'll continue to look into it. Well, the office sent out Farr to join De La Torres, and when Prettyman came out—which was about half an hour later—Farr took him on. He drove down to Main and went into a bar there—Anselmo's—not a very hot reputation, been closed down a couple of times for serving juveniles and getting caught with unlicenced stuff. In Farr goes after him, having his teeth in by then, and Prettyman had teamed up with another fellow at a table. They stayed there awhile, and Prettyman was calling the other guy Denny. Farr got as close as he could, but there was a lot of noise in the place, as usual, and he just got snatches of what they said. Until in about half an hour they started out together. Neither of 'em was drunk, he says, just high, at the back-slapping all-buddies-together stage.'

'Has this story got a tag-line?'

'Wait for it, I'm getting there. Farr ambles

126

out after 'em, and when they get to Prettyman's car round the corner—darker side street—he gets close enough to listen. And they're talking about Keats—'

'Now look,' said Mendoza. 'I've got no time to listen to interminable accounts of the funny dream you had last night. Tell your wife, she has to put up with being bored.'

'Will you *wait* for it, damn it! I don't mean Keats who wrote poetry, I mean—or I think *they* meant—one Walter William Keats who's a burglar. At least, most of the time he is, he did a three-to-five stretch for it awhile ago, but he's also been picked up for armed robbery and assault. This I got from Burglary and Theft, I'd never heard of him myself, but what they call the context kind of led both Farr and me to guess what his lay is. Prettyman and Denny, whoever *he* is, were talking about Keats' bad luck, getting in bad with the best fence in town, and—I'm coming to it now, you can start listening—Denny said, maybe he oughta try Frank's old boss, the Greek, *he* was kinda getting into that business himself. And Prettyman said, *Yeah*, was *that* so? And then—'

'The Greek. Same one Prettyman had just been visiting?'

'For what it's worth, Farr—who didn't know any of this background—said he sort of got the impression Prettyman was surprised and wanted to ask questions, but this Denny

127

started in talking about something else and he didn't have a chance then.'

'Mmh. Every time I acquire a little more suggestive information about this thing,' said Mendoza, 'it just makes it more complicated. Do I unravel this hearsay evidence right, that Denny was implying the Greek was turning fence? *Skyros?*'

'Maybe. And I haven't finished. Then Denny—who was a little higher than Prettyman—said, let's go see Amy, nice girl, Amy, and maybe take a bottle along. And Prettyman said Amy didn't got much for guys in his line of work, and Denny said, sure, she wouldn't mind, look at Angie, she liked *him* all right, didn't she? It was just, *you* know, Frank had been in it when he got his and it kinda reminded her, but Amy was O.K.'

'Wait a minute, let me get this down ... Yes?'

'You've almost got it. Finally they spotted Farr and he had to go on past to his own car. In a minute they both climbed into Prettyman's, and went on down Main to Daggett Street. Ended up at 341. Farr put all this down in his notes while he sat outside. After awhile Prettyman came out alone and took himself down to a joint called the Elite at Daggett and San Pedro. I may add that this joint we're looking at lately, because a user we picked up last week let out that he'd been told you could get a fix there. And a while

128

after that Prettyman went home, which is a cheap room in a Main Street hotel.'

'Well, well,' said Mendoza. 'This is a little something to think about, isn't it? But what a funny combination—burglary and dope—and what lay do you suppose this Denny's on, fraud or something? Unless it's one of those masterminded crime rings, as per the detective stories of thirty years back, all this rigmarole doesn't make any sense at all.'

'I can't help that, I'm just giving it to you as it came in. On account of your corpse. You said maybe the corpse knew something about Skyros, and likelier something about some crooked work in his regular business than any outside deal—but this seems to indicate that there might *be* some kind of outside business. Something funny, anyway. If he is the Greek.'

'I don't deny it. What about 341 Daggett—pro house?'

'If it is, Vice doesn't know it. Aside from that I know nothing about Amy. How much do you want? I only had this thrown at me half an hour ago.'

'I appreciate your good intentions,' said Mendoza. 'All you've succeeded in doing is arousing my curiosity to fever pitch. I really think I'll have to look into this myself—I couldn't explain to anybody just what to investigate. Thanks very much, I'll let you know if anything comes of it.'

'Always happy to co-operate,' said Callaghan.

Mendoza looked at his scribbled notes while he finished his cigarette, and then got up and reached for his hat. He had, he supposed, no business wasting time over such vague clues, on such a nebulous affair; but if he'd admit it to himself, he always hated to delegate authority. Now and then it made a little change, a little interest, to get out on the street again, at the core of a case, doing the work a sergeant or his underlings usually did, while the lieutenant waited to have all the loose ends handed him for tying up into neat knots. He might just begin the cast here, anyway.

Daggett Street, he thought. Twenty-three years ago he had lived on Daggett Street, down there the wrong side of Main...

★   ★   ★

Hackett came in late because yesterday had been his sister's birthday; he'd had to go out there for dinner and it was quite a little drive back and forth, clear out to Arcadia; he hadn't got in until after midnight, and had overslept.

Sergeant Lake told him Mendoza had been in and gone out again, leaving a note for him. The note said, '*Inmediatamente*, contact Driscoll and find out what his interest is in

Skyros.' Hackett felt unreasonably exasperated; that was Luis for you, like a dog with a meatless bone. There wasn't anything *in* this Domokous business.

But he dutifully called Driscoll's hotel, which he knew from the tail on him. Driscoll was out. Hackett left a request for him to call when he came in, and looked over the tail's report on him in desultory interest.

Mendoza had sized Driscoll up all right: the saga of his wanderings in the last thirty-six hours sounded remarkably like one of those pieces of fiction in which the emphasis was on pace rather than plausibility. He had visited the local office of his company on Wednesday morning, when his tail was first attached; had, as the tail reported laconically, drunk lunch at a nearby bar, and then driven out to the County Museum in Exposition Park. He hadn't stayed there long, but gone on out Wilshire to the Beverly-Hilton. Stayed there about half an hour, come out, driven back to Hollywood and gone to another bar, where he made a phone call which, the tail deduced by the fact that he'd got a ten-dollar bill changed into quarters first, was a long-distance one. He had then had dinner and taken himself to what the tail reported was a damned stale burlesque show down on Main. Came out about nine-thirty ('Thank God,' the tail appended, 'enough to put a man off women

131

for life') and sought out another bar. Subsequently the tail had had to load him into a taxi—perfectly safe, as he had already passed out—and send him back to his hotel. On Thursday, not unexpectedly, he had stayed in all morning: emerged about one o'clock, looking about as you'd expect, and had again driven out to the County Museum. This time he stayed a couple of hours, and from there went to the Times-Mirror Building and stayed another couple of hours. The tail had been unable to track close enough to find out where he'd gone inside. He came out at about six o'clock and had a sandwich and several drinks at still another bar. And then he went back to Hollywood to a much-vaunted live-revue theatre.

Bound to enjoy himself if it kills him, deduced Hackett. The night tail reported in just as he finished reading, and said Driscoll hadn't shown before the day man came on, but he'd been middling high when he came in last night and maybe was nursing another little hangover.

Yesterday afternoon Mendoza had decided to put a tail on the exotic brunette, and since Callaghan had taken over Skyros, Hackett had transferred Dwyer, Reade, and Higgins to her. Higgins' report, up to midnight, was here. Madame Bouvardier had dined at her hotel, and had then been driven up to Hollywood by her hired chauffeur to an

132

address near Silver Lake. She hadn't stayed there long, only half an hour or so, then returned to the hotel.

And what was there in all that? Exactly nothing. If Driscoll's movements said anything, they said he didn't seem inordinately interested in Mr. Skyros. And as for the woman—well! Jewellers, hairdressers, the hotel dining room, and probably some acquaintance in a good residential district—kind of thing you'd expect.

Nymphs and dolphins, thought Hackett. Once in a while one of Mendoza's hunches paid off, but a lot of them were duds too, and this looked like one of those all right.

About then Dwyer came in to report, on his way home; he said Hackett might have given him a break, and let him see something of this dame, on day duty—it wasn't, after all, often that a respectable married man had the chance to follow a skirt like that all over town on his legitimate job. As it was, she'd already been in her suite when he took over from Higgins, and he'd only had a brief look at her this morning before Reade showed up.

'Still in the hotel?'

'Was when I left. I kind of wandered in after the place woke up a little, you know, and around on that floor. About nine o'clock, just when I was expecting Reade, the door opened and out came the maid. It's the damndest thing,' said Dwyer, yawning, 'I don't figure they teach you right—I don't know—I took two years of French in high school, but they might as well have been talking Chinese, for all I could get of it. Except "*cabriolet*"—maybe she was telling the maid to take a taxi, I don't know. Seemed to be sending her on some errand, anyway, by all the gestures—and you shoulda seen the bathrobe, Sergeant, or I guess that wouldn't hardly be the name for it—'

'Negligée,' suggested Hackett.

'Or even something fancier. Pink, and a lot of lace. I guess the maid didn't like the idea of going, nervous about a strange town and all, they seemed to be having quite a little argument and the dame said an address over three-four times, finally wrote it down for her.'

'All this with the door open, or were you hiding in the bathroom?'

'Around the corner in the hall, sure, the door was open—like I say I didn't get any of the talk but it looked to me maybe the maid got cold feet at the last minute, you know, tried to back out. Anyway, finally she went off, and by that time Reade was there, he heard some of it too.' Dwyer yawned again and produced a slip of paper. 'I wrote down the address the dame said.'

'O.K.,' said Hackett, and Dwyer went off. The address didn't say anything to Hackett: just an address, in Hollywood somewhere, he thought. But as long as Mendoza was so set on looking at every little whipstitch ... He called Driscoll's hotel again; Driscoll was still out. Probably wandering the County Museum again, thought Hackett: or no, it wasn't open in the morning; he was probably at a bar. Oh, well.

He looked at a map, went downstairs and got his car, and drove up to Hollywood. It wasn't a classy street, and it wasn't by any means a slum street: just an ordinary run-of-the-mill district, and mostly lined— along this block—with middle-aged apartment buildings. The name of the one he wanted, as near as Dwyer had been able to transcribe it, was the Blon-shair Arms. There wasn't one by that name, but there was, in the middle of the block, a Blanchard Arms, and he deduced that was it. Apartment 406. He went around the block hunting a parking space, finally found one, walked back, went into the lobby and examined the rows of locked mailboxes with their little handwritten name slots.

And then he said aloud, 'I *will* be damned! I will be *damned*!' What the hell was this?

The name on the box marked 406 was *Miss Alison Weir*.

Hackett straightened and stared at the blank wall opposite, feeling as confused as he'd ever felt in his life. Alison Weir?—what did she have to do with the elegant, expensive visiting Parisian at the Beverly-Hilton? Who also knew Mr. Andreas Skyros, employer of Stevan Domokous? It didn't make any sense. But there it was: Madame Bouvardier had known her address. Why?

Hackett debated looking up the address of her school and going to ask her; but on second thought reflected that it might really be said to be Mendoza's job.

He drove back downtown, and fidgeted around the office waiting for Mendoza to come in. No, Sergeant Lake said, he hadn't said where he was going. Nor when he might be expected back. He wouldn't be in the building because he'd taken his hat.

Where the hell had he gone? Hackett had a feeling he ought to know about this right away: and yet, what could it mean? He couldn't settle to any routine work; every time the phone rang he jumped at it.

But it was nearly noon before Mendoza called in. Hackett, belatedly wondering how he'd take it, relayed the extraordinary news. There was a moment's silence at the other end of the wire, and then Mendoza said, '¡Qué demonio!—¡aguarda un momento!—I wonder! By God, I wonder! Listen, Art—you there?'

'I'm still here.'

'Por Dios, it'd be an incredible coincidence—or would it?—coincidences do happen, after all, and surprisingly often too.

136

Listen, call down to Traffic and get hold of a Sergeant Rhodes. I want to ask him some questions. What time is it? ... Look, bring him to lunch with us. I haven't got the car, come and pick me up, will you?—I'm at the corner of Daggett and San Pedro, the drugstore. O.K.?'

'Well, O.K.,' said Hackett, and started to ask what he was doing down there, but Mendoza had rung off.

So he called down to Traffic and got hold of Rhodes. It had been some time since he'd had anything to do with Traffic, and for a few minutes he thought they must be scraping the bottom of the barrel all right these days, because Rhodes couldn't seem to take in what he was saying. 'L-lunch? L-Lieutenant Mendoza?' he kept stuttering, and then apparently pulled himself together and said, 'Oh, yes, sir, *yes*, sir, of course, I'll meet you at the front door in five minutes, sir—' And was off the phone before Hackett could remind him he was just talking to another sergeant.

CHAPTER ELEVEN

Mendoza had rather enjoyed himself that morning. In all the places he'd be going, the Facel-Vega would earn him too much attention, and he'd walked from headquarters down Main, out of the Civic Centre. It wasn't often he had occasion to be on foot down here. Wasting time with a vengeance in a way, he thought as he turned into Daggett Street; but he didn't feel guilty at all.

Daggett Street hadn't changed much in twenty-three years, he'd noticed recently driving down it. Walking he thought the cracks in the sidewalk might be the same. Different faces, that was all. He enjoyed the walk. Along here, you turned to look at anyone speaking English; these couple of blocks were all business, and the store-front signs said *Comestibles abarrotes*, *Ropas de Mujeres*, *Zapatos*, *Vino y licores*, and also, *¡Gangas! Venga Ud. y mire!—¡Venta por quiebra!* Always *bargains*, always *bankrupt sales* ... And the old and the new cheek by jowl: the old ones in rusty black, sometimes ankle-length: the young ones in the same bright this-year's fashions in the shops uptown.

In the middle of the third block he looked across at the sagging old frame apartment, wondered if Mrs. Gonzales still owned it; such very good *torrijas* she had made, and always one to spare for a hungry boy: she'd had a son in medical college ... '*Los años, se pasan rapidamente*,' he muttered ruefully to himself.

Then it changed, the street: signs in
138

English, and presently an even frowsier look, something about the houses, the business blocks, not only shabby, but furtive and stagnant. Rooming houses, cheap hotels, bars, pool halls. And here was 341. Once a single-family house, with the third storey for servants: now bearing a sign, *Rooms Cheap*, but the fancy fretwork round every inch of eaves and porch was good as new.

He didn't think this place would be too particular, either about strange males calling on the female residents or about names; he smiled persuasively at the dispirited-looking woman who opened the door and asked simply, 'Which room'll I find Amy?'

He was right; she never asked a question, but said, 'Second floor, left front,' and went clumping away down the hall without a back look.'

So he climbed up to the second floor, knocked, and was rewarded with the sight of Amy in negligée—an affair of pink chiffon, not too clean, showing glimpses of a dancer's blue-mottled legs. The remains of last night's make-up were also visible as well as a dark parting in the silver-flax hair, and the burgundy-coloured nail polish was chipped and ragged. She leaned on the doorpost and said coldly, 'Yeah?'

Mendoza gave her a hopeful leer and said, 'I'm looking for a couple of guys, and I been told they're friends of yours. Angie and

139

Denny. You know where I could find either of 'em?'

Her expression didn't change. 'Sorry, mister, never heard of 'em.'

'Oh, yes, you did,' said Mendoza. 'Look, I got a favour to do this Angie, see. You do him a good turn, tell me where I can contact him.'

'Is that so?' said Amy. 'Well, that's just too bad, because I still don't know. And I don't like your looks much, mister.' She stepped back inside the room and slammed the door.

Mendoza sighed and went back downstairs to the street. Nothing there, except the implied fact that the woman knew what kind of business those two were in—whatever it was and whoever they were—and that it was on the wrong side of the fence, whether she was personally mixed up in it or not. And, now he came to think, he should have stopped at that Anselmo's bar first; it was on the way here and now he'd have to go back.

He walked back to Main and found Anselmo's. A hole in the wall, dirty, ancient, and cheap. He wondered if the liquor was safe, but went in and ordered rye. It was raw, but well-diluted—what pro slang called baptized. The bartender, sole occupant of the place at this hour, was a hairy young fellow running to paunch already and with a pair of shifty eyes. Nice if generalizations were all true, thought Mendoza: most crooks had exceptionally honest faces, and most

140

bartenders, honest or not, developed the shifty eyes from continual watching of customers.

'I'm looking,' he said, 'for a fellow named Angie. Know him? I got the word he comes in here sometimes.'

'That so?' said the bartender. 'Couldn't say. What you want him for?'

Yes; Angie definitely a wrong one, if his friends and/or acquaintances were so chary of admitting they knew his whereabouts. But did this fellow know him, or was he just cagey by nature? 'Well, I might have a little job for him,' said Mendoza at random. 'Kind of a better deal than he's got now.'

'Is that so?' said the bartender without batting and eye. "Well, you don't know his last name, can't help you, mister—couple of Angies come in here, now 'n' then. Couldn't say at all.'

Mendoza left the rest of his drink and came out. The hell with it, he said to himself; anything you got on a wild hunt like this, you got with infinite patience. A man, several men, watching and waiting around corners sometimes for weeks before the one little word was dropped that told you something. It was time to turn this over to one of Hackett's men and get back to his office where he belonged.

Instead, he walked back up Daggett to San Pedro and found the Elite, which added to its

141

name the misnomer of Club.

Inside, it was a small square place with a minute platform at one end for a band, now holding only a battered upright piano. Someone, a long time ago, had decorated it ambitiously with black lacquered tables and chairs, a home-carpentered banquette along one wall, and dime store decals on the wainscoting, an Oriental motif. Opposite the banquette was the bar: at the bar the bartender, two men standing; five others sat at one table over a hand of poker, monosyllabic.

Mendoza went up and leaned on the bar, leaving his hat on in deference to local custom. 'Straight rye.' It was surprisingly good quality; he told the bartender so. This was a bald middle-aged fat man who nodded shortly at the compliment without a word. Mendoza looked the other customers over casually.

Next to him at the bar, a big bruiser in a green nylon shirt and black slacks; just missed being handsome, in a saturnine rugged way: about forty. A smaller, older man, dark, needed a shave, lank black hair falling over one eye. At the table, the dealer was cadaverous, bushy-haired, young; the edge, a flashily dressed, very clean and pleasant-looking twenty-year-old; two of the others nondescript men in their thirties, who looked disconcertingly like respectable

142

citizens—one in brown slacks, one in grey. And the fifth man was a pale brown Negro with the regular, handsome features of the West Indian, a soft British accent.

Mendoza half turned back to the bartender. 'By the way, I'm looking for Angie. Where's he hanging out these days?'

Green Shirt glanced sideways at him; Bushy Hair hesitated the fraction of a second in picking up a card. The bartender might have been carved out of wood for all the expression he showed. 'Sorry, mister, never heard of him.' He turned away to answer the phone.

Mendoza finished his rye and came out. A wasted morning. But maybe some discreet looking around this place, and Anselmo's, and at Amy, might turn up something interesting eventually. Piggott, he decided. It was surprising how like a small-time pro Piggott could look and act, for a pillar of the Free Methodist Church and a cop with a spotless record. Let him mix with the crowd in here, and at Anselmo's, for a few nights.

He was tired and hot, and he'd begun to want his lunch. He went into the drugstore next to the Elite and called his office; and what Hackett had to tell him effectively took his mind off food ... Now what the hell was the connection here? That woman—*Lydia*? That Bouvardier female out at the Beverly-Hilton? Could it be, it must be, the

143

theft of the car: it had to be, the only possible thing. Find out what there was to find out about the car, obviously. He told Hackett to get hold of Rhodes.

Leaving the phone, he realized what a scorcher of a day it was: must be up around a hundred and ten. And these squalid streets, these old buildings, airless and fetid. There was a fan turning above the door, but it only stirred the stale air. However, hotter out on the corner in the sun. He was out of cigarettes, and bought a pack from the rat-faced druggist, opened it and lit one, drifted over to join a couple of women looking at the magazines. But he didn't see them very clearly; his mind was working furiously at this new, curious feature of what he wasn't too sure he could call a case ... He looked up automatically when the door opened, though it was too soon to expect Hackett—

Green Shirt and Bushy Hair came in together, spotted him and looked pleased. Grey Slacks and Brown Slacks, behind them, collected the two women and trundled them out to the street. 'This store's closed, ladies, come back some other time.'

'Hey,' said the druggist weakly, 'I ain't either closed—'

'You are now,' said Green Shirt, and slammed the door, locked it, and pulled down the shade. 'Get in the back room, buster, and you didn't see or hear nothin' or nobody.'

The druggist looked at him, licked his lips and backed away. 'That's right, I didn't,' he said. 'I sure as hell didn't.' He vanished into the rear of the store.

'Castro must be feelin' his oats, friend,' said Bushy Hair to Mendoza, 'send his errand boys round in broad daylight. Anyways, he sure looks like one o' Castro's boys, don't he?—cute li'l moustache an' all. This ain't healthy territory for you, friend. Castro oughta know that. Castro ain't took over from Pretty yet, or leastways he hadn't when we all went to bed las' night, an' I don't guess it'd happen without us knowing, hah, boys? He oughta send a bodyguard along with you anyways, if he wants you back any shape to do business for a while. Maybe he wants t' get rid of you, though, sendin' you out alone over here, askin' for Pretty's best boy to offer him another job? Kinda a shame, you so innocent 'n' all—nice li'l gennelman like you—and *ain't* he a fancy-dressed one, boys?'

'Real sharp,' said Green Shirt, grinning.

'Pore fella,' said Bushy Hair, poking a bony finger into Mendoza's chest.

Mendoza had the depressing suspicion that this was one of the occasions when he would wish he habitually carried a gun. *Ehtre la espada y la pared*, he thought in exasperation, between the sword and the wall!—haul out his I.D. card, fine—they didn't like cops any
145

better than who they thought he was, but more important, he had no intention of letting it be known that a cop was asking around for Angie—whoever Angie was. ('Pretty's best boy'—well, well.) In that case, Piggott and every one of the rest of Mendoza's men could go on looking from now till Christmas: no Angie.

He smiled at Green Shirt and said, 'Castro? Afraid I don't know him, you must have me mixed up with somebody else.' There was, of course, Hackett—and Rhodes—on the way, and not very far to come, a matter of blocks.

'Oh, boy, he's a fancy talker too,' said Grey Slacks admiringly.

'He sure don't belong in this crummy neighbourhood,' agreed Brown Slacks.

'But we don't want to send him back to his boss,' said Green Shirt, 'without a little something to show what we think of him—do we, boys?' He produced a short weighted sap from an inside pocket and tested it thoughtfully on his palm.

'Oh, we sure as hell wouldn't want to do that,' said Bushy Hair, and by legerdemain there was a flat black thing in his hand: a little click, and the switchblade shot out long and wicked.

Mendoza was alarmed by the thought that he must be getting old, to slip up on a thing like this. That phone call at the Elite bar had been the hairy fellow at Anselmo's, of

146

course—or just possibly Amy. He'd been thinking too hard about Angie and Denny, and all the rest of this thing—too damned single-minded, that was always his trouble. He also remembered bitterly that he was wearing a new suit. But these things happened. He dropped his cigarette, gave Green Shirt a very nervous smile, and backed away; he said, 'Now listen, mister, I haven't done anything—'

They were pleased, as this kind always was, to find the victim timid and fearful. They began to close in on him and he backed another few steps, brought up against a counter, and with his hands behind him felt around cautiously: cards of something, combs, and—ah—a large bottle. 'You got me all wrong,' he said.

'We got him all wrong, boys,' said Brown Slacks. 'Ain't that a shame!' He reached out, clicking open another blade, and took hold of Mendoza's tie. 'I seem to remember I forgot to sharpen this, and me, I'm fussy about that, I don't like no dull knives—let's just see,' and he sliced off a clean strip of the tie halfway up.

Brown Slacks didn't know it, but the tie was a Paris import and had cost twelve dollars two months ago. Mendoza was considerably annoyed: so annoyed that he forgot all about using delaying tactics until he should see Hackett's black sedan slide past the window, or Hackett's shadow on the shade, trying the door.

He said gently to Brown Slacks, 'Now *that* you shouldn't have done, you bastard,' and just on the chance, before beginning operations, he fired the bottle in his hand accurately at the big front window. It went through with a satisfactorily loud crash, but by then he was too busy to notice.

Brown Slacks, closest to him, was taken sufficiently by surprise to leave himself open, and Mendoza made a little room by a solid right to his mouth, staggering him back into a glass case. Bushy Hair came up in a hurry, knife straight out and low, but he came at such a convenient angle—possibly he had a higher-class background than Daggett Street and didn't expect it—that he walked smack into a nicely-timed kick in the groin, and went down flat on his back and dropped the knife. Mendoza dived after it and was helped on his way by Green Shirt falling on him from behind; he twisted away from the sap, heard it thud on the floor, missed the knife, rolled over and took the second blow of the sap glancingly on the temple. He heaved off Green Shirt desperately, staggered up on his feet again, and dodged as Grey Slacks swung at him.

He had no illusions about taking all four; all he wanted was to clear them out of the way to the door. There was a saying very

148

apropos—*Más vale qué digan, Aquí corrió, y no, aquí murió*—Better they say, he ran here, and not, he died here.

He took a nasty slash on the arm from Grey Slacks' knife; Brown Slacks was picking himself up from the shattered case, swearing, and Mendoza kicked him down again, simultaneously dodging Green Shirt's vicious swing of the sap. Bushy Hair, groaning steadily and clutching his stomach, sat up obligingly just in time to trip Green Shirt, who fell into Mendoza's left hard enough to make him think something was broken, and sprawled flat—but he was up again, and coming back for more. Mendoza heard the door rattle and Hackett's voice outside—the Marines had landed. He shouted, 'In, Art!' and saw Grey Slacks' knife slashing up for his stomach with a practised wrist-motion. He lunged for the wrist and got the blade first; it sliced deep across the ball of his thumb and palm, but a second later he had the arm in both hands, brought his knee up for leverage, leaned on it and heard the armbone snap.

As the man yelled, the door-panel smashed open and Hackett came in like a big bull, head down. He took in the situation as he came, and fell on top of Green Shirt, who was coming up behind Mendoza, and put him out of commission with the butt of his gun. Rhodes followed in time to collide with a blind swing from Brown Slacks, just up

149

again; he let out a bellow of surprise and knocked Brown Slacks into the third glass case and unconsciousness.

Mendoza sat down on the end fountain-stool and wrapped his handkerchief round his left hand. 'Very nice timing, Art,' he said rather breathlessly.

Hackett put his gun away, looked at the havoc, and asked, 'Is that an artery?'

'No, but it might as well be, the damage it's—I couldn't get to it right away. *¡Valgame Dios!* look at this suit! Three hundred bucks a month ago!'

'What the hell goes on here?' asked Rhodes, bewildered. 'What—suit? Lieutenant—' But training held; he didn't wait for an answer, went back to the door to stand off the crowd collecting, while Hackett found the phone and put in a call for a patrol car and an ambulance.

While they waited, he came and added his handkerchief to Mendoza's. 'One of these days, my latter-day *conquistador*, you're goin' to do this just once too often—tackle a gang armed with switchblades and knuckledusters without so much as a cap pistol on you. And why I should do any worrying about it, the good God above knows, because it's probably the only way I'll ever get to be a lieutenant.'

'*¡Quiá, imbécil!* You don't think this was my idea, do you? You think I took on four at once so everybody can say, That Mendoza,

150

¡que hombre!—a lion-eater! All I wanted was out, boy, but they were between me and the door, so it was *por malas o por buenas*—no choice.' He struggled out of his jacket and cursed, feeling the slash in the sleeve. Most of that sleeve and a good deal of the front panel was generously blood-stained, and the other sleeve half out of the shoulder seam. 'Three hundred bucks,' he said bitterly, 'and twelve for the tie!'

'My God in heaven,' said Hackett, and went to meet the precinct men arriving.

CHAPTER TWELVE

The druggist sidled out of the back room and gazed mournfully at the wreckage, and Mendoza, who'd followed Hackett to the door, said in an urgent undertone, 'Arrest me, Art—take me out all official-looking, nobody here must know who I am.'

'Games, yet,' said Hackett, grabbed him by one arm, and shoved him out. Mendoza sat in the ambulance while the interns bandaged him temporarily, refusing to go along to the General for stitches in his hand immediately; he'd have it seen to sometime today. He was publicly pushed into the back of Hackett's car.

'Tell the precinct sergeant somebody'll be

down to give him details on this. Don't be a fool, I'm not much damaged, I'll see a doctor after lunch, and lunch I've earned.' He looked at Rhodes, peering at him from the front seat still wearing a faintly astonished expression, and added, 'And we've things to talk over. Let's be on our way, Arturo. Though how the hell I can go into a—oh, well, they know me at Federico's, and it's a hot day.'

The head waiter, however, looked very surprised to see him with no jacket, no necktie, collar unbuttoned; and still more surprised when Mendoza demanded a drink before lunch. 'I'm going to wash, I'm filthy—don't sit down, Art, go and call Pat Callaghan and brief him on this. Those four, I think, are more his business than mine, and he'll want to see them. He's the one sent me down there in the first place.'

'That I want to hear about. I thought Callaghan was a friend of yours.'

'He didn't know I'm getting senile,' said Mendoza, 'to walk into a thing like that—like a fool I had my mind on something else. And probably nothing to show for it but the wear and tear.—And get me an aspirin somewhere, that sap connected once and I've got a headache.'

'What were you doing down there without a gun, Lieutenant?' asked Rhodes. 'I mean, I'd think—'

'Oh, his tailor won't let him pack a gun,' explained Hackett. 'It spoils that nice shoulder-line, you know.'

'That little joke I'm tired of. *¡Zappe!* Go and call Pat!'

'I'm going, I'm going.'

'You mean you never—why, that's asking for trouble, Lieutenant,' said Rhodes earnestly. 'Why, anyway?'

'Oh, I don't like loud bangs, they make me nervous,' said Mendoza irritably, and vanished to seek soap and water.

Hackett joined Rhodes at a table before Mendoza reappeared. Rhodes, who was a big fair farmery-looking young man, still wore a bewildered expression. 'I never heard that one,' he said to Hackett. 'About his not packing a gun. I mean, Landers—'

'You know Landers?'

'Yes, sure, and he—you know, talks about Lieutenant Mendoza sometimes, but he never mentioned that. Why doesn't he, anyway?'

'I'll tell you,' said Hackett, and broke off to demand coffee and offer Rhodes a cigarette, 'he's got this crazy idea, police exist to prevent violence and we ought to set an example. He says sure, out on patrol, anywhere you're apt to be in danger unarmed, O.K., but anything you got handy you're going to use when maybe it isn't strictly necessary. And a lot of perfectly good honest cops are still a little too quick on the trigger, if they've got it there six inches from their hand. He liked Wes Rich, thought he was a smart boy, but he got him broke from sergeant last year after Rich shot that Prince kid—remember the one killed his uncle because the uncle used to get drunk and beat up his wife and the kid? Prince tried to run on the way to the station, and Rich shot him. Sure, he didn't aim to kill, but it isn't exactly like target-shooting for a score, is it? Luis said he needed another little spell as an errand boy to think it over.'

'Well, my God,' said Rhodes, 'but it's not common sense to walk into the tiger cage without a whip and a kitchen chair.'

'How right you are,' said Hackett. 'That Luis doesn't say. Just that it's a good idea to try other methods first, and if you never move a step without the whip, you never have to think of any other way of doing it.'

'I see,' said Rhodes thoughtfully.

Mendoza came up, looking slightly more presentable, looked at the rye the waiter had left for him and said, 'I shouldn't have that, I've had two drinks already this morning—unprecedented, and you know what it does to me.'

'I guess you've had enough of a workout already you won't be spoiling for another fight in the next half hour,' said Hackett. 'Live dangerously for once, drink it.'

Mendoza did, said, 'Ah, coffee, that's

154

better. Did you get me some aspirin?'

Hackett gave him one and said Callaghan extended sympathy but was pleased to hear some of those boys from the Elite could be arrested for something, even common assault. He'd go right down to look them over, *and* their places of residence, and it might just be they could eventually be charged with something more, which would be very useful.

'They won't be charged with assaulting me, not by name anyway,' said Mendoza. 'I'm not appearing in this round. If there is any connection with this Domokous thing I don't want them to know I know it. Not that I know much, and God knows that.'

'I want to hear about this little adventure. What took you down there?'

'Take too long to tell—it's very complicated: briefly, I got some names from Pat, I went to do some sniffing around myself, and while I had my mind on the names I inadvertently gave these boys the impression I was doing something else they didn't like . . . yes, suggestive in a way, and I want to hear what Pat thinks. But meantime—' He told the waiter to bring him anything edible and more coffee *inmediatamente* 'Rhodes—this *is* Sergeant Rhodes? What with one thing and another we don't seem to have been introduced—'

'Yes, sir, I'm Rhodes.'

'I must be losing my grip, come to
155

think—you couldn't answer questions without your records, I don't suppose you remember much about it offhand. Car theft. Miss Alison Weir, a week ago last Sunday, and you found the car and returned it a week ago yesterday.'

'Miss Weir—oh, yes, sir, I do remember. I mean, I'd better explain, I know Landers in your office, you see, and he—that is—Miss Weir's a friend of yours, isn't she, and I happened to notice the name—'

'I see,' said Mendoza. 'And they say women are the gossips. Well, I want to hear everything you know about that business. Pretend I don't know anything about it—I don't, much—and give me all you remember, we can check your records later.'

'Well,' said Rhodes blankly. 'Well, it was kind of an ordinary thing, Lieutenant. Probably kids—you know how much of that sort of thing we get. The car was pinched from Exposition Park that Sunday afternoon, I heard later Miss Weir and a friend of hers 'd been to some art show at the County Museum—'

'¡Quiá! Now that I'd forgotten, if I ever heard it. The County Museum—what the hell has it got to do with this? A dignified, dreary spot like that—'

'Oh, I don't know, I kind of like museums,' said Hackett. 'But don't look at me for the answer. This much I'll

156

contribute—Driscoll has gone there twice in the last two days. I don't know why, the tail was too far behind and lost him inside.'

Mendoza laid down his fork and put a hand to his temple. 'I'm in no condition to be given shocks, Arturo. And I'll never, by God, make any more jokes about implausibly complicated detective fiction. I wonder what kind of exhibitions they've got on at the moment. Anything in the nature of nymphs and dolphins?'

'You've let nymphs and dolphins seduce you away from any solid facts in this thing—the few we've got,' said Hackett. 'I don't think they've got a damn thing to do with it.'

'I won't argue, I'm out of ammunition. Go on, Rhodes. What time and where from, exactly?'

Rhodes, who had stopped eating to follow this exchange with a furrowed brow, said, 'What? Oh, the car—why, it was early afternoon when Miss Weir left it, I seem to remember—and I think the call to the precinct went through about five o'clock. You know those little narrow winding streets all round the park buildings—it was somewhere along the one goes in front of the main museum building, a block or so down. I figured it afterwards, Sunday, you know, a public park with no admission fee—it was probably some teen-agers, just decided to take a joy ride. You get an awful lot of that. I don't know what you think, sir, but I put it down to people not being at home with their kids more, and maybe some of this progressive education. Because a lot of 'em we pick up, they're not what you'd call delinquents—it's just, my God, they don't seem to know any better, don't see any reason at all why they shouldn't take anything sitting around loose, if they've got a yen for it at the moment. You know? And what with the big areas public schools take in, there's bound to be a few real delinquents in a lot of them, and quite a few kids from ordinary respectable homes pick up little tricks, like how to do without an ignition key.'

'Yes, all that I grant you. But most kids, this sort or that, go for something new and classy.'

'Well, not always,' said Rhodes. 'Some of 'em who go in for drag-racing—But most of what we get from kids is just picking up anything handy to ride around in a few hours. Another thing that comes into it is taking a dare. My God, these kids!—it makes you wonder. I mean, one of 'em says, Bet you haven't got the nerve to swipe a car, and the other one's ashamed to chicken out. And mind you, both of 'em might be from respectable homes, raised to know better.'

'Also true,' said Mendoza patiently, 'but evidently whoever took Miss Weir's car kept it longer than a couple of hours. Where and when did it turn up?'

'I don't remember the exact address, sir, but it's in the records. It was that Thursday, about noon, around there—a fellow called the local precinct to report this car'd been sitting out in front of his house almost two days. So the boys went and checked, and of course it was on the hot list so they brought it into the headquarters garage. It was a new tract street somewhere out in Compton, I think, and the fellow said he'd first noticed it when he left for work on Wednesday morning, early.'

'Mmh. Abandoned there late Tuesday night. Did your boys go over it?'

'Well, sure,' said Rhodes. 'The way we usually do, you know—I mean, we didn't tear it apart looking, it's run-of-the-mill, stuff like that. We looked for prints on the wheel and so on, in case we could match them up to somebody in Records. I seem to remember that everything a driver'd touch had been wiped clean.'

'Which does not,' said Mendoza, 'look like a bunch of kids out for a joy ride.'

'Well, I guess not,' admitted Rhodes. 'But a pro—I mean, there isn't anything *in* hopping shorts unless you keep them, fake up new plates and so on, and sell them. We get a certain amount of that, of course. But a thing like this—car used a little while and then abandoned—it's practically always kids.'

159

'Unless it's a getaway of some kind,' said Mendoza. 'Somebody on the run in a hurry, maybe his own car stalled or—'

'Somehow,' said Hackett, 'I got the feeling that if there'd been a job pulled at the County Museum—one of their Rembrandts missing, or an Egyptian mummy maybe, or the dinosaur skeleton—there'd have been a line or two about it in the papers. They might even have called in the police.'

'All right, all right,' said Mendoza. 'I can do without the sarcasm. You didn't find anything in the car, nothing to point to who'd taken it. What about the mileage? Any way to check?'

'Well, it didn't seem very important, Lieutenant—I mean, why should we? I suppose there'd have been a check of some approximate kind, if there's a garage record on the doorpost as usual, for oil changes, and if Miss Weir could say what it was when the car was taken—'

'Which is very doubtful. Yes. And it's past praying for now, anyway. Damn. And what could it have told us? Nothing.'

'Sir,' Rhodes had been looking uneasy. 'I don't know what this is all about, but if there's something more to that business than just—I mean, something important—maybe you ought to—or maybe you know—'

'That little thing she found, yes,' nodded Mendoza. 'I know. I don't know how it ties in, or what it means, but it seems to mean something, because somebody seems to be anxious to have it back. And to be pretty sure it was lost in the car.'

Rhodes looked uneasier than ever. 'My God, do *you* think it was something to do with that? Miss Weir called in—twice—and I thought—I told her—'

'Yes, and you were quite justified,' Mendoza soothed him. 'Don't look so worried. Exactly the kind of thing a nervous, scatterbrained female might think up. Persecution—or wishful thinking, I suppose the head-doctors would say—big bad man pursuing her. But there are females and females, and as it happens Miss Weir is quite a level-headed one ordinarily, and not given to seeing ghosts.'

'Well, my God, I'm sorry, sir, I never—'

'No, not your fault, don't apologize, you couldn't know that, and I don't say it's an absolutely sure thing even now. *I* may be seeing ghosts. Maybe it was just kids broke into the garage, random mischief. But, damn it, unless the car had something to do with it, how has Alison got into this thing? That mysterious female out at the Beverly-Hilton—and what has *she* got to do with Skyros? ... Wait a minute. Have I had an inspiration? I wonder ... Well, one thing I must do first is see her—Alison, I mean—and get the key to her mailbox. Because it's fifty to one that French maid left a note in it.'

'Now that never occurred to me,' admitted Hackett. 'But it's not the first thing you're going to do, *chico*, you're going to visit a doctor and get some stitches in that thing.'

'Who's the lieutenant here? Listen, Rhodes, you copy down all your records about that business and send them up to my office, O.K.? Thanks very much. And Art, you keep after Driscoll—that boy I want to have a talk with, and some straight answers from! And I'll check up on the note. And all right, Auntie dear, I'll go and get stitched up first.' Mendoza grimaced as he got up. 'Damn it, I kept telling myself I should have sent you or one of the boys instead, on that little jaunt this morning. I'm out of condition for that sort of thing.'

'So the exercise was probably good for you,' said Hackett. 'Maybe I shouldn't have ambitions to be a lieutenant, it's a sedentary job. Come on, grandpa, you can lean on me.'

★　　★　　★

Mendoza saw a doctor and had eleven stitches taken in his hand, went home and took a bath and changed into a whole suit and a clean shirt. He then discovered that it was impossible to knot his tie with one hand and the tips of two fingers on the other, did some cursing, investigated that floor of the

162

apartment to see who else was home, and met Mrs. Bryson just going out. She laid down her purse and gloves on the bottom step, exclaimed over the bandage, and made a firm nautical square knot for him, explaining ingenuously that she had a nephew in the Navy, as he knew. Getting back into the car, Mendoza felt it uneasily and hoped he wouldn't have to get her to untie it for him when he came home.

He stopped at Alison's school on Sunset on his way downtown, and was surprised to find it closed. No class, no sign on the door—nobody there, and the door locked. He felt ridiculously uneasy over *that*, and sought the nearest public phone to call her apartment. He let the phone ring a dozen times, but got no answer. The school closed on a Friday, a weekday, and if she was ill she'd be home. Unreasonably he felt annoyed with Alison: where was she, just when he wanted her?

Well, it couldn't be helped; he'd check back later. He went on downtown, and straight up to Callaghan's office at headquarters. Callaghan wasn't there, and he fumed about that; hung around for ten minutes or so, and was just about to go down to his own office when Callaghan came in. He regarded Mendoza fondly, shepherded him into the inner office, and installed him in the one comfortable chair.

'Once in awhile you really earn your keep around here, Luis. You've been real helpful today—you've got no idea how helpful. I think those four thugs you ran into are all pushers, it gave us an excuse to get a warrant to go through that Elite joint, and we came across quite a little cache of stuff—including about a thousand made-up reefers—in a back room. *And* a few decks on Prettyman and one of the others.'

'Oh, Prettyman was one of them, was he? We weren't formally introduced.'

'The big fellow in the green shirt was Prettyman. I understand you're acting coy, don't want to show in the business by being named victim of assault. Well, that's O.K., we got these two, Prettyman and Flores, charged with unlawful possession, and we can run through the assault on the others with a John Doe if the judge co-operates. Everybody else at the Elite had been warned by the time we got there, of course—not a soul in the place, more's the pity ... And now I'd like to hear a blow-by-blow account of how you got into the hassle in the first place.'

'And there are some suggestive points in it,' said Mendoza, and obliged ... 'Castro—they thought I was working for him. As a pusher? If Prettyman and these others are on that lay, it rather looks like it, doesn't it? Can we build it up that Prettyman is a head pusher for somebody?—let's not say

Skyros until we've got more evidence, but maybe. And he's supplying these others, his boys as they put it. And if they leaped to the conclusion that this Castro was trespassing on Prettyman's territory, and resented it so much, where does that put Castro? You know about Bratti, of course.'

Callaghan blew smoke at the ceiling and said thoughtfully, 'One thing this job's taught me is a lot of respect for the capitalistic system. You'd be surprised how much these little trade wars help us sometimes. If there wasn't the opportunity for competition, we wouldn't get to know about half these bastards—whether we can get evidence on 'em or not, it's nice to know their names. And when a couple of minor territory-bosses get into a little war—maybe one of 'em trying to encroach, you know, hire a boy away to his string, or sometimes something right outside the business, jealousy over a woman or something like that—it makes a grudge, and that gives us an in. None of 'em are very smart on that level, you know, they can't think far ahead. I've known 'em get into street fights, yet, one little gang against the other, and all get hauled in—ruin a ten-thousand-a-week business for some damn-fool little personal grudge. And afterwards, under questioning, you'll get the same thing sometimes—with luck, and if they're fools enough. Tell you anything they

165

know about the other gang, to take them along on the skids too.'

'Have you got anything like that from these?'

'It's early. I hope we will. I've seen all of 'em once. They're all still damn cocky, especially Prettyman. I'd better warn you, he's saying it was a trumped-up job, you were planted to give us an excuse to drag 'em in. But I don't think that'll do him any good with the bench, because he did have the stuff on him. I don't think we'll get much useful out of him, he's a little too smart. But I've got him well separated from the other three, he can't brief them, and they're still convinced, probably, that you were this Castro's boy. By what they said to you, sure, there's one of these little trade wars going on between Prettyman and Castro, and that does indeed put Castro as another head pusher—Prettyman's opposite number. For which middleman, I wonder?'

'Bratti,' said Mendoza. 'You want to bet? Skyros' opposite number.'

'No bets with you. I got a wife and family to support.'

'Yes, and also—look—that might say something to us about why Skyros tried to steer us onto Bratti. Heads or tails—either he didn't know Castro was Bratti's head man, and couldn't name him to us, or he thinks we're so dumb we wouldn't know Bratti

166

wouldn't be out working the street himself. As I—mmh—divined at the time, he just wanted to get Bratti in trouble.'

'Could be. Yes, it's kind of tempting to think, isn't it? And if so, naturally Prettyman's middleman supplier—let's commit slander and say Skyros—wouldn't have much use for Bratti. The grudge might even have come from there originally, personal fight between middlemen passed down to the lower level. Cut-throat competition. I hope by the time these three have stewed awhile, we may get some revealing remarks out of them ... Oh, sure, Prettyman yelled for a lawyer right away, and there'll be bail—but that gives us a little time to hang onto them, they won't come up until Monday probably, and meanwhile we may get to hear some more about Castro.'

'And Angie,' said Mendoza. 'Who is Pretty's best boy. And who knows Denny, who from somewhere got the information that the Greek is turning fence. I didn't acquire these bandages in a spirit of altruism, you know—I was looking for something on my end of the business.'

'Oh, granted,' said Callaghan. 'I'll keep my ears open, and issue instructions to the jailers ditto. I think maybe about tomorrow it might be helpful to move two of them in together and hear what they have to say to each other. Inadmissible evidence—self-condemnation—

but very interesting sometimes, and points to other places to look for legal evidence. I'll keep your corpse in mind. And I'm also going to do a little looking at Amy.'

'Who is, or was, this Frank that Prettyman and Denny mentioned?'

'No idea, I'll have a look at Records and see if we can turn him up.'

'Well, I wish you luck.' Mendoza stood up. 'I hope you realize I've wasted most of the day doing your job. So far I've got nothing out of this at all.'

'Patience, maybe you will. I'll keep you posted.'

CHAPTER THIRTEEN

Mendoza returned to his own office and called Alison's apartment again. No answer. Now where the hell was she? Off on a painting jaunt somewhere? Not on a weekday: she wouldn't close the school just for that.

He tried to remember the names of friends he'd heard her mention, and came up with only one whole one, Patricia Moore—hadn't he met her once?—dowdy Englishwoman, a commercial artist of some kind. He looked her up in the phone book and called there, but again drew blank.

It was four o'clock. His head was still

aching, and he kept hitting that damned hand on everything in reach—the left one, praise heaven for small mercies. Hackett called in and said Driscoll had disappeared somewhere with his tail. 'Hell and damnation!' said Mendoza, and sent Sergeant Lake out for coffee for both of them.

At four-thirty he tried the apartment and the school again. No luck. The night tail for Driscoll came in and asked whether the day man had called in to say where to pick him up. He hadn't. They waited around awhile for that, and nothing happened.

At five o'clock Mendoza said he was going home, he'd had a full day. He was to be called at once, *pronto*, when Driscoll was located or if anything else interesting broke. On the way home he stopped at Alison's school and apartment, and found both empty and silent. Maddeningly, through the slots in her mailbox he could see several envelopes.

He couldn't say he was exactly worried about her—Alison could take care of herself quite well—but he didn't like it. He went on home, to the haven of air-conditioning and an affectionate welcome from Bast; he managed to untie Mrs. Bryson's knot, made some coffee, and lay down to ruminate in peace, or in as much peace as possible with Bast curled up on his stomach. He woke up at a quarter of eight, decided it was too much trouble to get dressed and go out for a meal, and made himself an omelette. He fed Bast. He called his office: hadn't Driscoll been located yet? Yes, the day man had called in, the night man gone to relieve him, and Sergeant Hackett had been briefed when he came in after dinner, but by the time Hackett got there—to a restaurant on Fairfax—they'd both gone.

'¡*Fuera!*' said Mendoza. 'Keep me informed, as soon as the tail calls in.'

He had another cup of coffee. Bast lay purring steadily on his lap, and the clock-hands moved slowly around to nine-thirty. When the phone rang he jumped for it, and then had to stop to apologize to Bast, so rudely discarded. 'Yes?'

'Myers just called in, sir. Driscoll's gone back to his hotel and looks like staying in.'

'Ah,' said Mendoza. 'Thanks very much.' He flung off his robe, dressed hastily, and this time carried his tie upstairs to Mr. Elgin. 'By the way,' he said as Mr. Elgin pulled the knot tight, 'do you really think that precocious tom of yours—?'

'Well, I must say it looked that way to me,' said Mr. Elgin, and elaborated.

'You can have first choice of the litter,' said Mendoza generously, and Mr. Elgin looked alarmed.

'Oh, well—er—we *have* four already—'

'I might have known you'd disclaim responsibility. It's legal enticement, if you ask me. Why you had to bring home a tom—this

170

oversexed delinquent with rape in his eye—'

'Now really, Mendoza—she's been acting pretty coy with him, too—enticement on the other side, if you ask *me*. And he's not just *any* tom. It might be worse. Abyssinians are sort of first cousins to Siamese, they ought to turn out quite interesting kittens.'

Mendoza said Elgin was a traitor and a coward, but he hadn't time to argue about it now. The night had begun to cool off a little, thank God. He drove down to Driscoll's hotel and found Myers in the lobby. 'Is he sober?'

'Depends what you mean by sober, Lieutenant. Say, I heard you got banged up a little today, that looks pretty nasty ... Well, he was feeling pretty good when I picked him up, but dinner settled him down a little. He went out to see that dame at the Beverly, and Dwyer and I strolled up and down the hall outside—you know—and we gathered there was some sort of hassle going on ... Oh, the usual thing, you might say—not that I got any more of the French than Bert did, but it wasn't hard to figure. You can recognize swearing—even, er, ladylike swearing—in any language. She did most of the talking, and most of it after she had the door open and started ordering him out. By the gestures.' Myers looked gravely amused. 'Not very polite gestures. We figured he'd been trying to make her, maybe with not much finesse if you get me, and she said No nineteen

171

different ways—at the top of her voice—and ended up by slapping his face. Good and hard—sounded like a shot.'

'*¡No me diga!*' Mendoza laughed. 'That I'd like to have seen. How'd he take it?'

'Oh, mad as hell. Insult to his vanity, like they say. He went straight down to the bar, but after a couple of drinks it probably dawned on him what kind of mark-up he was paying for the atmosphere, and he came back to town and found a cheaper place. When he left and came back here, he was high, but not quite passing-out high.'

'And that might be just the way I want him,' said Mendoza. 'What's his room number? Come up with me.'

He knocked on the door, waited, knocked again. A stir inside; Driscoll asked without opening, 'Wha' the hell you want?'

'Open the door, Mr. Driscoll. This is Lieutenant Mendoza from headquarters, and I've got some questions to ask you.'

'You go to hell,' said Driscoll.

'Open the door or I'll get the manager to open it for me.'

A long pause; then Driscoll fumbled at the lock inside and the door opened slowly, halfway. 'Listen, why the hell you got to come round at this time of night? What d'you want with *me*? *Cops!* I'm a law-abiding citizen, you can't—'

'That's fine,' said Mendoza. 'Let us in, and

we'll discuss this in private.' He pushed Driscoll aside, went in with Myers and shut the door. The room was strewn with discarded clothes, careless: the bed a tangle of sheet and blanket. 'You seem to be interested in a business way in a couple of people we're interested in too, and I'd like to ask your co-operation in the matter. Just what *is* your interest—or your company's interest—in Madame Bouvardier and Mr. Andreas Skyros?'

Driscoll looked at him blearily. 'I don't have to tell you one thing. It's private comp'ny business. Nothing to do with cops—'

'But we think it has, Mr. Driscoll, and you should know that you're bound, both as a private citizen and an investigator, to co-operate with us when you're asked, give us any information you may have.'

'You can go to hell!' said Driscoll, uneasily belligerent. 'Smart boy cop—sure, take all the credit if I—By God, clean it up m'self, no *co-operation* from you smart boys—tell Howard so too—Go ahead, beat me up, why don't you—two of you, tha's jus' the way you boys like it, isn't it, two t' one!' His eyes focused momentarily; he laughed. 'You been in a li'l ruckus already, Lieutenant?—wha' happen, you run up against somebody a li'l tougher, like maybe a five-year-old kid? Go on, jus' try—dirty Mex bastard—'

'That one I've heard from tougher ones than you, Mr. Driscoll,' said Mendoza. 'Just a little tougher. And we really don't operate that way, you know—it's not such a good idea to give the public reason to confuse us with the thugs. Do I understand you're refusing to give us any information you have?'

'You got it in one—bingo!' said Driscoll, and attempted another laugh.

Mendoza looked at him a moment more and said, 'O.K., if that's the way you want to play it.' He turned and came out, Myers behind, and Driscoll slammed the door after them.

'A real tough baby,' said Myers. 'Oh, my.'

Mendoza grinned. 'Suppose you hang around this floor while I go down and phone in for a warrant. Just in case he gets any ideas.' He went down to the lobby, called his office and requested a warrant—material witness—as soon as possible. 'I'll wait here for it.'

It didn't take long. One of the night-duty sergeants brought it up, and Mendoza took him back up to where Myers was holding the fort. They had to make a little noise, banging on the door and threatening to get the manager, and an interested crowd had collected by the time Driscoll finally opened to them. Mendoza charged him formally and added, 'You've got five minutes to dress, make it snappy.'

'*You can't do this to me*—'

'Famous last words,' said the sergeant. 'In, buddy, and get your pants on. You're going for a joy ride ... I'll bet they turned him down for the Army, Lieutenant, he'd've learned a lot fancier cussing than that in the service.'

*   *   *

The telephone brought Mendoza out of deep sleep, shrill and imperative. Mechanically he reached out to the bedside table, only half awake, and hit his hand on the edge; swore, coming further out of sleep, and turned over to reach the phone with his right hand. Bast, who was curled in a ball alongside him, uttered faint protests at being so rudely wakened.

'Mendoza speaking.'

'This Lieutenant Mendoza of headquarters?'

'Yes.' He was fully awake now. 'Who is this?'

'Sergeant Polaski speaking, sir, Kenneth Street precinct, Hollywood. We just had a call to a break-in and assault up here, and the neighbours seemed to think you ought to be informed—say the young lady's a friend of yours. A Miss Alison Weir, it's the Blanchard Arms on—'

'I know the address, what's happened?'

175

'Just got here ourselves, sir—somebody broke in and attacked her—'

'All right, I'm coming, you carry on!' He swore steadily at his hand as he flung on some clothes: a damned nuisance. It was five minutes before he left, leaving the light on behind him. Bast looked at it plaintively, uttered a philosophic sigh, curled up with her back to it and her tail across her eyes, and went to sleep again.

On the way across town Mendoza was absently interested to notice that the Facel-Vega was apparently capable of what the manufacturers claimed for it. A good many automatic signals were off for the night at this hour, and he ignored the ones that weren't. The force was shorthanded, but he'd have a word to drop to Fletcher in Traffic: despite the comparative emptiness of the streets after midnight, it wasn't until he was within a mile of his destination that a patrol car picked him up. He didn't stop, and it was a minute behind him when he pulled up at the kerb. He got to the elevator before a patrolman caught him up, breathing wrath, to be calmed down and presented with identification.

There'd been another patrol car ahead of where he parked, and on the fourth floor there was quite a crowd. People in dressing gowns standing in their doorways, interested and excited; a very young patrolman taking notes as a pretty grey-haired woman gabbled at him; another on his knees earnestly studying the open door of Alison's apartment; a sergeant looking at something on the floor inside.

Mendoza snapped out his name and pushed past the kneeling man. 'Sergeant—'

'Lieutenant Mendoza? Good evening, sir, I mean good morning, isn't it? I'm Sergeant Polaski.' What he was looking at was a weighted short sap lying there near the door. 'The—Miss Weir, she got a nasty crack on the head—doctor's with her now, he didn't think it was necessary to take her into hospital, but—The guy evidently got scared off in a hurry, before he could do much real damage. Woman across the hall, Mrs. Corder—by what we've got so far—she and her husband were just coming home, heard Miss Weir call out, and when the guy heard *them* coming, he ran, knocked the woman halfway down the stairs to get by, and of course the husband was so busy helping her up he can't give a description—and the stair light was out of commission anyway.'

'*Vaya, vaya,*' said Mendoza, and sat down in the nearest chair and took off his hat. 'Out of commission. Or put that way. All right, Sergeant, that's good, you can carry on here just as you ordinarily would, but whatever you get I want sent downtown to headquarters to my office, O.K.?'

177

'Yes, sir.'

'And I'll have some of my men up now to look around too.' He went to the phone and called downtown, asked for a man from Prints and one of his own night staff. He discovered he'd come away without cigarettes, and emptied the box on the coffee table into his pocket, lit one. He dialled Hackett's number and was rewarded by an outraged voice.

'Don't you ever sleep? I'd think after the day you had—'

'I'm one of those people when I can't sleep I like to wake up everybody else. Now listen.' He told him briefly what had happened. '*Pronto, inmediatamente*, go and find out where they were—call the tails—'

'Who?'

'*¡Pedazo de alcornoque, imbécil!* This is the Domokous business—I think—it could be. And damn it, would either of those we know about do it themselves?—hired men—nevertheless, we'll look. The Bouvardier woman and Skyros. Were they at home thirty minutes ago, and if not, where? We'll check where we can, at least.'

'You mean I'll check,' said Hackett bitterly. 'All right, I'm on it. How's Miss Weir?'

'She has survived, I can hear her talking. You don't kill a woman until you kill her tongue. I'm about to hear what she has to say.

178

Get busy, and call me here,' he named the number, 'when you've got anything.' He hung up and went into the bedroom. The doctor, a thin sandy young man, was bending over Alison on the bed; he looked up sharply.

'Who are you? Here, young woman, you lie still, better not sit up just yet.'

'Why, Luis,' said Alison in a faint voice, sounding pleased, 'you came out without a tie.'

Mendoza said, 'It's this damned bandage, I can't manage a knot.' He sat down on the foot of the bed.

'Both been in the wars, have we? What happened to you?' She propped herself up to look at him.

'A little cut, nothing. I want to hear all about this, now. What—'

'You can't question her much now, Officer,' said the doctor. 'She's had a severe blow on the head, there's no concussion but she must have sedation and rest, and take things easy for a day or so. I understand you must know a few details, but five minutes is really *all* I can allow—'

'*¡Qué va, qué va!* Don't be stupid, she's a big strong healthy girl and not much hurt!' said Mendoza robustly.

Alison sat up straight and glared at him. 'Of all the insulting things to—you—you— *¡Monstruo diabólico!* I might have been *killed*—'

Mendoza grinned at the doctor. 'You see? She's half Irish, she can't resist a fight. You ever want to insult a woman, call her healthy.'

'I'm *not* all right, I have a horrible headache—'

'Those tablets should take effect soon, Miss Weir, *if* you are allowed to rest.'

'You haven't been in practice long, have you?' asked Mendoza. 'You or me, yes, but she's female—do her much more good to talk about it. A nice cup of coffee and cigarette—'

'No caffeine or tobacco!' said the doctor, looking as if he had suggested cyanide. 'If people would only realize, the most dangerous drugs easily available to—I cannot recommend—'

'Coffee sounds fine,' said Alison. 'If those pills *do* take effect. You go and make some, Luis. I refuse to answer questions before I comb my hair and get into something decent.' Her silk dressing gown had been ripped down the front, one sleeve torn away; she got off the bed unsteadily, clutching the torn edges together.

'Really, I *cannot* recommend—'

Mendoza took his arm and led him out. 'Thank you very much for your services, Doctor.' Spluttering, the doctor went away. Mendoza started water heating for coffee, thoughtfully making enough for everybody, and cast around in the refrigerator for something to make a sandwich of; he was hungry. The men from downtown arrived and he set one to printing the door, the other looking around generally here and downstairs.

Twenty minutes later he installed Alison in the biggest armchair with a cup of coffee, passed cups and a plate of sandwiches round to the sergeant, the very young patrolman who was ready with his notebook and pencil, and his own man Williams, who was yawning steadily, and sat down opposite Alison. 'Very cosy, *¿no es verdad?* Do you want a cigarette now, *querida?*'

'Yes, please. Doctors!' said Alison. 'If you were going to ask, I feel better, thank you. Though there's an awfully tender soft spot—' She fingered the back of her head and winced. She had combed her hair, powdered her nose, and put on lipstick, another house-robe, and looked reasonably herself.

'I should say there is a soft spot! I told you to put the chain up and keep the windows locked, damn it!'

'Well, but Luis, it just didn't seem possible—Oh, all *right*, I know it was careless, but I was tired, and after everything *else*—Coming in to find that note I couldn't make head or tail of, and *then* that the apartment had been searched—'

'*¡Por el amor de Dios!* The apartment—and *that* didn't tell you to take extra care—*¿para*

181

qué, what's the use? Females! And where in hell have you been all day? I—'

'And where were *you* when I tried to get you *then*? I called—Well, I wasn't sure, Luis, nobody could be, it was just little things, you know—'

'I don't know, but I'm going to hear every last little thing about it right now—come on, come on, tell!'

The young patrolman looked uneasily astonished at this peremptory manner of examining a witness, so contrary to the regulations in the police manual, but set down his cup and poised his pencil. 'Aren't you feeling tactful tonight!' said Alison. 'The cave-man technique.'

'Don't be obtuse, I had the hell scared out of me and this is reaction, the way a mother spanks her lost tot she thought was kidnapped. Real redheads, they're not picked up on every street-corner, it might be all of a couple of months before I found another. Let's take this in order, now. Where have you been and what time did you get home?'

'I went to the Vesperian exhibition. It was only on today, he's really quite an impossible autocrat, you know, does things just as he pleases and if it's inconvenient for other people that's just too bad. I had to close the school for the afternoon, I wanted to see it, he had all sorts of things never on view before ... The museum? Certainly not, I'm talking

182

about Vesperian the dealer—gallery out on Santa Monica Boulevard. I picked up Pat about one o'clock and of course we met various other people there, and afterwards— about five-thirty it'd have been—some of us went on to the Bradleys', and then just as it was breaking up Tony Lawlor came in wanting to talk about it all over again—really some very intersting things—and the upshot was we all went out to dinner in a crowd, to that Swedish place—'

'Yes, yes, this Bohemian riffraff you associate with, I know the kind of thing. What time—'

'That's a very old-fashioned view,' said Alison kindly. 'Bohemians are a good thirty years out of date. And we went back to the Mawsons' because Sally wanted us to look at a new thing Andy's just finished. It was about ten-thirty when Pat and I left, and I dropped her and came straight home. There was some mail, and I brought it up with me and looked at it, and this note—left by hand—I couldn't make out *what* on earth it was—'

'Yes, and you've left your prints all over it, I suppose, and maybe some of the sergeant's men have too—where is it?—the bedroom—' Mendoza went to get it, brought it back delicately balanced on his palm, and laid it on the desk. 'We'll have to isolate the extra prints, if possible, that's all. Yes. *¿Qué mono*, isn't this pretty? Ladylike fancy stationery, a
183

very fine-pointed pen, and a mysterious message. *You will tell your Irishman gangster that since he does not come in touch with me to conclude the bargain, all is cancelled, for his dishonourable greed—I do not buy, I pay him nothing! Let him come and ask now for his original price, perhaps I think about it, but if not by tomorrow, I seek the police and tell them his name.'*

'Exactly like Agatha Christie,' said Alison. 'Isn't it? And of course, I thought of that Lydia right away—'

'So do I. *Caray*, yes, and so we know who Lydia is—and, *de paso*, I'm vindicated. A lot of names I've been called by a lot of people, but nobody ever accused me of being an Irishman. Yes, well, I want this gone over for prints—oh, hell, Hellenthal's gone with the rest of what he picked up—have you got any wrapping paper?' He went and got it, and covered the note carefully in an improvised folder with its envelope. 'All right, go on.'

'Well, I couldn't make head or tail of it, but I thought you'd better hear about it, so I called you at home, and you weren't there. So I thought I'd wait until morning and then I noticed that the top drawer in my dressing table wasn't closed. And that's a sort of complex with me, you know, drawers left open—I never do—I may stuff things away all untidy, to keep it neat on the surface, but I don't like clutter, and I always shut drawers

184

properly. Even if I'd been in a particular hurry when I left—and I wasn't, today. I—Luis, you *devil*, is this that Special Roquefort I had in the—? It was for a *party*, I'm having some people in on Sunday—'

'You can get some more, it's good. Yes, go on.'

'At a dollar and a quarter—'

'I'll buy it, I'll buy it! Go on!'

'Well! I felt a little uneasy about it, and I looked around—and there were two drawers in the desk not quite shut, and I thought I'd left the closet door closed—I usually do. But I couldn't swear to any of it, it just made me wonder a little. There isn't anything missing, not that there'd be much of real value to take, but the only good pieces of jewellery I have, my grandmother's topaz ring and a few odds and ends like that, weren't touched. I wasn't sure, I just felt—you know—a little queer about it. And you needn't remind me I was warned, I couldn't leave the chain up when I went out, could I? And I couldn't see that the door had been forced, and those windows onto the fire escape *were* locked.'

'With plenty of time, he could try this and that master key or even take an impression and get a key made. It wasn't forced, no, but it might have been manipulated in some way. We'll take it off and have a look, and you'll have a new one installed anyway. What about that thing, that little coin? Where was it?'

'As a matter of fact I had it with me. I wanted to show it to Vesperian, he knows a little about a lot of things and I thought he might be able to say what it was. But I didn't get a chance to talk to him, as it happened. It's still in with the change in my coin purse, in my bag.'

Mendoza went to find it. 'This I'll take charge of. Yes, he came when you'd be gone and he could expect enough time to search thoroughly, for such a little thing. All he was after. And he did search, and didn't find it. So he figured you must be carrying it, and he came back to get it after you were home ... What the hell is its importance? But fifty to one, that's the answer.'

'Yes, I thought of it, of course. But I wasn't sure, as I say, and it seemed incredible—even after the garage business—and I didn't see any reason to call the local precinct, there wasn't anything missing and I'd feel a fool—you know how they looked at me before! And I was awfully tired, all the talk and confusion in a crowd like that, you know—I thought I'd just call you about it in the morning, there wasn't anything to do at that hour. So I went to bed. That was about midnight. All right, so I was a fool not to think of the chain—but after all, he'd *been* here, how did I know he was going to come back? I've no idea what time it was when I woke up—'

186

'The call came through at one-forty, miss,' contributed Sergeant Polaski.

'Then I suppose it'd have been ten or fifteen minutes before. I don't know what woke me—some little noise he made, maybe—but all of a sudden, I was awake, and I *knew* there was somebody in the apartment. I lay there for a minute, telling myself not to be a nervous idiot, you know how one does, and then I did hear something for certain, just a little slurred sort of sound in here—footstep on the carpet, I think. I got up as quiet as I could, and put on my robe—I had some vague idea of waiting until he came into the bedroom, if he did, and then slipping out to reach the phone and yell 'Police!' at least. I was terrified, it's a wonder he didn't hear my heart pounding. I waited for what seemed like ages, and then he *did* come in—I was over by the window, I just saw a big dark shadow move through the door. He had a pencil-flash—he was awfully quiet—and he just stood there inside the door, as if he was waiting for something. I thought—'

'That sounds,' said the sergeant thoughtfully, 'like an experienced man. He wanted to be sure you were sleeping sound. He could tell by your breathing.'

'At the moment, I sounded to myself like a steam engine. I see. I suppose that was what gave me away—he heard me from the wrong place, not the bed—and maybe I made some

187

noise moving. Anyway all of a sudden he switched on the flash and swept it around, and saw me—I was almost to the door—and made a lunge for me. I was too frightened to scream, I didn't think I could make a sound to save my life, but I did try—I called "Help!" or something, that was what the Corders heard—and I managed to pull away from him and ran in here—I thought if I could get to the phone, just to knock the receiver off and yell—and of course he came after me, and he must have knocked me out the first blow, because that's all I remember. When I came to, the Corders were dithering around and the police just getting here.'

'He didn't even have time to snatch your bag afterwards—he heard the Corders coming, and was afraid he'd be trapped—maybe he lost his head a little, dropping the sap he'd used. Yes, I see.'

'Corder,' said the sergeant, 'he said something about there having been some other trouble lately—garage broken into—and he seemed to think Miss Weir'd want you called, sir—'

'Yes, I told him all about it that morning, you remember,' said Alison.

'Well, sir, if this is mixed up with some case you're working, as I gather it is, it's out of our hands,' said the sergeant, looking interested. 'And if that's all the lady can tell us,' he heaved himself up—'we'll be getting back to the station.'

'You've been *very* kind,' said Alison, smiling at him. 'Thank you so much.' The gracious effect was marred by a sudden wide yawn. 'Oh, lord, I'm getting sleepy now, those pills—'

'Well, it's our job, miss, glad to oblige,' said the sergeant gallantly. 'If you'll be O.K. now, alone—'

'Oh, I'll be here,' said Mendoza. 'It's almost morning anyway—three o'clock—and I told my sergeant to call me here. She'll be O.K., and a new lock can be put on tomorrow.'

The sergeant looked rather doubtful, but took himself and the patrolman out. Williams was nearly asleep in his chair; Mendoza shook him awake and sent him back to headquarters with the note to deliver to Prints. 'And you are going to bed. With another of the doctor's pills.' He steered her into the bedroom. 'You'd better stay home and rest tomorrow.'

'Yes, thank heaven it's Saturday,' she said through another yawn. 'Were you really worried, Luis?' she aded sleepily, untying the sash of her robe.

'Oh, terrified—terrified. But then I scare easy.' He kissed the corner of her mouth lightly. 'Go to sleep.'

She kissed him back drowsily. 'Don't forget the Roquefort.'

'*¡Qué joven*, what a woman! Good night,

189

gatita.' As he came out to the living room the phone rang. It was Hackett, relaying the information that both Skyros and the Bouvardier woman had been as far as was humanly ascertainable, virtuously in their own beds at the crucial time.

'Or at least, in their beds. Now can I go back to mine?'

'For what's left of the night. I could wish the bastard—whoever he was—had carried on this little caper tomorrow night, I've had a full day. However! Yes, I'll see you at ten o'clock, that gives you an extra two hours to get the rest a growing boy needs.'

Hackett groaned and hung up. Mendoza carried all the dishes out to the kitchen and stacked them neatly, unable to wash them with one hand; struggled out of his jacket, took off his shoes and stretched out on the davenport, and thought some more through the last of Alison's cigarettes. Then he switched off the light, hitting his bandaged hand on the stiff parchment shade, and went to sleep.

CHAPTER FOURTEEN

Mr. Andreas Skyros had been a worried man even before he had those two phone calls. He would have said he could hardly have been more worried.

In the first place, there was the County Museum. He had seen Jackie Donovan yesterday evening, and Donovan had let it out to him—in the most casual way, as if it was a bargaining point!—how he had found out about the insurance. These low-class crooks!—one would think that anyone with the intelligence God favoured a dog would realize—! Donovan saying stupidly, 'Well, hell, they wanted to buy it before, didn't they? If they'd bid higher'n she would—only sense to go an' ask!' Sense!

The County Museum ... Mr. Skyros was not acquainted with its director, but he could vividly imagine what reception Donovan had had. And doubtless they had instantly called the police, or at least the insurance firm—God in heaven, yes, of course, that was how the insurance people had got onto it! For all he knew, they might have been quietly working away and found out everything—

No; stop; foolish to be so pessimistic. They could not—could they!—really have discovered anything. The insurance fellow had come to see Lydia Bouvardier, but unless she was lying, the insurance people had not seemed to know that she had actually been approached as yet. A crazy female, but not so crazy as to give that away, or Mr. Skyros' name, or Donovan's. Naturally not. And no one else *knew* anything about this, except

191

Donovan's brother—

Mr. Skyros had a moment of quite violent regret. If only Jackie Donovan had not got out so soon! Another month in San Quentin, and the whole deal would have been over and done. Denny was another matter entirely than Jackie. An amiable soft man, and stupid—even more stupid than Jackie—and very easy to handle. Denny, of course, had *needed* Mr. Skyros to advise him in the business—and it had again pointed the moral to Mr. Skyros of that proverb about casting one's bread on the waters. He was a man who liked to be pleasant and friendly whenever possible, and it had been only a thoughtless polite remark, that day after poor Frank's funeral, when Denny called to thank him for sending the money...

'I knowed it was from you, sir, I hope you don't mind, but I sort of felt like I ought to thank you—Frank thought you was a swell boss, he—'

At the time Mr. Skyros had been angry and alarmed; he was always so careful to keep his name and face right out of any provable contact, and here was someone entirely outside the business, someone with no interest in preserving secrecy—only because he had happened to be Frank's brother. Well, one could not prevent people from having relatives, of course. But this lout, Frank's brother, what line was *he* in?—Mr. Skyros

192

had heard, but could not recall now. But Denny sounded humble and anxious, and automatically Mr. Skyros had been paternally friendly, with an eye to winning his loyalty. And inevitably had said, 'If there's ever any way I can help you, my friend—'

And had it not paid off! Not two months later, Denny coming to him with this—money for nothing, you could say. And agreeing to the price at once, so astonished that they might get such a price for it; *and* to the cut, fifty-fifty. It was, of course, a reasonable price—and a reasonable cut. After all, it was a rather delicate matter to handle, it required just the right touch, and Mr. Skyros was the man to handle it. He had, of course, no intentions of revealing himself as in touch with the original thief—he did not then know Lexourion's daughter; she might be an honest woman who would immediately go to the police at the mere suggestion.

He was quite pleased with the artistic little idea of the advertisement in the paper ostensibly to get in touch with the thieves. It had convinced her that he was only the helpful friend of her late father's, as he had represented himself; and of course it had been easy to persuade her to let him make the contact in that way—a lady could not be allowed to have such dealings with a criminal, when there was a gentleman willing to substitute. It had delayed matters, inevitably;

there had to be plausible time allowed to give it the appearance of—of verisimilitude.

But all so very easy and smooth. And then this one, this Jackie, must show up, just a little smarter—smart enough to see that Mr. Skyros had tied himself into it and must get his cut, but greedy for a higher price in consequence.

The County Museum, my God...

And this crazy woman, bent on defrauding the insurance company. Madness. Nothing out of Mr. Skyros' pocket, but could she not see that in a matter of this kind one must give a little in order to gain? True, two hundred thousand dollars was a respectable sum of money: Mr. Skyros could appreciate the temptation, to get it back twice. But it was *not* such a thing as cash, or nice bearer bonds, or a handful of diamonds—anonymous, unidentifiable. Wherever this thing showed up, it would be known; and it could not be sold piecemeal, its actual intrinsic value was as a whole: split it up, and it was worth nowhere near that amount. If she wanted anything out of it, the pedigree, so to speak, had to be clear. Men to buy in secret, she said: nonsense: anyone who laid out that kind of money wanted to boast of it.

So, this nice plausible little story for the police and the insurance men, one easy to believe, for they too would know it was nothing a thief could sell to a fence. Perhaps

194

to make them think—it was an idea—that the thief had aimed for her all along, to hold it at ransom, as it were. A nice story about this telephone call, this meeting with a disguised fellow—no, not to be identified, so little she'd seen of him—the exchange of cash for the collection. And there she was with it in her legal possession, able to sell it openly.

Everybody made a profit that way. My God, she had no guarantee the old man would have left her anything at all: had he lived longer, the thing would have been sold, and heaven above knew she had plenty of money already; he might very well have left everything to some society or college, who knew? The ten thousand profit to Mr. Skyros (though she need not know he had a piece of it, of course) and the Donovans was the little price she paid for clear title to it, for being able to realize something from its sale.

He had thought anyone would see that, even a scatter-headed female. A thing like this, my God, the insurance people would be like starving tigers on a manhunt if they suspected—and of course they *would* suspect, not being fools. But she did *not* see, she was determined to keep that money: Mr. Skyros, sitting at his desk that Friday afternoon worrying, mopped his brow agitatedly. Bring them all down on her like—like the Assyrians in that poem, she would, and eventually on Mr. Skyros too. Because she would naturally not hesitate, come to the point, to name him, believing he was an innocent upright businessman with all his ways open to inspection.

And, oh, God, this Domokous business ... He had thought the police were quite satisfied about Domokous, but were they? Were they still investigating? God only knew. Mr. Skyros had just returned from the funeral, where he had received another little shock—Domokous had been engaged, the girl was there. The girl—a sullen-looking young woman—now what might she want, asking if she could come to see him tomorrow afternoon? He would tell her, he decided, that Domokous' salary had been due, and he felt she should have it in lieu of any family. Yes. The picture of the kind, friendly employer he had presented at the funeral. Maybe she only wanted to ask him for a job or something.

Domokous ... Really a chapter of accidents, *that* had not been necessary at all. These violent people—no finesse, no understanding! Domokous had known nothing; Mr. Skyros had seen at once that he was only too anxious to believe it a misunderstanding, and any halfway plausible little story would have sent him away satisfied. But *not* after he'd been knocked unconscious from behind. Or even before

196

that, after the little argument with Donovan there—

Suddenly Mr. Skyros sat bolt upright in his chair and called upon God. He had remembered something. He saw Domokous with that list in his hand, picked up from the desk, and Donovan swearing, reaching for it—he heard the little snap of tearing paper. Part of it had torn away—had it? If so, what had become of it? Did it include anything which might be dangerous?

He must ask Donovan about it.

These terrible violent men. Killing, that *was* dangerous: a prudent man found other means, did not get into situations which might lead to such actions. But circumstances, as the saying went, alter cases. There Domokous *was*, knowing that something wrong was going on, and what to do with him? He was not the type to be bought off, *that* Mr. Skyros knew: a most tiresomely honest young man.

Two birds with one stone. Involve Bratti. One could hope, at least. But Mr. Skyros had not at all liked anything about that business; he had had as little to do with it as possible . . .

He had been worried then, sitting there in his office thinking about it; but three minutes later his worries increased. The phone rang and he took it up to hear the voice of one Eugene Castro, whom he had once known well.

197

'Listen,' said Castro, 'the boss don't like fancy tricks played on him ... You know what I mean. Big joke, hah, telling your Frog lady-friend about how Bratti's a real old-fashioned gangster, hot cannon man at his elbow night 'n' day—hah?—so she tries to hire him to take off a guy she don't like. That's a dilly of a joke, Skyros—real belly laugh!'

'What? My friend, I don't know what you're talking about—'

'Skip the friend. It kind of annoyed the boss, an' I wouldn't say but what it's maybe give him ideas. You *can* still buy it, you know just where to go an' who to see, contact a dropper for rent. You pull another one like that, an' the boss just might go lookin', Skyros.' The receiver thudded in his ear.

Mr. Skyros clutched his temples. Heaven above knew he was not sorry that Bratti was annoyed, but—! 'Your Frog lady-friend'— what had this crazy woman been up to now?

And then the phone rang again, and it was Angelo, with the news that Prettyman and three of his boys were in jail, and the Elite raided and the entire month's supply confiscated.

★   ★   ★

Jackie Donovan was worried as hell, and the worst of it was, it wasn't the kind of worry he

198

could share aloud with anybody. Not even Denny. God, Denny least of all—Denny always looking up to him as the boss, Jackie the one knew all the answers, called all the shots. Always *had* been. So, sure, it was just this first little while, kind of getting back on his feet after that long a stretch—but he didn't like this funny feeling, not being *sure*.

Doing things a ten-year-old kid—

Like a nervous kid on his first job.

That sap. Dropping it like that. And of course he'd had gloves on, but he'd handled it before without, and he didn't know whether the holding it with the gloves after would have maybe wiped out all the prints.

He sat in the park thinking about it, worrying about it, but worrying a lot harder about something else. About a feeling he'd been having since he remembered about the sap, a feeling he hadn't even dared admit to himself until just now.

That sap, maybe with a print. So they'd know. And they'd put him back inside.

And he didn't care—he wanted to be back inside.

No! Acourse that was a crazy damn-fool thing, just part of being first out after so long. He'd be feeling his old self, thinking like his old self, pretty soon now, and looking back to all this and laughing. Private-like, to himself.

Some guys did get that way. So they felt—lost—outside. Inside, you *knew* about everything. Just what was going to happen, when. You didn't have to think, and plan, and worry. Some guys got so they didn't like it outside; it was easier in.

Jackie Donovan, my God, wasn't one of those. Fifteen years or fifteen hundred, he'd never be one of those!

Better think about that little thing. How the hell to get it back. Not in the car, that he was sure of, and so he'd figured she must have found it. He'd been surprised it turned out to be a dame, the name such a funny one; but all the easier, in a way—he'd had plenty of time, go through the apartment careful, and he'd swear it wasn't there. So then he'd figured she had it on her—and *that* had gone all wrong . . .

Everything, God, going wrong. He thought vaguely maybe be oughtn't ever to've let Denny and Frank get to where they just waited for him to give the orders: if they'd had to think out things for themselves, maybe they wouldn't have got into such messes when he got sent across, wasn't there no more. Well, so O.K., they'd made out all right, in a sort of way, but just no sense about looking ahead. Getting tied up to pushers . . . That Angelo. Well, all right, Angie'd been a good guy once, lot of fun sometimes, a nice little guy, and dependable too: jobs he'd done with them, Angie'd maybe pulled them out of a spot, couple of times—good driver, then, he'd been. You could figure it was old times had held Denny to Angie, and that was fine, ordinarily: nobody liked a guy ran out on his pals. But the minute Angie had got onto *that* lay, and started taking sleigh-rides himself, Denny ought to've dropped him but quick. Instead, he let Angie take Frank into it, and—

Water under the bridge. You had to think about here and now. Damn fool Denny bunking down with Angie—just have somebody to talk to, after Frank was gone! Jackie hadn't got the straight of this business yesterday, if somebody had talked or the cops had just found out something on their own, and he didn't much care. It'd given him the excuse to pull Denny out, anyways. To say, maybe if somebody's talked, the cops knew about all of them, about Angie too, and better they split up. Angie'd seen the sense in that. Didn't matter where Angie'd gone; let him go his own way from now on, forget him. Angie said, now this other guy was inside, and marked, probably he'd get his job—specially as he knew the middleman Skyros. Well, knew who he was. That kind, like Skyros, was usually leery of getting known much, but Angie happened to know him, account of Frank—way Denny's got in with him too, on this other deal.

And what a deal. Of all the crazy things: Jackie'd got to feeling a little like how Denny did, better get shut of it any old way.

When you came down to it, anything they got off it was profit, like Denny said. Ten thousand for *that*. But it really griped him that Skyros had to get a fifty percent cut—sure, so he'd set it up with the dame, but what was there to that? My God, if he'd got out sooner himself, before Denny made the deal he could have set it up with her just as good, and the ten thousand between him and Denny. Skyros, this chiseller...

So what about that little thing he'd lost? He was wondering now if maybe that other dame had ever had it at all. He'd thought of the car, first place, because things did slip out of your pockets sometimes, sitting down; but it could have happened other ways. When he came back to the Caddy, that day, he'd been feeling kind of mean—way that guy in there had looked down his nose at him—and you didn't notice things much, feeling like that. Maybe when he reached to get the keys, it had dropped out. Could be. Dropped onto the grass in the parking there, or in the gutter. Could've been laying there ever since—unless they cleaned up, a gardener with a rake or something—but a little thing like that ... If it was in the gutter, other shorts'd gone over it, it might be covered up with leaves and muck—Not awful likely anybody would have found it.

But, God, how could he go and look? He
202

thought he could remember just about where, but in a place like that, everybody noticing ... He could say he'd dropped his keys or something—yes, and ten to one a gardener, or some kids, wanting to help look. Oh, the hell with it—if he did find it, no need let anybody see, stick it in his pocket and pretend to keep on looking for what he'd lost. Nobody would notice.

If he didn't get it back, *that* would be noticed all right.

That damned sap. If there was a print—Didn't want to get Denny in trouble. Just as well Denny didn't know anything about it; he could say so, if—

Donovan got up and walked out of Pershing Square, down Sixth to Main, and down Carson to the cheap rooming house where they'd moved last night, him and Denny. There wasn't a garage; the Caddy was sitting on the street. The Caddy Denny'd gone and got back for him. He got out his keys slowly, got in and started her. He felt a little bit easier with her now.

He drove out Exposition to the park and into the grounds, found a place to put the Caddy, and walked up to where he'd parked that day, near as he remembered. There were parked cars almost solid here, damn it, couldn't go crawling under every one to see. But he did what looking he could, peering along the gutter between cars.

After awhile, just as he'd figured, a guy came along and stopped and asked what was wrong. 'I dropped my keys somewheres,' said Donovan, 'somewheres right along here. I *think* it musta been—damn fool thing to do, but you know how these things happen.'

'Oh,' said the guy, 'that so? Hope you find 'em, damn nuisance all right. You don't, you better go and ask at the Lost and Found desk in at the museum—maybe somebody's turned 'em in.'

'Gee, yes, maybe so,' agreed Donovan. The guy got into the car by the kerb there and started the engine. Donovan realized maybe he'd been suspicious he was looking her over with an eye to hopping her. But it left a space free to look at ... He waited for the guy to jink her out into the street, and all of a sudden he noticed something and his heart dropped.

The car didn't have fender aprons, and as it pulled out he could see the threads of the back tyres; and on the left one, there was an old bent metal slug of some kind half-buried in the rubber, sticking there ... This damn hundred-and-ten weather, the asphalt going all soft, your shoes'd stick to it sometimes, crossing the street—a little thing like that, sticky with asphalt, getting glued onto a tyre easy, carried away God knew where. Or more likely ground down into the asphalt when tyres went over it.

For half a minute there he felt like he could cry, just sit down on the kerb and bawl like a kid. He felt the sweat trickling down his back, in the merciless muggy heat; and he knew for sure that thing was gone for good, he'd never get it back. He thought of what trouble *that* would make.

He thought of Angie saying, anything to do with an ace of spades, bad luck. And maybe Angie was right.

And all of a sudden, again, he felt kind of homesick—for the place you didn't have to worry what was going to happen tomorrow . . .

★   ★   ★

Driscoll lay awake miserably on the hard cell cot and worried over his sins. What the hell Howard would say to *this*—well, all right, he knew what the hell Howard would say! And damn it, you could say all Howard's fault in the first place—*picking* at him, criticizing—so he wanted, by God, to show Howard just how good he was—

Damned cops. All bullies, taking any excuse to—

And unless he was the hell of a lot luckier than he'd been lately, this would mean his job.

All right, so he'd just have to do what he could on it, now. Tell the damned cops what they wanted to know, all pals together, apologize all over the place for how he'd acted—personal troubles, he'd say, he knew he'd been drinking too much—lay it to that—give a guy a break, I didn't mean to—So they wouldn't go sending any official complaint to the company. Howard needn't ever hear a word about it, with any luck. O.K.

His head was aching and his stomach felt queasy; he groaned, trying to get into a comfortable position. Ease up on the drink, sure, after this. Better try. But God, he'd like one now, get him through, help him—

He couldn't sleep, and it seemed morning would never come, so he could start to get this all straightened out—as straight as he could, anyway...

CHAPTER FIFTEEN

Lydia Bouvardier was feeling not so much worried as irritated. She was irritated at Mr. Skyros, at this Donovan, very much so at that insurance man, and at the situation in general. A good deal of her irritation was occasioned by the fact that nothing seemed to be as she had thought—as it *should* be.

She applied lipstick carefully and said, 'Go try to get this Skyros at the telephone again,

Berthe ... More and more I have the feeling that he is not to be trusted! All these fine excuses why he cannot put me in touch with this Irishman—no business for a lady, he says. And in any case he does not know where Donovan is. Which is absurd, of course he knows. If I could but again meet Donovan face to face, ah, I see he makes the bargain quickly!'

She made a little exclamation of annoyance and snatched up a tissue to wipe away the minute ragged speck of lipstick on her excellent white teeth ... It was not only irritating, but puzzling. She had thought it a brilliant inspiration, about the jewellers. One gathered from the *romans de policiers* that that kind of thing was quite common here; it was well known that Americans would do anything for money. Very probably the owners of the place robbed had been in the affair with the robber, in order to defraud the insurance firm—the jewels taken they would then have back, and recut and remount to sell them. So, naturally, they would know the thief *and* where he was to be found. A delicate little matter, to speak frankly to them, explain that she had no care for that aspect, it was their own business, but if they would be so obliging to inform her where Donovan was staying ... Once they understood clearly that she knew the ins and outs of the affair, and were reassured of her tolerance in the matter—

One was aware that it was nothing out of the way here, all Americans were quite lawless. But it appeared that she had been wrong. The gentleman there in the shop, introducing himself—the same name as that on the door, one of the owners then: he had positively exuded respectable integrity. That she had recognized almost instantly: one might as well suspect the present Minister of Finance of robbing the national treasury.

In fact, when it came to the point, that was far more likely.

That red-haired woman ... It had looked to be a respectable apartment, very poor of course, but—Not probable that Donovan was actually living there. And he had ignored her messages.

And when one thought twice, it would be foolish to have Donovan shot, or his mistress, for in the one case he could not conclude the bargain, and in the other he would only be more annoyed. But perhaps to let him see that she was *not* a fool, to threaten him convincingly—And so she had been very practical, remembering the name Skyros had said, a cheap gangster (which was just as well, she did not want to lay out too great a sum on this), and looking it up in the directory.

But, *zut!*—he was not a gangster at all. He did not wear a black shirt, or leave his cigarette in the mouth-corner like an *Apache*,

208

he spoke quite grammatical English, and at first he had been very polite. Later he had been annoyed, which of course was understandable if he was not a gangster.

'They say Mr. Skyros is not in his office, madame, but he is expected there after lunch.'

'Ah, how provoking!' exclaimed Madame Bouvardier. 'All this, it leaves me exactly where I have started! Since this Irishman makes no reply to my messages, which he must have had by now, he is evidently determined to remain obstinate. Perhaps he and Skyros have made it up between them to be obstinate, yes. Well, this Skyros shall have some plain language from me today, that I can promise!'

★　　★　　★

Mr. Skyros did not sleep much on Friday night. He got up very early, pleading business to his wife, and arrived at his office before eight o'clock, before his employees. He locked himself in and went to the small safe he kept on the shelf of the filing cupboard; from this he took five twenty-dollar bills. Then he put on the gloves he had brought with him, sat down at the desk, and addressed an envelope to one Mr. Chester Scott, attorney-at-law. He cut a strip of paper from a clean page and printed on it in

209

carefully disguised letters, *In account with M. Prettyman*, and attached it to the bills with a paper clip. He put this small parcel into the envelope, sealed and stamped it, unlocked the door and left the office.

Outside, he sought his car and drove down to the main post office, and mailed the envelope at the kerb box without leaving the car. Heading back for the office, he left just a trifle more cheerful; there was one little matter off his mind, at least. But from the few details he had heard, no lawyer could get Prettyman off the hook, with the stuff found on him—a year at least ... Mr. Skyros was not much worried about the lawyer. He was not a very scrupulous lawyer, he was used to dealing with such clients as Prettyman, and he would not bat an eye at receiving this anonymous retainer. It was necessary to guarantee the Prettymans such services, of course, for otherwise they might feel a grievance and talk a bit too much while they were inside. No reasonable man could object to paying out a moderate sum for loyalty.

By the time he arrived back at his office the staff had come in, and the pretty bookkeeper gave him a cheerful good morning. 'Gee, it's going to be hot again, Mr. Skyros—even this early you can tell.'

'This time of year, one wishes maybe to live in Alaska, isn't it?' returned Mr. Skyros genially. 'I bet all your friends, they envy you in a nice air-conditioned office. Maybe I ought to cut something off your salary for the advantage!' He passed on into his office, sat down and worried a little more, waiting for the phone call.

When it came, he had thought of a place. Sometimes it was inconvenient, going all round to get somewhere, but it was only sense to be careful. About the cops you never knew: they could be almost cunning sometimes, and if they did know about others besides those they'd taken, and were watching . . . 'Come to the airport,' he said. 'Municipal Airport, isn't it? In the men's room, the main building.'

Such a nice public place, and perhaps—if he was ever asked about it—he'd been thinking of a little holiday somewhere, inquiring about fares. Yes.

He told the bookkeeper he'd be back after lunch, and drove out to the airport. A terrible drive in traffic in this weather, but these things always came up at inconvenient times. He sought out the men's room and waited; whenever someone else came in he pretended to be washing his hands, straightening his tie. And presently he was joined by the man he waited for, but, my God, he had this stupid lout, this Denny, with him.

'We kinda figured I maybe oughta come along, Mr. Skyros, on account you never met Angie before and I could say he *is*.'

'No names, for the love of heaven,' implored Mr. Skyros. 'All right, I am assured, this is he himself.' And then they all fell silent, as a pair of men came in. Mr. Skyros washed his hands industriously, looking at Angelo Forti out of the corner of his eye. No, him he had not met before, but he knew a good deal about him from Prettyman. A useful man—for the time being—because he was, by what Prettyman said, such a very persuasive salesman. A specialist in the high school kids, looking a little like a kid himself, though not young—but a small, frail-looking man, a man nobody could ever be afraid of, a little not-unhandsome man with dreamy dark eyes. And of course, also the profit was higher on Angelo, since he was a user himself. But for that very reason Mr. Skyros much disliked having any dealing with him, and *that* was going to pose a little problem . . .

'It was Castro,' said Angelo, turning his soft dark eyes on Mr. Skyros as they were left alone. 'Way I heard it. One of his boys come around askin' for me, probably an offer get me into that string, see, and Pretty and some o' the boys, they just figured rough him up a little. You know. No trouble. But it kinda went wrong—I don't know, seemed the guy was a little bit tougher than he looked—there was quite a ruckus, and somebody called the cops.'

212

'Such a thing!' said Mr. Skyros crossly. 'All over such a little business!' There were times he wished he had never had a disagreement with Bratti, and actually that had been unnecessary too, looked at calmly. A little matter of a thousand dollars or so, and it was quite possible that it had not been Bratti or Castro who had waylaid Hogg and taken the stuff from him. Hogg had not been able to say, he had been riding high himself at the time—madness to get on the stuff, these irresponsible people!—and Mr. Skyros had perhaps leaped to a conclusion. But that was past praying for now, the quarrel established.

'I figured,' said Angie, 'I take over for Pretty, and maybe so, you tell me now where to pick up the stuff and when? It'd be just fine, you got some stashed away maybe now, on account the cops got everything at the Elite.'

Yes, and here was the problem. Mr. Skyros had no desire at all to put Angelo in Prettyman's shoes; you could not trust any man who was on the stuff himself. Angie might be worth his weight in gold as a pusher, but to take any responsibility—my God! To know dangerous information—one never knew what that kind would do.

He gave Angie a genial smile and said, 'Well, now, you see, my friend, I haven't just made up my mind, I've thought maybe it's a good idea to lie quiet awhile. If the cops know some more than it looks like—dropping on the boys so—'

'Ah, that was just the breaks,' said Angie. 'They don't know nothin'. Just happened find the stuff on Pretty, after that ruckus. Everything's O.K. I can get you three-four new guys, no time at all, to take over. Find a new drop, the Elite closed up. No trouble.'

'Well—' said Mr. Skyros. 'I take a little time to think it over.' It was awkward: very awkward. There would be all the nuisance of contacting someone else to take over. Someone reasonably trustworthy. And Angie would hear about it. And Angie knew—

'Time,' said Angie, and he smiled very sweet and slow at Mr. Skyros. 'Not too much time, because I'll be needing some more myself pretty much right away. And I done favours for you, big favour not so long back, didn't I, and I'm right here to take on where Pretty left off. No trouble. I don't want no trouble, you don't want no trouble, nobody wants trouble, Mr. Skyros.'

Dear heaven, no, thought Mr. Skyros, turning away as another man came in. He straightened his tie at the mirror with a shaking hand; the genial smile seemed painted on his face. Angie knew—Speak of dangerous information! Angie knew too much entirely already. Really he had Mr. Skyros at bay . . .

'Big favour I done you. Acourse there's this

214

deal o' Denny's—and Jackie's—kinda hangin' fire, ain't it, maybe you've been kinda worryin' over that. And can't say I blame you,' said Angie thoughtfully. 'This deal with the ace o' spades. Anything to do with an ace o' spades, bad luck.'

Ace of spades—a widow, that was what they called a widow, these low-class crooks, remembered Mr. Skyros distractedly. All about that Angie knew, too. When things got a little out of hand, they very rapidly got a lot out of hand—it seemed to be a general rule. All just by chance, and in a way tracing back to poor Frank, all of it, because naturally—brothers, living together—and Angie—

Mr. Skyros did not at all like the look on Angelo's regular-featured, almost girlishly good-looking face—or indeed anything about Angelo. Mr. Skyros was not a man who thought very much about moral principles; he found money much more interesting; but all the same he thought now, uneasily, of the way in which Angelo earned his living—and paid for his own stuff—and eyed the soft smile, and the spaniel-like dark eyes, and he felt a little ill.

'Look, my friend,' he said, 'in my life I learn, how is it the proverb says, better an ounce of prevention to a pound of cure. I stay in business so long because I'm careful. Two weeks, a month, we talk it over again, and maybe if nothing happens meanwhile to say the cops know this and that, then we make a little deal, isn't it?'

'That's a long while,' said Angie. 'I tell you, you want to leave it that way, I don't fool around with it. I go over to Castro and get fixed up there. I can't wait no two weeks.'

And Mr. Skyros didn't like Angie, but what with Prettyman and three of his boys inside, and not likely to come out—And Angie such a valuable salesman, Prettyman said—All the nuisance and danger of getting in touch with practically a whole new bunch of boys—Why did everything have to happen at once?

Denny said stupidly, 'Why, you ain't turning Angie down, are you, Mr. Skyros? I mean, we all figured—I guess anybody'd figure—Angie—'

Angelo gave him an affectionate smile. 'Mr. Skyros too smart a fellow want to get rid of me,' he said. 'It's O.K., Denny, everything's O.K. Ain't it, Mr. Skyros?'

Oh, God, the name repeated over and over, anybody to hear—Not being a fool, Mr. Skyros knew why. But aside from everything else, it would scarcely be pleasant to have dealings with one who was nominally an underling and actually held—you could say—the whip hand. And all because of Domokous! If Mr. Skyros had dreamed of all

216

the trouble that young man would eventually cause—

Of course, there was another factor. Angie was worth his weight in gold right now, but these users, they sometimes went down fast. Who knew, Angie might not last long . . . The sweat broke out on Mr. Skyros' forehead as he realized he had been actually thinking—hoping—planning—perhaps—

Good God above, had not Domokous been enough?

He patted Angelo's thin shoulder paternally. 'Now you don't want to go talking that way,' he said. 'Sure, sure, you're the one take over for Pretty, soon as I get the supply, get started up again, isn't it? You don't need worry, Angelo. I tell you, I know how it is with you, my friend, I sympathize, and I'll make it a special point—a special favour—get in touch, and get some stuff just for you. I don't know if I can manage it tonight or tomorrow, but I'll try my best, my friend. You see, you got to remember, we all got schedules, like any business! My man, he won't be around a little while, he just fixed me up with this stuff they took out of the Elite. It's awkward, you see that, isn't it?'

'Well, that's your business, Mr. Skyros,' said Angie, and his dreamy eyes moved past Mr. Skyros' shoulder to gaze vaguely out of the ground-glass window. 'I appreciate it, you do that. Sure. We don't none of us want no trouble . . . I'm in a room over the Golden

Club on San Pedro, you just ask for me there, you want see me. Or maybe I call you—tonight? About nine o'clock, I call and see if you got any. A couple decks for me, Mr. Skyros—and ten-twelve to sell, see, I like to have a little ready cash.'

'Oh, now, I don't know about that much,' said Mr. Skyros. 'And you know, Angelo, Pretty, he always keeps it a strict cash basis, like they say—'

'Sure,' said Angie. 'Sure, Mr. Skyros. Fifty a throw, that the deal? Sure. I bring you the cash, say five hundred for ten decks. Never mind how much I cut it, how much I get,' and he smiled his sleepy smile again. 'Standard deal, Mr. Skyros. You go 'n' have a look round for it.'

'I do my best,' said Mr. Skyros earnestly, 'just for you, my friend. This is awkward for everybody, isn't it, we all got to put up with inconvenience sometimes. But I do my best for you.' He got out of there in a hurry, brushing past another man in the door, mopping his brow.

The expedient thing—yes, very true, one must make do as one could, in some situations. It could all be straightened out later. Not very much later, but when things had settled down a little. After this deal with the Bouvardier woman went through. An ace of spades . . . He was not a superstitious man, but he felt perhaps there was a little something in that, indeed. He rather wished he had never got into the business, and still—scarcely to be resisted, a nice little profit with not much work involved, easy money...

★   ★   ★

Katya Roslev, who would be Katharine Ross so very soon now, rang up her first sale of the day and counted back the change. She did not notice that the customer seized her purchase and turned away without a smile or a word of thanks. Usually she marked the few who did thank you, you didn't get that kind much in a place like this; and she played a little game with herself, seeing how downright rude she could act to the others, before they'd take offence, threaten to call the manager. Funny how seldom they did: used to it, probably. The kind who came into a cheap store like this! Grab, snatch, I saw that first! and, Here, I'll take this, I was before *her*, you wait on me now or I don't bother with it, see! This kind of place...

She'd be through here, just no time at all—leave this kind of thing 'way behind. Off at noon, and she'd never come back. Never have to. Money—a lot of money, *enough*. She'd be smart about it, get him to give it to her in little bills so's nobody would suspect—maybe couldn't get it until Monday

219

account of that, the banks—But that wasn't really long to wait. Not when she'd waited so long already.

No need say anything at all to the old woman. She had it all planned out, how she'd do. She'd say she didn't feel good on Sunday, couldn't go to church—there'd be a little argument, but she could be stubborn—and when the old woman had gone, quick pack the things she'd need to take, all but the dress she'd wear Monday, and take the bag down to that place in the station where you could put things in a locker overnight, for a dime. Then on Monday morning—or it might have to be Tuesday—get up and leave just the usual time, and last thing, put the money in an envelope under the old woman's purse there in the drawer. She wouldn't be going to get that for an hour or so after Katya had left, go do the daily shopping. No need leave a note with it, either—or maybe just something like, Don't worry about me, I'm going away to make a better life.

A better life. Escape. It wasn't as if she wanted *much*. She didn't mind working hard, not as if she figured to do anything *wrong* to live easy and soft—all she wanted was a *chance*, where she wasn't marked as what she was. To be Katharine Ross, and work in a nicer shop somewhere, at a little more money so she could have prettier clothes, and learn ladies' manners and all like that, and get to know different people than up to now, not just the ones like her here, with foreign-sounding names, the ones went to the same church and—Different place, different job, different people, she'd be all different too. Prettier, she'd do her hair another way; smarter, and wear different kinds of clothes—she'd be Katharine Ross, just what that *sounded* like.

'You've given me the wrong change,' said the customer sharply. 'Think I can't count?'

Katya made up the amount in indifferent silence. She was listening to other voices, out of the future. Some of those vaguely-imagined new, different people. *Oh, Katharine's awfully nice, and pretty too, I like Katharine—Let's ask Katharine to go with us, she's always lots of fun—Katharine—*

Soon, very soon now . . .

CHAPTER SIXTEEN

Mendoza didn't wake until nearly nine-thirty. It was going to be another hot day; already the thermometer stood close to ninety. Alison was still sound asleep; he made fresh coffee and searched through all the desk drawers for more cigarettes before thinking of her handbag, and found a crumpled stray cigarette at its bottom, which tasted peculiarly of face powder. He left a note propped on the desk asking her to call him sometime today, and drove home.

After he'd got out fresh liver for Bast, he paused to look at her crouched daintily over her dish. Surely she *was* just a trifle fatter around the middle? He seemed to remember reading somewhere that Abyssinians had large litters, and suffered a dismaying vision of the apartment overrun with a dozen kittens. '*¿Y qué sigue despues?—*what then?' he asked her severely. 'A lot of people are so peculiar that they don't like cats, it's not the easiest thing in the world to find good homes for kittens—and, damn it, you know very well if I have them around long, impossible to give them away! And I suppose now that you've finally grown up, if a little late, you'd go on producing kittens every six months or so. Yes, well, it's a pity to spoil your girlish figure—which all those kittens would do anyway—but I think when you've raised these we'll just have the vet fix it so there won't be any more . . . I wonder if the Carters would take one . . . And it's no good looking at me like that,' as she wound affectionately around his ankles. '*Todo tiene sus limites*—a limit to everything, *¿comprende?* We will not keep more than one, and there'll be no more!'

He had a bath and shaved. He looked up the number and called Miss Champion, the receptionist-bookkeeper at Alison's school, and told her to go round to the apartment in an hour or so; explained. Miss Champion twittered: she'd put up a notice and go *right* round, what a terrible *thing*, and—what?—oh, yes, she'd take some cigarettes with her. Mendoza looked in the book again and called a locksmith, told him to go and install a new lock, but not before eleven o'clock. Then he folded his tie to take with him and drove downtown.

He found Hackett already there, reading a report. 'You've got an excuse,' said Hackett, taking the tie from him, 'but I'll bet you've never checked in so late since you made rank. Hold your head up, I can't get at it with—No, I know it's not as pretty a job as you'd do, but I didn't join the force to learn how to be a valet. This is from Callaghan. I don't know how much it'll say to you—it doesn't say much to me.'

Mendoza sat down and took the page. It was a copy of an official card from Records, and it sketched in the person and salient points of career of one Francis Joseph Donovan. Five-ten, one-seventy, hair black, eyes grey, complexion medium, Caucasian, male. One short stretch in reformatory as a minor, for car theft: one three-year term seven years later for burglary: picked up several times for questioning on various occasions thereafter, but no more charges or sentences after he'd got out from serving that one eight years ago. Suspected rather recently of having turned pusher, considering known associates. Callaghan had appended some notes to the terse concluding sentence of the record. A little over three months ago, Frank Donovan had been pointed out to a traffic patrolman, by a high school boy, as the man who had approached him and made some pitch the boy thought was leading up to offering marijuana or some other dope. There'd been lectures at school about these guys, he said, and a movie—and this one acted kind of like that. So the patrolman had gone up to ask some questions, and not being satisfied with the answers had searched Donovan and come across a handful of reefers; whereupon Donovan had tried to run, the patrolman had gone after him, shouted warning, fired once over his head and once at his legs—but it was hard to take careful aim when you were running, and he'd got him through the spine. Donovan had died that night in the General.

'Mmh, yes,' said Mendoza. 'And I don't like that kind of careless business as a rule—it gets in the papers, the public talks about trigger-happy cops—but once in a while it saves everybody a lot of trouble. This kind, a year inside for unlawful possession, what is it? They can't be cured.' He turned the page over and read a further notation in Callaghan's big scrawl. *I think this is the Frank*

224

those two meant. He left a widow, Mrs. Amy Donovan, address you know on Daggett. She works at a joint on Main, the Golden Club, singing with a cheap combo. No record. 'Well, well. Don't tell me we're beginning to straighten all this out. At least place some of the people, even the ones on the outside edge of the business. Like the house that Jack built. Prettyman who knows Skyros who knows Lydia.'

'I don't know Lydia. Suppose you bring me up to date.'

Mendoza obliged. 'The only way I can figure it is that this part of it goes back to the theft of Alison's car. Somebody dropped this thing in it'—he brought it out, looked at it, passed it over—'and is anxious to have it back. So anxious he's made several elaborate attempts for it. Which reminds me,' and he reached for the phone, called down to Prints, and asked if they had anything on that sap or the letter he'd sent in. Nothing but a confused mess on the sap; a variety of prints on the letter. As was only to be expected, damn it. He called the lab and asked if anything had turned up on that lock. Marks inside, little fresh scratches, where the thin arms of the stiff-wire tools from any complete burglar's kit had groped for the right combination of pressures. 'There you are. An experienced man. Not, of course, Lydia—somebody else. Which fits in, in a way, you know, because Lydia apparently thought Alison was—mmh—somebody else than she is. *Caray*, what a series of little accidents! Yes, I *think* Lydia had a ride in that car while the thief had it, and noticed the registration slip, and leaped to the conclusion that the car belonged to the thief's girl-friend. I can see that happening, can't you? And she also tells us that the thief is an Irishman. Donovan is an Irish name.'

'You aren't supposing,' said Hackett, 'that Frank Donovan got up out of his grave, where he'd been peacefully decomposing for a couple of months, and stole Miss Weir's car out of the park?'

'*No hay tal*. But the Irish are a prolific race,' said Mendoza. 'And just what has that got to do with Stevan Domokous? So, we can say for maybe ninety per cent sure that Skyros is a middleman dope-runner, on Bratti's level, and a rival of Bratti's—that Domokous somehow found out about it, couldn't be bought off, and had to be killed. And on the principle of killing two birds with one stone, Skyros told us a nice little tale about Domokous mentioning Bratti, hoping to tie Bratti up to it. That I see. But who and what is Lydia? I thought I'd had an inspiration yesterday, I had a little vision of Skyros being more important than a middleman, importing the stuff himself, cunningly stashed away in the hollow insides

226

of his foreign bric-à-brac—say inside this nymph and that dolphin, you know. But on second thoughts, I realized that the customs boys surely must know about that old dodge, it'd never do.'

Hackett agreed absently, still looking at the coin. 'Funny-looking thing. Looks damned old, doesn't it? There's a fellow down in Records, O'Brien, I ran into him at lunch one day awhile back—he's an amateur what-you call-it—numismatist. I wonder if he'd know anything about what kind of thing this is.'

'No harm to go and ask. Take it if you like ... Yes, of course it looks like a straightforward pro business—whether it was murder or not, legally speaking. From the little we've got on it. And yet, Lydia—'

Hackett was still turning the little coin over in his fingers. '*I* think,' he said suddenly, 'you've got hold of a couple of different picture puzzles, and're trying to fit pieces from both into one picture. It could be that Domokous is just exactly what he looks like—and Skyros didn't know one thing about it, but took the little opportunity it offered to mention Bratti's name in connection, hoping it'd take root, so to speak. And whatever business this is about Miss Weir's car, and whoever took it, and about this thing, and this Bouvardier woman, it hasn't anything to do with the dope-peddling.'

'*Eso es lo peor*,' said Mendoza, 'that's the worst of it. I have a feeling that's so, it's something different entirely. But both Skyros and Lydia are tied up to both ends of it.'

Hackett eyed him exasperatedly. 'Sometimes I wonder why I don't put in for a transfer to some nice quiet routine place like Traffic or Records. Where I'd have a chance of getting a superior officer with just an ordinary bright I.Q., who didn't go off at tangents after ghosts nobody else can see.'

'So why don't you?'

'I'll tell you. Just one reason. It's always helpful towards promotion if you've got another language besides English, and I'm improvin' my Spanish quite a lot working under you ... Does that blank stare mean you've had another idea?'

'A brilliant one,' said Mendoza truthfully. It had just occurred to him that by what Mr. Elgin said those kittens should be due about the middle of next month: which meant that they'd be ready to leave home and mother just around Christmas. Such an excellent excuse for the unsolicited gift. Of course one would want to be sure of choosing people who liked cats, would provide good homes—but so much easier to present the seasonal gift than chase all round asking the hopeful question, Wouldn't you like—'

It was definitely an idea. 'Well,' and he stood up, 'if I'm going to get anything done

228

today at all—my God, look at the time, nearly noon, the whole morning wasted. I want to see Driscoll and find out where the insurance comes in, if he's chastened enough to tell me.'

'I'll go hunt up O'Brien. I called Callaghan's office, by the way, just before you came in—he's over at the jail questioning your thugs. Maybe he'll get another little piece for you to fit in.'

'I'm not,' said Mendoza, 'nearly so interested in the thugs as I am in Lydia—'

'¡Naturalmente!' said Hackett. 'She's female!'

★   ★   ★

Mendoza met Callaghan just emerging from the inside block of the county jail. 'Anything new?'

'This and that,' said Callaghan. 'Come and have lunch with me, I'll brief you. I've earned it, God knows, been hammering at these boys most of the morning.'

'I haven't got time. Owing to various excitements I was up half the night and I've wasted half today already. I've got some hammering to do myself. Tell me here.'

They sat down on the bench along the wall and lit cigarettes. 'Prettyman isn't coming out with anything. He's a smart boy. Also there's probably a deal set up—usually is—about his boss getting a lawyer for him, and in return he keeps his mouth shut. The lawyer—we see a lot of him and a couple of others the same kind—knows what the setup is, but so long as he gets his fee he figures what the hell. Somebody's got to represent the Prettymans in court, and he might as well get a piece of what's going. From the other three I've got a little useful talk about this Castro, but they don't know who his immediate boss is, of course—they're just punks. I did also hear a few things about this Angie.'

'Ah,' said Mendoza.

'It seems to tie up in a sort of way, but I don't see what it ties up *to*. What they dropped about Angie—I had to put two and two together on it, because they're trying to be awful damn cagey, you know—I gather he's another pusher like we figured, in this same string—'

'Yes, Pretty's best boy.'

'And he's been sharing quarters—maybe still is, but it's on the cards when we hauled these four in and went through the Elite, the rest of 'em'd scatter quick in case we had 'em spotted—with one Denny. That is, if it's the same Denny that Prettyman knows. Seems likely. And from a couple of little things, I don't think Denny's on this lay at all.'

'That figures. Denny. For Dennis? Another Irish name.'

'Well, we come all sorts like other people,'

230

said Callaghan. 'Does that say anything to you?'

'I don't know. Maybe. That's about it? Well, I'll go and ask my questions and maybe this'll mean a little more.' Mendoza went on in and requested admittance to Driscoll.

Driscoll was a sorry sight after his hours in a cell; he was dishevelled, he needed a shave, his eyes were puffy and bloodshot, and he was probably suffering from a headache and a bad case of indigestion—he looked it. He almost fell on Mendoza, babbling eagerly at him the minute he came in sight.

'Lieutenant, say, I certainly owe you an apology, way I've been acting—don't know what got *into* me, I know better than to act that way—you've got to make allowances, I've been drinking kind of heavy, had some personal worries on my mind, you know how it is—'

The jailer banged the cell door shut and Mendoza surveyed Driscoll leisurely. 'So you're ready to co-operate now, Mr. Driscoll? Yes, I rather expected you'd take it like this. You have been a nuisance, Mr. Driscoll—I might say a damned nuisance. Ordinarily men in your job are quite co-operative and polite, we find—especially those associated with as large and well-known a firm as yours. Despite popular fiction, it usually does pay an investigator—public or private—to remember his manners, you know. At least I've always found it so. There's an old saying that one

231

catches more flies with honey than with vinegar.'

'Listen, Lieutenant, my God, I know all that, I said I been worried, drinking a little heavy, and you know how it takes some—couple of drinks, they're spoiling for a fight, pick a fight with anybody looks at them—I'm kind of like that—'

'So am I,' said Mendoza conversationally, leaning on the door, 'so I don't drink much. It saves a lot of trouble.'

'I want to apologize, I know I've made you mad, and no wonder. Don't know what got into me, I know better—listen, you'll give me a break, Lieutenant, you look like a regular guy, you won't complain to the company, will you?—swear I never acted like this before, and—'

'I am not so constituted,' said Mendoza, 'that I enjoy being fawned on, Mr. Driscoll. I don't give one damn for your relations with your company, but I should doubt that you keep your job much longer whether or not I issue an official reprimand. All I'm interested in right now is some straight answers you should have given me three days ago.'

'Yes, sure, I *know*, Lieutenant, be glad to tell you whatever you want to know ... Skyros ... Well, I'll tell you, maybe I better just let you have it from the start, see, tell you just how it was ...' Driscoll went on talking for some time, going into elaborate details.

And that built-in sense of order somewhere inside Mendoza, that thing that was rendered so acutely wretched by the wrinkle in the rug, the picture hanging crooked, the untidy scattered pieces of the jigsaw puzzle—it began to settle down into peace and cease to nag at him. It was satisfied. So that's how it is, that's the pattern, or a large part of it; just the background to fill in. Oh, very nice—pieces dovetailing into each other neat and meaningful. Yes. He felt better than he had all week, since this had been on his mind. He even began to feel slightly benevolent towards Driscoll.

At the end of what Driscoll had to say, he saw to the necessary forms for his release and drove happily back to headquarters. His mind was busy filling in background details, and of course there were a few little things he still didn't know—

Such as who *had* killed Stevan Domokous—

But such a large part of it unravelled now, the rest ought to be untied easily . . .

*   *   *

He stopped at First Aid and had his hand redressed, thinking that he'd probably be too busy the rest of the day to bother with it. And he was not wrong.

Sergeant Lake greeted him with relief. 'I

was hoping you'd be in pretty soon, knowing how it's on your mind sort of, Lieutenant. One of Callaghan's office men just called down, said they had orders to relay any news about this Skyros. The tail they've got on him had just called in, said there was the hell of a ruction of some sort going on in his office, and a call out to the precinct—'

'For God's sake, what about? All right, I'd better go and find out,' and Mendoza snatched up his hat again and made back for the elevator.

CHAPTER SEVENTEEN

Mr. Skyros had had only one brief moment of alarm. Of all the little shocks and worries he had suffered lately, this was the easiest to handle, because he knew about Domokous. Earnest young Domokous saying, 'A little it worried me, sir, I don't like to think bad things about you, and maybe I just misunderstood some meaning—'

Domokous had known nothing definite, so obviously the girl knew nothing.

Really a most unattractive girl: that long sallow face, tangled black hair—and she was staring at him with bright-eyed vindictive triumph, as if she actually thought she had said something meaningful.

234

'My dear young lady,' he said, smiling, sure of himself, 'first I say I'm very sorry to see Stevan's girl with such thoughts in her head—it's not a nice thing. And you're all wrong, you know, this is a very silly little business altogether, you have got this funny idea from Stevan, I know, yes, but it was just a little mistake.'

'It wasn't no mistake!' she said. 'He told me all about it—he'd found out just what you're up to—that's why you killed him, I know! I know about *everything*, Mr. Skyros—but you won't hurt me, you won't dare, see? I've got it all wrote down, just like I say, black 'n' white, an' I got it put away in a box at the bank, where nobody can't get at it but me. See? But you give me the five thousand dollars an' I won't tell—that's fair, isn't it? I'd promise never to tell—'

Mr. Skyros laughed. 'Miss Roslev—really, I don't know what I should say to you, this silly little thing, this nothing! I don't want to call the police, tell them this bad thing, how you have such crazy ideas—'

'You wouldn't dare—I know!'

'But that's just what I tell you, young lady, you *don't* know, isn't it? You don't know anything at all. Come now, what is this bad thing I'm supposed to do, eh? I steal from somebody, I break in a house to rob, maybe? And you say, my good God, me, I murder Stevan? Now this isn't funny, I don't like it.'

'I know what you done! And it's all wrote down—'

'Then you let me in on the secret, eh? What is it all about?'

'Stevan *told* me—he'd found out—'

'But nobody tells me,' said Mr. Skyros. 'Now you listen to me, young lady. Yes, sure, poor Stevan, maybe he tells you how he hears a little something one night, makes him think bad things about me. This I don't doubt he says to you, because he comes to me and tells me, he's worried for it—such a nice honest young man he was, isn't it?—and I have set his mind at rest. It was a little mistake was all, he don't know some of the words we use in a business way, you see. And I straighten it out in his mind, so he knows everything's O.K., I'm no big public enemy like the papers call it! That's all it was, a little mistake, you see? This you didn't know, that we'd talked it over—poor fellow, he's dead before he sees you again, I suppose. And I'm patient to explain, tell you how it was, because I'm sorry for you, such bad ideas in your head.'

She stared at him stupidly, across the desk there. 'That's not so, that's a lie! I *know*—about a lot of money—there, that tells you I know! An' I'll tell *everybody* if you don't give me—'

'Oh, my good God in heaven,' exclaimed Mr. Skyros. 'This is a comedy, like in the

236

films—only maybe not so funny. Very good, young lady, you go to the police and say, this Andreas Skyros is a bad man, he's figuring to steal a lot of money—you tell everybody just how and where and when, isn't it? Only you can't tell, nothing you've got to tell, and this *I* know! Now be sensible, Miss Roslev, go away and put these crazy ideas out of your head.'

'No!' she said, and she leaned forward, gripping the edge of the desk hard, fingers pressed bone-white. 'It's all lies—I do too know—everything about it! And I'll tell—you got to give me five thousand dollars right now—then I won't—'

'Oh, go away, young woman!' said Mr. Skyros crossly. 'I'm a very patient man, and I don't want to make a big fuss about this little nonsense, call in the police and tell them you put these silly little threats on me—poor Stevan's girl, it wouldn't look nice at all!—but I don't put up with it all day either. A lot of craziness in your head is all. You stop bothering me, go away, forget it.'

'You just wouldn't *dare*—the cops—I do *too*! You *got* to. I'll tell—'

'Now look,' said Mr. Skyros, and stood up. He knew it was scarcely a chance at all he was taking; the girl knew nothing in any case, she was only bluffing, and how she had thought to get away with it was beyond his understanding. But she would not go to the police, and it would not be necessary that he

237

carry out a threat to do so. Of course he could not do that—it was only that she must be made to understand her ridiculous position. 'Now look, young woman. I'm patient like I say, I explain to you how it happens, this little mistake. It's nothing, you know nothing, because there's nothing to know—and that's all to say about it. I don't like to do such a thing, but I can't be pestered like this, and you don't leave my office, then I call the police and tell them how you try to blackmail me—over nothing, just a silly idea—'

'—Wouldn't *dare*—'

'Now, who do they listen to, I ask you? Me, I'm a respectable businessman, an honest man, my own place, never in any kind of trouble, and no—no axe to grind I got, like they say—' He shrugged. 'Why should I tell lies about this unimportant girl—some kind of cheap job, a cheap little couple of rooms somewhere, a girl nobody knows or cares about much, isn't it? Nobody pays any attention to you, Miss—'

'*You old devil!*' she screamed at him suddenly. 'You *got* to give me that money, you *got* to—you—' She sprang to her feet, still gripping the desk, leaning across it. 'You *got* to, you *know* you got to,' she panted. 'I *got* to have—'

Suddenly Mr. Skyros felt just a little nervous. It was absurd, of course, but her

238

eyes were quite wild, she sounded—And nobody else in the building, so far as he knew: the office staff had all gone off, Saturday afternoon ... 'I don't got to do anything,' he said. 'You go away and calm down, or I call the police.'

'You—you—*I got to have that money! I'll kill you—if you don't*—' Her hand darted out like a snake, snatched up the letter-knife from the desk. It was a miniature Indian dagger of brass—Mr. Skyros had a fancy for such things—with a curved blade, and while it was not quite as razor-sharp as a real dagger would be, it could probably inflict some damage—its point was sharp enough. Mr. Skyros stepped backwards involuntarily, tripped over his desk chair, and half fell sideways clutching at the desk.

'Now, young lady, don't you be foolish,' he started to say.

'Kill you—I just *got* to—' And she was on him like a cat, rushing around that side of the desk. Mr. Skyros felt the knife-point bite deep into his upper chest and let out a shrill yelp, staggering backwards towards the window with some idea of calling for help. She flew at him again, sobbing with fury, and then the door opened and a nondescript man ran in, got her from behind by the arms, said, 'What the hell's going on here?' and blew a whistle out of the window.

Mr. Skyros collapsed into his desk chair

and squinted fearfully down at his chest. There was some blood; he tore his shirt open and was rather disappointed to find only a minute puncture in the pink soft flesh. 'This—this fiend of a female,' he gasped to the man, 'she—'

Running footsteps pounding up the stairs, a uniformed patrolman. 'Darcy, headquarters,' said the other man. 'Attack of some sort, you better call the wagon. Listen, sister, you just calm down and stop trying to fight me, you're goin' nowhere right now.'

Mr. Skyros sank lower in his chair and moaned to himself. Police—having to hear all about it—and no telling what this terrible woman would say—These crazy females!

'That's right, sister, you take it easy for a change,' said the man. The girl subsided suddenly into a straight chair, and crouched there bent forward, hair falling over her face, silent and sullen.

★ ★ ★

Mendoza got there in time to follow the patrol car in to the precinct station. He took Mr. Skyros along, volubly protesting. Mr. Skyros' little wound was given first aid, and he was asked if he wanted to charge the young woman formally with assault.

'Look,' said Mr. Skyros earnestly, 'let's not make the big thing out of this, isn't it? I'm sorry for the young lady, that's all. She's this poor Domokous' girl, going to marry him she was, and maybe she's a little lightheaded—a little crazy, you know—with the grieving for the poor boy. You see what I mean, gentlemen. She's got some crazy idea in her head—I don't know, don't ask *me* how females get ideas!—that it's, somehow, because he works for me he gets himself killed like that, you see? *I* don't know how she figures, gentlemen, she comes, says a lot of crazy things that don't make any sense at all, says it's all my fault poor Stevan dies—don't ask *me* why she thinks like that! It's a terrible thing all round, poor Stevan and now this girl acting like she's crazy—but I don't want any big trouble about it, bad for everybody, isn't it? I'm sorry for this poor girl, she don't know what she's saying, you know. She don't hurt me much,' said Mr. Skyros bravely, 'just a little scratch like, and I don't hold any grudge on the poor girl. You let her go home, get calmed down, maybe see a doctor—I don't charge her with anything, gentlemen.'

But it wasn't quite as simple as that. Mendoza let Skyros go; he had a pretty good idea of what was behind this, and there wouldn't be anything more to be got out of Skyros. The last couple of remarks the girl had made in his office that day—he could add two and two and figure she'd had a second thought; maybe the little Domokous had told her that time might be material for blackmail. It could just be that Domokous had told her more, though it didn't seem likely when what he'd told the priest added up to nothing, really. And what was it worth if he had—hearsay evidence? Still ... So he let Skyros go, and saw the girl there in the precinct sergeant's office.

'You went to Mr. Skyros' office to threaten him, Miss Roslev,' he said. 'What did you have to threaten him with? ... You can tell me, you know, and I can see he's punished for it, if it's something very bad.' Almost instinctively he spoke as one would to a child, for her blank stare. She had made no attempt to tidy herself, comb her hair, refasten her blouse where its buttons had pulled apart in the little struggle.

She just stared at him vaguely. After a moment she said, 'Five thousand dollars. He's *got* to pay me. I *know*—I do so know.'

'What do you know, Miss Roslev?'

'He's *got* to,' she said. 'Just *got* to. Or I'll tell. A lie, say I don't know nothing. I do too. An awful lot o' money—Stevan said—about an awful lot o' money. Five thousand dollars, I thought.'

'Yes. What about it, Miss Roslev?'

She looked at him a long moment, and her eyes focused on him, and then she smiled a small, scornful smile and said, 'That's not my name. I'm Katharine Ross. I'm *Katharine Ross*, I don't have nothing to do with these people, funny foreign-sounding names, nothing I got to do—my name's Katharine—Katharine—Katharine—I'm Katharine Ross and I—'

Mendoza went out and told the sergeant it might be a good idea to call in a doctor to look at her, also to notify the grandmother as next of kin. Maybe she was shamming, maybe she thought Skyros had charged her and she'd get out of it playing crazy, but he didn't much like her looks.

And it didn't matter a damn, it wouldn't be legal evidence anyway; but he hung around to hear what the doctor said. And of course that didn't mean a damn thing either: a lot of double talk! Thus the doctor—shock, perhaps temporary amnesia, perhaps an unstable personality; one could not really say definitely without intensive psychiatric examination, and naturally one was not equipped—oh, well, as to *competent*, one would not like to say—

Mendoza said a few things to himself about modern psychiatric theories, and went out to the charge room. The grandmother was there by then, and the priest had come with her. Any man in the force ran across both attitudes his first day in uniform, but Mendoza had never much liked meeting either one: the old woman saw Authority to be feared, always tyrannical; the priest, Authority to be ultimately relied on, always knowing all the answers.

Mendoza didn't know all the answers any more than another man. He told them what he knew. And because one day it might be legally important (though he didn't think so) whether Katya Roslev really knew something or didn't, he went with the old woman and the priest back to the room where she sat slouched in a chair, silent, under the doctor's eye.

'Katya, the gentleman, Mr. Skyros, he is kind and don't ask the police to shut you in jail,'—the old woman, timid—'you can come home with me now, I know you don't mean anything wrong, whatever it is you do. Katya—'

The girl looked at her blankly. 'Go home?' she said. 'Home—with you? I don't know you. My name's *Katharine Ross*. Good American name. I don't know you—funny old foreign woman, can't even talk English good—I don't know *anybody* like you, I never *did*—'

'Oh, Katya, you don't say such to me—me who raises you from a baby, tries to teach you all how to do right—how is it you say, you don't know me? It is your own great-mother speak to you, my dear—it's not to matter, what you've done, you know I don't stop loving you—it's all right, Katya—' She went

244

off into her own tongue then, probably saying it all over.

'*I don't know you or your damned foreign talk, you old bitch!*' screamed the girl at her, harsh and sudden. 'Go away—go away—go away!'

The priest exchanged a look with Mendoza and led the old woman out; she had fallen silent, looking stunned. 'Perhaps it's foolish to ask what you think, Lieutenant? Such a distressing—'

'Not for me to say. They'll take her into hospital, of course—the General.'

'But always I am kind with her,' whispered the old woman. The priest shook his head and shepherded her away.

And it was, that, very much a side issue; Mendoza switched his mind back to the main problem, driving back to headquarters.

★   ★   ★

Hackett had wandered through Records looking for O'Brien in vain; he didn't know him well. Finally he asked, and was told that O'Brien wouldn't be in until afternoon, off on some special job. Hackett swore mildly and took himself out to lunch. Coming back, he just missed Mendoza, heard about the undefined excitement at Skyros' office and wondered about that. He looked over the tails' reports on the Bouvardier woman, which contained nothing of interest at all.

About two o'clock he went down to Records again and found O'Brien, who looked more like a school principal than a policeman, half-hidden behind a stack of file-size record cards. 'Heard you were asking for me,' said O'Brien.

'Nothing official.' Hackett pulled up a chair. 'It's this little thing. I remembered you saying your hobby is coins. It's cropped up in something of Luis Mendoza's, and we wondered if you could give us any idea what it might be. If anything. For all I know, it's just a souvenir medal from a midway shooting gallery or something like that.'

'Let's have a look,' said O'Brien. He took the thing in his palm, weighed it, whisked out his handkerchief to polish it and then stopped, looked at it again, made a little clicking sound with his tongue, and put the handkerchief away without using it. He said, 'But it can't possibly—it must be a replica—' He opened a drawer, brought out a magnifying lens, and bent over the coin laid flat on his desk; presently he turned it over very delicately and examined the other side.

'Well?' said Hackett.

'Where'd you get this?' asked O'Brien.

'Apparently somebody lost it in a hot car.'

'Jesus H. Christ,' said O'Brien in an awed small voice. 'And you or Lieutenant Mendoza

246

have been carrying it around loose in your pocket—'

'Why not? What is it, anyway? Is it worth anything?'

'Worth anything,' said O'Brien. '*Worth*— well, I wouldn't like to guess what, offhand, I'm not a real expert—and besides, you wouldn't often find a thing like this in such good condition. Not *fine* condition, but technically very good, and of course you could hardly expect anything better. I'll be damned. I will be damned. Carrying it around loose—'

'What *is* it?' asked Hackett. 'I thought it looked pretty well beaten up myself. I suppose you could polish it, if it's silver—'

O'Brien clutched the magnifying glass like a bludgeon and asked if any vandal up in Homicide had tried to polish it.

'No, of course not, and why the hell all the excitement about it?'

'I'm not an expert,' said O'Brien, 'as I say. But my own interest has always been mostly in the older foreign stuff, and I can tell you just a little something about this, Sergeant. Though I've never seen anything like it outside a museum, which is where it ought to be. This is a Greek coin, I wouldn't say from which city but most likely Athens or Elis or just possibly Syracuse, and I'd place it as dating from somewhere around 400 B.C.'

'What? You don't mean—'

'That's what I said. It's a silver *stater*, the

common currency of the Greek city-states. Probably one of the oldest Greek coins extant, and in wonderful condition. It can't have circulated much—those early coins wore down very rapidly, you know, not being milled—and not so much alloy, either. All made by hand—you can see it never was a true circle—and stamped with hand-made dies. The eagle with the hare in its talons, here on the obverse, that's a device you find rather often on Greek pieces of the period—never seen one before, just photographs—really marvellous detail, considering—and this thing on the reverse is Zeus's thunderbolt, stylized of course, but beautiful—beautiful work. I can't imagine where this came from, such condition—just dropped in a *car*?—but—' Suddenly O'Brien fell silent, mouth open, bounced straighter in his chair, stared excitedly from the coin to Hackett, and finally said again, '*Jesus* H. Christ. Listen, Sergeant—I wonder—listen, there was a big collection of Greek coins stolen just about a month ago, the most important collection, and the biggest, in existence—the Lexourion collection—and one of the things makes it so valuable, all the pieces are—were—in wonderful condition, not *mint*, you couldn't expect it, but very good. The County Museum was angling to buy it, I remember reading it in the *Times*.'

'I'll be damned,' said Hackett, and now he

felt almost as excited as O'Brien looked, 'I wonder—this could be a big piece of the story! Thanks, we'll check that—thanks very much, O'Brien,' and he reached for the coin.

'No, you don't, you Goth,' said O'Brien. 'Wait just a minute, now.' He rummaged in the drawer. 'Whether this is part of the Lexourion collection or not, it's worth the hell of a lot of money and a lot more than that in historical importance—you're not going to ruin its condition. Have the owner suing you for damages, you don't want that, do you? Here,' and he stowed it away, carefully wrapped in Kleenex, in the little paper-clip box.

CHAPTER EIGHTEEN

When Hackett came into the office he found Mendoza there, standing at his desk, hat still on, which meant he was slightly excited about something, talking on the inside phone.

'*¡Válgame Dios!* What use are your files to me? I want to talk to the man who worked the case, I want Goldberg! ... Where? *¡Fuegos del infierno!* What the hell is he doing in San Francisco? Isn't he working here any longer? ... You send a full-fledged lieutenant to ride herd on a two-bit mugger? ... Yes, Sergeant Gomez, I am annoyed. Doubtless Burglary

249

knows its own business, but ... Well, what time does the plane get in? Four-fifteen, *muy bien.* I'll be here to catch him—I presume he'll be bringing this desperate criminal to headquarters *pronto*—when he's delivered the goods. I might even buy him a drink if he can tell me some things I want to know. About four forty-five? ... What? *¡Vaya por Dios!* All right, all right, if it's midnight I'll be here, I want to see him. *Gracias* very much for nothing.' He put down the phone, swept off his hat, and flung himself into his chair. 'Fates conspiring! They must send Goldberg off to escort this mugger home for indictment, just when I want him. And of course some special Air Force manoeuvres or something have routed the San Francisco flights to land at Municipal instead of Burbank—another hour's drive in traffic, he won't be here until after six at a guess ... You've missed some excitement, by the way,' and he told Hackett about Katya Roslev.

Hackett scarcely paid attention, full of his own news. 'Listen, Luis, I've got something—it might be a lot—I got O'Brien to look at this coin, and he says—'

'I can guess,' said Mendoza. 'Maybe part of the famous Lexourion collection. I've heard about it from Driscoll. Why do you think I want to talk to Goldberg?'

'Oh, hell, and I thought I'd got ahead of you for once. So what did Driscoll part with?'

'A lot of the story.' Mendoza lit a cigarette and shouted to Sergeant Lake to bring in some coffee. 'The Lexourion collection, it seems, is one of the largest and most valuable collections of ancient Greek coins in existence. It was amassed over a period of many years by one Alexander Lexourion, whom I somehow see as one of those amiable fuzzy-minded professors, but actually I believe he was a hard-headed businessman. About two months ago Lexourion came here, with his collection, to negotiate with the L.A. County Museum, which was thinking of buying it. And he'd no sooner got here than it was stolen, under funny circumstances too, which I trust Goldberg can tell me more about. And Lexourion gets such a shock hearing about it that he has a stroke and passes out. Now, the collection is insured for two hundred thousand bucks, and naturally the insurance company sits up and takes notice—'

'And wouldn't they,' agreed Hackett. 'But what in God's name could a burglar do with a thing like that? I mean, it'd be like stealing the Mona Lisa or—'

'And I hear even that's been done once. Yes, of course, that was the first thing in the insurance company's collective mind. Nobody could sell such a thing to a fence. There are, I understand, about seven-hundred-odd coins altogether, and separately

251

they'd be worth something but not nearly so much as in a collection. And also, a thing like that, there's what you might call a pedigree attached, you know—anybody who'd be interested in buying it would want to be assured that it *is* the Lexourion collection. Well, the same thing leaped into my mind as the insurance company thought of, both of us having some experience of human nature—'

'Fraud,' said Hackett. 'But Lexourion didn't know, if he died of the shock.'

'Ransom,' said Mendoza. 'Steal it and sell it back to the original owner. And the owner just might try—being understandably annoyed at having to pay for his own property—to figure out a way to hang onto some of the insurance money. Sure, a little awkward, but I suppose even today you'd find a few private collectors who might buy the thing secretly, if they were assured of the pedigree, and very possibly—if it was smuggled out of the country—the insurance company'd find it hard to follow the transaction *or* do anything about it. Now!' He regarded with pleasure the coffee Sergeant Lake had just brought in, and drank some. 'This may be years getting settled legally—not our business—probate and so on. Lexourion died intestate, and therefore his legal next of kin comes in for whatever he had to leave. And who, Mr. Bones, do you suppose is his legal next of kin? One Madame

252

Lydia Bouvardier, his only child. Lydia Bouvardier. Such a romantic-sounding name, isn't it?'

'And isn't that nice to know,' said Hackett. 'But what's it got to do with Stevan Domokous dead of heroin in a Carson Street alley?'

'*Tenga paciencia, allá veremos*—with time all will be clear. I hope. A little something I've tied up, at least. Driscoll, damn him, delayed us on this thing nearly a week—longer—he should have come in and laid the facts on the line the minute he landed here, and I'd take a small bet Goldberg will want his hide nailed to the door of his office for keeping it secret. Though you can also say the director of the museum was lax—but I'd take another little bet that Driscoll let him think *he* was in touch with the police, so the director didn't do anything about it himself. These glory boys, out to play to the grandstand ... About three weeks after the collection was stolen—in fact, Arturo, on the same Sunday afternoon that Alison attended that exhibition at the County Museum—the museum director had a very odd and mysterious visitor. About this I'd like to know more than Driscoll passed on secondhand, but I expect Lieutenant Goldberg will be even more passionately interested, and do the direct investigating. Now my curiosity's beginning to be satisfied,

253

I'm rather liking this case, you know—it encroaches on other people's jobs, and they're doing so much of the work ... This visitor asked the director if he'd be interested in buying a collection of Greek coins, and even hinted at the Lexourion collection. The price mentioned was fifteen thousand dollars, which—not surprisingly—struck the director as a little suspicious, considering that if it *was* the Lexourion stuff, that was insured for two hundred thousand. By the sample the visitor produced to show him, he said, it might have been the Lexourion stuff. Naturally, since the museum had been interested, he was tolerably familiar with it. And from what he said to Driscoll, I gather that the visitor didn't seem exactly the type to go in for collecting ancient Greek coins, and the director instantly put two and two together and wondered if he was, so to speak, being offered hot goods.'

'A *sample*,' said Hackett. He got out the little box and looked at the silver *stater* O'Brien said was twenty-three hundred years old. The thunderbolt of Zeus ... 'Could be, just possibly, this little thing?'

'Could be, very possibly,' said Mendoza in dreamy satisfaction. 'I can't say why he might have hopped Alison's car. Ridiculous sort of thing to do—but there it is. I think he did. After he left the director. The director thought it over, and then he made a little mistake. Instead of calling us, he called the

254

insurance company. I deduce he was thinking of avoiding publicity. Handle the thing nice and quiet, just in case he was wrong and the visitor was a *bona fide* collector. Anyway, the insurance people shot Driscoll out *pronto*, of course—because why? Because Lexourion's daughter had come over from Paris—legal business, I suppose there's miles of red tape to untangle about the estate even though he wasn't a citizen—and this looked as if the thief was maybe getting bids on the collection.'

'Now wait a minute,' said Hackett. 'You're not telling me that anybody—even the dumbest pro in business—would think he could sell it under the counter to the County Museum?'

'Just look back over your career, *chico*. Only nine years you've been in, compared to my seventeen, but you've met them—you know them. One of the reasons the paperback detective thrillers are so damn fantastic, to anybody who's had a little contact with the real thing. How often have you said to yourself, Nobody can be *that* stupid! Nobody but a pro—never mind what lay he's on, never mind whether he's a juvenile just starting out hopping shorts, swiping little stuff off dime store counters, or a very much ex-con just out from a twenty-year stretch for armed robbery and assault. They don't come any dumber, when it comes to—mmh—both the ordinary sort of knowledge almost anybody in any crowd has, or what you might call the nuances of ordinary human give-and-take. One of the reasons they're pros, Art—you know as well as I do—they haven't got even the rudimentary empathy, the little imagination about other people, that most people have ... The simplest things, the smallest things, they just don't *know*.'

'That's so, God knows. But you'd think anybody—still, of course, that *is* so.'

'Most of the reason we're kept busy,' said Mendoza. 'Well, as I say, Driscoll's sent out but quick to look into this. It would be Driscoll, of course. Water under the bridge—let it go—we know now, anyway. Driscoll pokes around, asking questions of the director, of our Lydia, and he reads what the papers had to say at the time about the robbery—damn fool way to investigate, half the time they get details wrong or some officious editor cuts out the relevant facts—and he comes to some conclusions. Your guess is as good as mine as to whether the conclusions were born of whisky or solid deduction. One of his methods seems to be trying to make any female involved in a case, possibly on the theory that women always speak the truth in bed—which, *de paso*, graphically illustrates his appalling lack of experience.'

'And what conclusion did he come to?'

'He thinks that our Lydia is up to something. I agree. She is,' said Mendoza, 'a widow. A romantic, young, beautiful widow. Her late husband was upwards of sixty when she married him, and an extremely wealthy man—land-rich and munitions-rich—and she was a tender innocent young thing of seventeen. I don't think. A young lady with her head screwed on very tight—take the cash and let the romance go. Very sensible, ¿no es verdad?'

'Oh, *absolutamente*,' said Hackett with a grin.

'He also thinks—and again I agree—that Mr. Andreas Skyros is not merely a social acquaintance of our Lydia. He doesn't know whether or not she's been approached about buying back the collection, but he thinks she will be if she hasn't been, and that she would probably be willing to dicker about the—mmh—ransom. One thing that emerges, by the information he has from his company, is that our Lydia disapproved of the intention to sell the collection in the United States, would prefer to see it, say, in the Louvre or somewhere like that, if they'd be interested. At any rate, Driscoll says, and quite reasonably too, that if Mr. Skyros was a purely social acquaintance—maybe somewhere she had a letter of introduction to—she'd be going to his house, entertained by his wife, whereas it looks rather like a

257

business relationship.'

'So it does. Where do you figure Skyros comes in? And still all this doesn't say one thing about Domokous.'

'I don't know,' said Mendoza. 'It's easy to build up stories about it—as Mr. Skyros would say, isn't it? I'm hoping Goldberg can add a few details to pin down which of the stories might be the right one.'

★　　★　　★

Lieutenant Saul Goldberg sneezed, groped blindly for more Kleenex in his breast pocket, and said thickly through it, 'It's the whisky, I'm allergic to it.'

'Then why drink it?'

'What, turn down a free drink?' Goldberg, his sinus passages temporarily clear, sat back in the booth and sipped cautiously. 'I'm allergic to so damn many things,' he said gloomily, 'that I've just given up doing anything about it. Life's too short, and the allergy specialist too free with my money. Everything in the house non-allergenic, yet—I'm surprised they don't tell me to get rid of my wife and kids as well as feather pillows and all the rugs. Have all the more money to hand them. And I've still got the allergies, so I say the hell with it, I just buy Kleenex. And besides the cat found her way home, and we hadn't the heart to give her

258

away again after that. You want a kitten, by the way, Mendoza? She seems to've stopped somewhere on the way. Four cute little grey and white fellows, one black.'

'Coals to Newcastle, I think I'm going to have some of my own ... So it doesn't show yet, very funny, now forget your sinuses and tell me what you know about that job at Shanrahan and MacReady's, where the collection of Greek coins was part of the loot.'

'Hey, you got something on that?' asked Goldberg, looking interested.

'Maybe. You tell me what you know first ... Damn it, Shanrahan mentioned it too, but how was I to know?'

'You're welcome to what I've got. Sometimes you got to sit on these things a while—that's what I'm doing now. That was a damn funny job, in some ways—'

'Stop a minute. One little thing that struck me funny: what was a collection of Greek coins doing in the safe of a fashionable jeweller?'

Goldberg grinned. 'That's one of the funny things. And ordinarily I've got no sympathy for pro burglars, do you know, I did kind of feel for the guy who pulled the job—it must've been quite a little shock, not to say disappointment, when he found out what he'd got away with. I'll tell you how it happened. This Greek, Lexourion, who owned the stuff—'

'Yes, I know about him.'

'He'd just landed here. He'd never been here before, it was on account of the possible deal with the County Museum he came, but it's like any of these hobbies—you know—there's speciality magazines, clubs, societies, and so on—and he did know somebody here: MacReady. MacReady is an amateur numismatist too. It seems they'd been corresponding, all enthusiastic and friendly, for some time, and so MacReady was all set to entertain the old boy when he got here, and of course to see his famous collection. Well, Lexourion got in by plane one afternoon. MacReady met him, and they go straight up to MacReady's house and spend a couple of hours looking at the collection. You know how these fanatic hobbyists are. And after awhile, when they're thinking about going out for dinner, all of a sudden Lexourion realizes it's too late to stash the stuff away in a bank vault as he'd meant to do, pending his interview at the County Museum. So MacReady, naturally, says there's no trouble about that, they'll just put it away safe in the store vault for the night—good as a bank any time, burglar alarm and so on.'

Mendoza sat back and laughed. 'I see—I see. How very embarrassed Mr. MacReady must have been.'

'That's an understatement,' said Goldberg.

'Especially when the poor old fellow dropped dead, hearing about it. Because of course that was the very night somebody picked to knock over Shanrahan and MacReady. It was a pro job, kind of routine. I wouldn't say it was sure just one man. He came in through the skylight in the back room, and of course he had to be damn quick. These burglar alarm systems,' and Goldberg looked rueful, 'they're just dandy if you've got old-fashioned cops walking a beat, and in a place where the precinct station isn't ten miles away. He had about ten-twelve minutes after he tripped the alarm, and that he knew, and he used it. He set a charge of Dinah on the safe door and blew her, and he scooped up what was on top, probably all he could carry, and got clean away before the patrol car got there. Didn't leave any prints, of course. It was a neat enough little job. And when I think how he must have felt, when he got home with the loot and looked it over—' Goldberg laughed. 'That's the reason I say one man; what was gone would just about make a one-man load, say in a ditty bag or something like that. This collection was on top of everything else in the safe, naturally, and I guess it must have looked impressive to him, way it was described to me. It was in an even dozen big square leather-covered boxes, each one about the size of a desk tray only thicker, because there are three tiers in each one, trays, you know. The trays are covered with velvet and have indented beds for each coin. And there was a manila folder in the lid of the top box with a complete list and description of every coin in the collection. You know, I'd love to've seen his face when he opened that first box and saw a lot of dirty old foreign coins instead of a handful of sparklers.'

'Crime doesn't pay,' agreed Mendoza amusedly. 'Did he get much else?'

'About ten grand worth of the real stuff, but he wouldn't get much for it, you know. Matter of fact I think I know what he did get for it, a little over thirty-five hundred bucks.' Goldberg finished his drink and got out a cigarette.

'Ah, now we get to it. You had a line on him?'

'I didn't,' said Goldberg, 'until I got hold of an excuse to search old Benny Hess's place. You might think we could've stopped worrying about Benny—he was over eighty and all crippled up with arthritis, *and* he had a nice little estate built up from the proceeds of a mis-spent life—a lot of it cannily transferred into his daughter's name, too—but they don't change, do they? I—oh, hell,' and he began to sneeze again, groped for the Kleenex. 'Damn cigarettes. Doctor says I shouldn't smoke at all. The hell with him. Benny was a fence, and a big one. He got inside for it just once—he was a pretty smart boy. Kept a junk secondhand store out on Pico Boulevard. Well, about ten days, two weeks ago, Benny's number came up and they hauled him off to the General, and seeing as he wasn't coming back to complain about the officious cops persecuting an innocent citizen who'd paid his debt to society, I got a warrant and went through his place but very thorough. There were a couple of other little things we were looking for at the time, of course. And we found Benny had a very pretty setup, just like the stories, you know: dug-out room under his living quarters, with a safe in it yet, and being a businesslike old guy, he'd kept records too—there was a ledger. Very abbreviated entries, but I could read between the lines—some of 'em. In the safe was about half the Shanrahan and MacReady stuff—the real stuff—he hadn't got rid of yet. And in the ledger, among other things, I came across this entry of thirty-five hundred and some-odd bucks, listed under *Donovan*, and that added up awful easy in my mind.'

'Donovan,' said Mendoza fondly. '¡*Venga más!*—the thing is clear—*y más vale tarde que nunca*, better late than never! Oh, very pretty. You knew the name?'

'Sure I knew the name,' said Goldberg, catching the waiter's eye on beckoning. 'I owe you a drink—I'll be sorry for this, those damn sinuses, but what the hell—same again.

263

Sure I did. And it kind of made a little sense too, because the Donovans always stuck pretty close together—'

'More than one?'

'Three. One down, two to go. There was—'

'Francis Joseph,' said Mendoza, smiling at his new drink. 'Poor fellow, executed without benefit of a trial, just because a high school kid paid attention to a lecture for once.'

Goldberg looked at him. 'And what's Homicide's interest now? You've gone into the Donovans?'

'He just showed on the edge of something. About the others I don't know. Tell me—tell me all, *amigo*.'

'Well—the Donovans,' said Goldberg. 'Pros from a pro family. The dad was a stick-up specialist. Died in San Quentin doing his third stretch, when the boys were in their teens, I'd guess—before my time. There's Jackie, and Denny, and Frank. All of 'em did time in reformatory for hopping cars, petty theft, and so on. Typical record sheets.'

'I've seen Frank's.'

'Then you've seen Denny's, except for the last line. Jackie—this is some fancy deduction of my own, he was one of my first arrests when I was a tender young rookie—Jackie was always the boss. Jackie was the one with a little more on the ball, as much as that kind of pro ever has. There was a time Jackie

Donovan was on the F.B.I. list of Most Wanted. Back there about twenty years, eighteen years ago, there was a little gang—reading between the lines, and by what a couple of desk men in Records and my own office tell me, men who were around then and remember. The three Donovan brothers, and a little Italian fellow named Angelo Forti. Stick-ups, a few, but mostly burglary. After they all got through being minors and getting slapped on the wrist for being naughty boys, we got Jackie twice—a one-to-three and a three-to-five—both times for . burglarly. Denny, a one-to-three—same first count as Jackie. On that one, the little Italian was the driver, and he was only just past eighteen and he said he didn't know what they were up to, didn't know nothing about nothing, and the judge listened to him and put him on probation. He's never done any time at all—I don't know where he is or what he's doing now. And—'

'Angelo,' said Mendoza. 'Angie? Oh, yes—very nice. Maybe I can give you a hint. Yes, go on.'

'The third time Jackie was picked up, he was either alone or the others got clean away. Pay your money and take your choice. I made that pinch, my first job after I ranked sergeant it was. Damn, the time goes ... Third count for him, they gave him the book and he got a taxi, fifteen years. He did the

265

whole stretch too, because the parole chief we've got in now is a tough one, *which* is all to the good and more power to him ... Reason I saw a little kind of logic in it, and hooked up the Shanrahan-MacReady job with that *Donovan* entry in Benny's ledger, it's because Jackie Donovan was just due to come out. About three weeks back, from that fifteen-year stretch.'

'Oh, this I like to hear,' purred Mendoza. 'But not soon enough to have done that job?'

'Uh-uh. I figure that was Denny. The way I say, these Donovans always stuck pretty close. Family feeling, you know? When I saw that entry in Benny's ledger, under the date which'd have been just about the time whoever did the Shanrahan-MacReady job was disposing of the loot, I had a kind of sentimental little vision, you know. Here's Jackie Donovan coming out after fifteen long years inside—and maybe his loving brother Denny figured on making a little celebration. I don't know what Denny's been doing since—God knows we get enough casual stick-ups and break-ins we never can get anybody for, it could be he's managed to support himself that way, just smart enough to take nothing but cash, you know. Anyway, I wondered. I've had a little bet with myself that the proceeds wrung out of Benny Hess went to arrange a celebration party for Jackie Donovan. *And* I might add,' said Goldberg,

266

'that I did a little private cussing that I didn't know about it until after Jackie *was* out, or I could've put a leash on him to lead me to Denny. If you see what I mean.'

'As it is, you don't know where either of them is?'

'I wish to God I did. That entry is enough to let me haul Denny in for questioning, at least. But ninety per cent of this is all in my mind—just like the head-doctors say—*and*,' added Goldberg bitterly, 'some of the allergy specialists . . . I haven't got anything to take to the D.A. And now I've bared my heart to you, what's your interest and have you got anything more useful to hand me?'

'Maybe you'd better have another drink,' said Mendoza. 'I'm going to tell you something that'll raise your blood pressure.' He told Goldberg about Driscoll and the mysterious visitor to the County Museum, and Goldberg invoked the Almighty, burst into a paroxysm of sneezing, called down curses on all stupid civilians, and emerged from fresh Kleenex to finish his second drink.

'Damn specialists. Tell me to avoid nervous tension. All in your emotions. What the hell do they expect, that I'll give up all my seniority and go and grow roses somewhere quiet? I will be damned. My God, these private eyes . . . I'll tell you, Mendoza, I can't say at that that it comes as a big surprise. Donovan I couldn't lay my hands on, but I'd

267

have taken a little bet there was some negotiation going on about that collection. We're reasonably smart these days, you know, and I can add one and one as easy as the next man. It was obvious no fence'd take on that kind of thing, and so I thought about it—along the lines of that one about the lost horse and the idiot boy—and—do you know that Lexourion's daughter is here?'

'My God,' said Mendoza, 'don't tell me I've been keeping three men busy on eight-hour shifts all to do work you've been doing too?'

Goldberg sat back and laughed. 'There you are, too many cooks. Dangers of a big organization. Sure I've had men on her. What else could Donovan—if it was Donovan—do with a thing like this collection? And at that, I've had moments of doubt. I mean, a dumb small-time pro like Denny Donovan—would he even read the papers next morning to know what he had? I had another little vision of him dumping all those boxes in a pawnshop for five bucks—only of course they haven't showed up.'

'I don't know for sure about Donovan,' said Mendoza, 'but whoever it was, he knew. That visit to the museum director—'

'Sure, and I'm going to be awful damn interested in what that one looked like,' said Goldberg. 'And the only surprise to me about that is the direction it took. Because I thought a little harder, after I had the word that the daughter was in town, and I asked myself how I'd handle it, say I was a middling-smart pro like Jackie Donovan stuck with that stuff—because Jackie was out by then—and I thought one like that might think it was just worth a five-buck investment—just on the chance, you know. So I sent a man down to look through the classified ads the last three weeks—'

'*¡Hijo mio!*' said Mendoza affectionately. 'A man after my own heart. Exactly what I'd have done. And did you come up with anything interesting?'

'I think so,' said Goldberg. 'In two ways, you might say. There was an ad run in the personals for five days—haven't got a copy on me, but I can supply you—an ad that said, quote, Concerning Greek money, party will negotiate, Box So-and-So, unquote. It makes you wonder sometimes, doesn't it? You'd think they'd realize after a while that even the run-of-the-mill rookie in uniform's got an I.Q. over seventy-five.'

'Isn't it the truth! And of course you went down and asked who'd placed the ad.'

'One Andrew Jackson placed it. I shouldn't think any connection of the late general. There were no answers to Box So-and-So at all.'

'None?'

'None. Which makes you think about a few

269

other things. I was kind of persistent, and finally got hold of the girl who had taken the ad in the first place, not that I had much hope of her remembering anything about Andrew Jackson. But she did. I don't think she could pass a standard Civil Service exam, she's the kind has to stop and think what comes after C in the alphabet, but she placed him because she's female. Sex, it's wonderful. She said he was an awful handsome young fella—just like a movie star—looked like that new fella in movies now, couldn't remember his name but he's Greek or Italian or something, just awful handsome. She—'

'¡Arriba!' said Mendoza. 'Goldberg, I could kiss you! I think we do arrive somewhere. Yes, we'll show her the corpse's photograph—but it does look open-and-shut. Very satisfying.'

Goldberg sneezed and said plaintively, 'Elucidate.'

'With pleasure,' and Mendoza lit another cigarette and began to talk...

CHAPTER NINETEEN

Time never meant much to Mendoza when he was working on a case; he chased Goldberg back to his office to get the name of the classified-ad girl, called the *Times*, he bullied

270

the editor of that department into giving him her home address. He had caught Hackett just on the point of leaving; he passed over the address. 'Go down to the morgue, get their file shot of Domokous and see what she says about it.'

'That one I don't see,' said Hackett, who had had a brief account of their joint deductions and got out the silver *stater* again to show Goldberg. 'If it was Domokous who placed that ad for Skyros, why didn't he say something to the priest or the girl when he was talking about—'

'I don't think he ever thought twice about the ad—connected it with anything else. There are several little excuses Skyros could have given him: it was an advertising stunt, say, or a business code of some kind, or a joke on somebody—can we even be sure Domokous read the thing? Skyros probably had it all typed out neatly, together with the false name and address as of the advertiser, all Domokous had to do was hand it over the counter and pay, and all the girl had to do was count the words. Just luck she happened to remember him, and in connection with the ad. Of course Goldberg'—Mendoza beamed on him—'did catch her immediately afterwards while it was fresh in her mind. I can see Domokous doing that as just a little errand for the boss, maybe on his lunch hour, and forgetting it by the next day. And of

271

course, damn it, he's not around to have his memory jogged and tell us it *was* Skyros' ad—but it's another little handle.'

'It all ties up, all right. This Denny pulled the break-in and found he was stuck with the collection—but how can we figure Skyros got into it?'

'He knew Frank,' said Mendoza. 'It's got to be that—use a little imagination on it. Frank wasn't his head pusher, of course—that we can say almost for certain—but maybe he'd got confidential with Prettyman, maybe Prettyman talks a bit too much when he's tight or something—if that's so, pity we can't slip him a bottle in jail—anyway, Frank knew Skyros' name if nothing else. And Frank was probably sharing quarters with Denny at the time. There's Angie too. Angie in the same string of boys. Guess at it—it always pays the ones like Skyros to be nice and friendly to the boys, if anonymously. Maybe he contributed some money to pay for poor Frank's funeral, something like that, and Denny knew who he was from Frank before and called up to thank him. Anyway, they were acquainted—if only just acquainted—somehow. I can guess at this part of it. You know what restricted circles, so to speak, the pros like Denny move in. He might not have known anybody—or *of* anybody—except Skyros, who might be expected to know a bit more about that collection than he did, who might give him a little advice about how to realize something from it. And of course it'd look like easy money to Skyros ... Considering that ad, and the fact that he hasn't attempted to hide his acquaintanceship with Lydia Bouvardier, I don't think she's been allowed to realize that he's anything but an ordinary helpful middleman—of the innocent variety, that is. Maybe he represented himself as a sympathetic friend of Papa's. Because no one actually answered the ad. It was a blind—it was to satisfy Lydia that that's how he got in touch with the thief.'

'That sounds reasonable,' nodded Goldberg. 'He's a canny one?—longheaded fraud artist?'

'Oh, very careful indeed of everything to do with Mr. Skyros ... Let's not fight about him, Goldberg. It may be, with luck, enough will emerge that Callaghan'll have something on him too, and unless he did the actual murder—which I very much doubt—that charge'd earn him a stiffer sentence—we may as well let Pat have him ... But for some reason the negotiations have been delayed. Mmh. That little visit Lydia paid to Alison—and the note—yes, I wonder. You said Jackie Donovan was the one with a few more brains, Goldberg.' Mendoza laughed. 'I wonder if maybe Jackie put a monkey wrench in the works, by wanting to change the price.

If he came out to find the deal set up, and told Denny he was a fool to take the first price mentioned—especially when they had to cut it with Skyros—and has been trying to hold up Lydia for more.'

'You're building bricks without straw there, *chico*,' said Hackett.

'Yes, first things first. With luck, we'll hear the details later! You go and see this girl, that much we'll get cleared up tonight. Goldberg is going to rout out the museum director—'

'I want to hear first hand what that visitor looked like,' said Goldberg. 'If it was either of the Donovans, I think I'd recognize a description. And that gives us another little something. I'll say this: Denny would probably talk. He wouldn't mean to get anybody in trouble, but he just can't help talking, and any kind of complicated little lie, he'd get all tangled up in it. If we get something to put out a Wanted on the Donovans, and pick them up, I think Denny would eventually give us a lot more of the story.'

'Which is very nice and helpful to look forward to,' said Mendoza. 'But it would be even more helpful if we can get somebody else to talk. And you know, if it's handled just right—scarcely worth while to trump up a charge on her, and it'd probably never stick anyway—she's got the money to hire a smart lawyer—'

274

'You needen't tell me,' said Hackett, 'what you're going to do. Somehow, all in the most innocent way, Goldberg, he always ends up with the good-looking females in a case—if any. If just to question. I know, you're going out to the Beverly-Hilton.'

'She's not my type,' said Mendoza. 'But yes, I'll take her on, because neither of you have anything like what's called the élan to appeal to her, and I'll get more out of her. I hope enough to add to a charge of some kind on Skyros.'

But he didn't get out there at once. Just as he was leaving the office the outside phone rang, and it was the Greek priest, apologetic.

'The old lady, she doesn't understand much about the law, Lieutenant. She has this conviction in her mind that you will say Katya was the one who killed Stevan, because you think she's a lunatic.'

'About that, who knows?'

'Indeed. But if you would be so kind to come by, just a few moments, let her hear you say it's not true—she won't believe me, she says I would not know what the police think. It would be a kindness—'

'What's the address?' asked Mendoza with a mental sigh.

It was a shabby old frame apartment on a side street off Main; the priest was waiting for him in the entrance. 'Very kind,' he repeated. 'Such a distressing thing—sometimes it's

275

hard to understand the ways of God, Lieutenant. I have been thinking of that passage: *From him who hath not shall be taken even that which he hath*. I know something of the story, you see: when she came here there was no Russian church near, she came to ours, and has been a faithful attendant. Not an easy or happy life—her husband deserted her long ago, and there were three children—two sons and a daughter. She could do nothing but domestic work, but she managed to raise them alone—it was a struggle. The older son was a sailor, and killed in an explosion at sea—his wife had died at Katya's birth—and the younger son was killed in the war. The daughter,'—the priest sighed—'perhaps malnutrition, or a hereditary disposition—she is in a tuberculosis sanatorium. There is, of course, no money but what Katya earned. She will be in straits if the girl—'

They climbed rickety, dirty stairs. 'Pass by on the other side,' said Mendoza. 'What else? You see a good deal of it—I see more. The innocent bystanders. I know.'

'But that,' said the priest, 'is not the terrible thing, Lieutenant. In this country, no one need starve, there is always charity. We have a church fund—No, it is not the material. If this poor girl is—incompetent, either temporarily or otherwise, there'll be these pompous doctors, I daresay, to say it is

276

all the fault of her childhood environment and such nonsense. Always a difficult, sullen girl ... And never any appreciation or gratitude shown for the struggle and sacrifice—not that the old lady wanted that—only a little love. And none of that either.'

'It's not a thing to be manufactured,' said Mendoza. They went into a bare, shabby room where the old woman sat huddled in a chair. He told her no one was thinking that her granddaughter had killed Stevan, she was not in prison; she was in the hospital, because it might be she was ill and needed treatment.

The woman listened in silence, her dark tragic eyes fixed on his. 'You would know this—you are of high rank in the police. Do you tell the truth to me? ... Yes, she's sick—sick she must be, to say such things to me—she doesn't mean it, you know, she doesn't know at all what she says—' anxious, turning to the priest.

'No, she does not know, she wouldn't say such things to you from her heart.'

'If they would let her come home, I make her well and strong soon ... But I should take her clothes? They would let me in to see her, if I go there?'

'I don't know,' said Mendoza. 'Perhaps not if she's very ill, but you could ask.'

'I will go,' she said on a little gasp; and he knew that she would be very frightened, seeking that place of impersonal Authority, but she would go bravely and ask, for the love she bore one incapable of loving. And again her glance on him was half fearful.

He got away from the priest as quickly as he could afterwards, feeling depressed.

★ ★ ★

'I apologize for intruding so late,' he said to Madame Bouvardier.

'It makes no matter.' Her eyes were busy, trying to sum him up. 'You come from Mr. Skyros? On your card you write his name—'

'Well, let's say about Mr. Skyros. May we sit down?' Mendoza offered her a cigarette, smiling, laying on conscious charm. 'You know, madame, it's not kind of you to come here and get yourself mixed up with criminals. You get yourself into trouble, and then you go home and say some very nasty things about these low-class Americans, which we don't deserve at all.'

'But what is this? Me, mixed up with criminals? Who are you? It's a joke, maybe—'

'No joke. Lieutenant Mendoza of the police, madame.' He produced his credentials. 'You've been making quite a little work for us lately, you know. Although if you forgive me, I will say that my men have found it much more entertaining than following some lout of a suspected thief.'

'I? Followed? What—' She was deciding

278

whether to be angry or frightened.

'I won't eat you,' grinned Mendoza. 'Sit down and we'll make a little bargain. I think'—and it was a lie, but the easiest way to handle it and the only way to get anything out of her—'you've been an innocent victim in this case. Of course, you don't know our laws, and obviously a beautiful young lady like you, she doesn't waste her time studying books—'

She smiled and relaxed a little, beside him on the couch. 'No, indeed I don't know about things here—imagine, I'm told the police are all uncouth *canaille* and look like farmers! Obviously also this is a lie.'

'You're too kind—I hope so, madame. And then too, you are still grieving for your late father and possibly—shall we say?—not in any state to judge clearly. But shall we also say, it wasn't very wise of you to accept the proposal to buy back your father's collection from the thief.'

'And now what has given you this idea?' She widened her eyes at him, wary, playing for time.

Mendoza laughed, brought out the little box, let her see the coin. 'You recognize it? Good ... No, we have not got the rest, only this, but we will have ... Now, it's late and there's no point in playing games, trying to trick each other. Cards on the table, madame. We know almost the whole story. Mr. Skyros has been negotiating for you with the thief, hasn't he? Very unwise to trust him—he is a professional criminal himself, you know—'

'But I do not know! What is this—Skyros? A—a gangster?'

'Well, that could be one word for it—'

'I have not trusted him, but this I did not imagine,' she said thoughtfully. 'How extremely odd.'

'He has it arranged with the thief, you see. We have evidence on him,' said Mendoza, hoping he told the truth, 'and on several others—including Donovan.' He watched her on that one, and saw that she recognized the name; so Goldberg hadn't been woolgathering, and they'd been right about that. 'It is, in other words, all off, madame: they're about to be arrested and charged, and I am afraid it will appear as if you conspired with them—you understand—unless, of course, you speak out and tell the truth. All the truth. How you met Mr. Skyros, and all about the negotiating, and so on. But whether you do or not, that deal is off. I should imagine, however, that you'll get the collection back in time, when it's recovered.'

Madame Bouvardier heaved a long sigh. 'Well, at least that is something,' she said practically. 'Although I do *not* understand why the insurance company is not liable to pay also. The insurance is against theft, among other things, is it not?—very well—it is stolen, so they should pay! That is only logical. Whatever should occur later, it is nothing at all to do with that.'

'Very logical,' agreed Mendoza gravely, 'but the ways of law are like the ways of God, madame—mysterious.'

'You will have a little glass of wine with me. Berthe! I see you are a gentleman, *très gentil*, you are sympathetic, and also I think most accomplished at persuading the ladies! I will tell you about it—I tell you everything—it is to be seen there is nothing else I can do in this situation, and one must be practical. You are *quite* right,' said Madame Bouvardier emphatically, rolling her eyes at him over her glass, 'that I am entirely innocent in this affair—that it is against the law to do such, this I never knew! I will tell you how it came about, and beg that you believe me—'

'But who could doubt the word of so charming a lady?'

'Ah, you are so *sympathique*—I think I am much relieved after all it should end so. I tell you how it began, this Skyros...'

*   *   *

It was past eleven when he got home. And it was about all wound up, all but the tiresome routine, the collating of evidence, the further questioning, the formal taking of statements.

281

He knew almost all about it now—though he still didn't know who had killed Domokous, but doubtless that would emerge—and he ought to be feeling pretty good about it. A little teaser of a business—some fairly complex details built up out of not much to start with. Interesting. Instead, he was feeling rather depressed.

That old woman, still a little on his mind. Nothing you could do about that kind of thing: there it was. In his trade he saw a lot of it. The innocent bystanders, as he'd said to the priest.

He sat up in bed smoking; at a little past midnight, on impulse and suffering a slight guilty conscience, he called his grandmother. The old lady was a night owl, up at all hours, but she told him instantly that he was extremely thoughtless to call at such a time, though it was something of a relief to know he was yet alive, not coming near her in all this long while. 'Peace, peace,' he soothed her, 'I'm a public servant, my time's not my own.'

'And so have you yet got a birthday gift for me?'

'You're too old for birthday gifts, my little pigeon.'

'Little pigeon indeed, you're disrespectful. And since I never had any whatever all my life to fifteen years ago, I am making up for lost time.'

'I'll buy you a box of handkerchiefs . . . I

can't promise when I'll come, I'm just winding up this case. Day after tomorrow, maybe. And I know very well in any case what cunning plans are in your head—new neighbours I must meet! With a fair-to-middling pretty daughter or niece or cousin, confess it!—and you trying to play go-between.'

'Wicked one, it's past time you are decently married. Are you so foolish at your age to believe in this Anglo-Saxon notion, true love for a lifetime, to base a marriage upon?'

'I was never so young or so foolish. I do quite well as I am. Have you visited the doctor about the stiffness in your knees?'

'Why should I pay money to the doctor to tell me I am getting old? That I know. There is nothing else wrong with me at all, I've never had a sick day in my life—'

'There is a great deal wrong with you, and you still running back and forth to the priests it's to be hoped you confess it now and then. You tell lies, for one thing—all these elegant forbears direct from a castle in Spain! I myself distinctly remember your telling me that your own mother was half-breed Indian from the backwoods and never wore a pair of shoes until—'

'*That* is the lie, you remember quite falsely, and you're very rude to an old woman ... Now what is wrong, Luis? You're troubled for something ... Yes, you are, and wouldn't

I know, that raised you from the nuisance of an infant you were?'

'It's nothing, a little something in this case is all ... now, you don't want to hear about such things ... well, it's only...'

She listened, and sighed in sympathy, and said, 'You lie awake with the sore heart for this poor, poor woman, it is understood.'

'Don't talk nonsense, it's well known I have a heart of flint.'

'Oh, yes, indeed, like feathers it is hard, I know that very well—you begging the table scraps to feed every mangy stray cat and dog in the neighbourhood! The poor soul, and one of these Russian heretics too, with only a false God to give comfort. Life, it bears hard, so it does. But God sends the burden according to the shoulder, boy. That, by what you say, she knows already—and her troubles have strengthened her. She will be all right, Luis, with time gone by.'

'Let us hope,' he said. 'That there is always plenty of.' When he put down the phone he felt better; he would sleep; and tomorrow, things to do—see the case wound up, find out all the details.

He drew his good hand down Bast's spine and she tured over on her back, four black paws in the air, and shamelessly showed him the very distinctly rounding pale brown stomach that began to say *kittens*. 'You know something, *chica*,' he said, 'it's the old ones

284

who are tough. They've had it before, they won't die of it over again.' He switched off the light and slid down beside her, and went to sleep while she still purred in his ear.

CHAPTER TWENTY

Mr. Skyros did not often attend church, but his wife did; he saw her off that Sunday morning, and retired to his den to mull over these various little awkwardnesses which had arisen. It seemed to him that one very good way out of the difficulty about Prettyman and Angelo would be to patch up the quarrel with Bratti. Doubtless he would need to fawn a little, own the fault entirely his own, that kind of thing, but Bratti was a sensible fellow, he would understand the position. And while it might seem on the face of it that Bratti would be only too pleased to see Mr. Skyros forced out of business, actually that was not the case. It was like any other business—it cost the wholesaler a certain amount to import the stuff, and the more steady customers he had, the cheaper he could afford to sell and still see his profits rise. Volume—always a determining factor in business.

It also seemed that the little trick Mr. Skyros had sought to play, planting

Domokous' death at Bratti's door, had fallen flat: the police had not been intelligent enough to take the hint. And that was just as well: as it was, that little matter Bratti had never known anything about. If he could patch up the quarrel with Bratti, throw himself on Bratti's mercy, rent a few boys from him temporarily until business was started up again...

Also, some time today he must see Donovan, see that tiresome woman, and once for all conclude that deal. It had turned out to be more trouble and worry than it was worth.

At that point the doorbell chimed, and he went to answer it, putting on his usual genial smile for some neighbour or a Sunday pedlar. The smile faded as he opened the door. 'You fool, to come *here*—all open—go away! You cannot—it's madness—' Oh, God, that he'd ever become known to such a one! Trouble, always trouble from this kind—

Angelo laid a hand on Mr. Skyros' chest, pushed him back gently, and walked in. He was smiling his soft smile. And behind him Denny Donovan babbled anxiously, coming in too.

'Now you take it easy, Angie—look, Mr. Skyros, I just had to bring him, state he's in an' all—come round sayin' such things to me, *me*—like he'll take a knife to me don't I drive him—why, Angie, boy, you know I allus do anythin' for you, but you got to take it easy,

286

don't do nothing to make trouble—listen, I'm sorry, Mr. Skyros, but he—'

'You fools, you must both go away at once! I will not have—'

'No trouble,' said Angie. He walked Mr. Skyros backwards another couple of steps; his little smile was fixed. 'Only you got to give me some stuff right now, Mr. Skyros. Say last night, very sorry, you couldn't get none, wait awhile, Angelo. That don't do, Mr. Skyros. Now I got to have it. Right now.'

'I haven't *got* any,' said Mr. Skyros irritably. 'Next week I get some, my man's around again then, Angelo. You be sensible now, go away and—and buy yourself a fix from somebody—'

'Retail prices,' said Angelo, 'why do I go 'n' do like that, Mr. Skyros? You're the supplier—you got the stuff, you always got the stuff—I pay you for ten decks, right now, an' so that way I got some to sell an' buy more—next week, tomorrow, next month— only I buy it now, Mr. Skyros. Fifty a deck, Mr. Skyros. You go 'n' get it.'

'I haven't *got* any, fool!'

'Now listen, Angie, you see it's no good, you better come away an' do like he says—you be sensible now, Angie—'

Angelo slid a hand into his breast pocket and took out a knife. An ordinary bone-handled bread knife it was, with a blade about nine inches long. Mr. Skyros stepped

287

smartly backwards. 'I don't want no trouble,' said Angie softly. 'Who else do I come to, who else'd have it? You're the supplier. Go 'n' get it. I need it right now, Mr. Skyros.'

'For God's sake,' Mr. Skyros implored Denny, 'do something, take the knife away from him—I can't, Angelo, I tell you there's none here, you understand plain English, isn't it?—you be good, sensible, now—'

'Yeah, it's no good, Angie—you—you let me take you back downtown,' chattered Denny nervously, 'find somebody fix you up O.K.—'

'No trouble,' said Angie, and put the point of the knife against Mr. Skyros' stomach. Mr. Skyros uttered a small moan and took another step backwards, and the doorbell chimed again. 'Needn't pay no notice to that, Mr. Skyros. You just go 'n' get the stuff. Right now. Because it's right now I got to have it.' His liquid dark eyes were fixed, staring, above the little soft smile.

Mr. Skyros took another step. If he could get into the den, the dining room, slam the door between—Suddenly and irrelevantly he realized the lost benefit of being an upright citizen, who could (if possible to do so) take up the telephone and call for the police. But Angie paced with him step by step, holding the knife steady. The doorbell chimed again.

'Now listen—' panted Mr. Skyros. He was across the threshold of the dining room now, and suddenly over Angie's shoulder he saw movement out there beyond the french window—someone on the porch—a man coming up to peer in. It was that Lieutenant Mendoza, that man from police headquarters: and Mr. Skyros had never imagined that he would feel so happy to lay eyes on a cop. He sidled towards the windows, drawing Angie with him, and so far as he was thinking at all he began to formulate a vague tale about this lunatic breaking in, threatening him—

'Not that way,' said Angie gently. 'In, Mr. Skyros. Wherever you keep it. Go—'

'*Help!*' yelled Mr. Skyros, and plunged sideways and took prudent cover under the dining table. The french windows crashed in, glass shattering, and Mendoza and Hacket were in by the shortest route. There was a little scuffle; Mr. Skyros peered out fearfully, saw Angie safe in the competent grasp of Hackett, and scrambled out on all fours.

'Oh, Lieutenant, so happy I am to see you—such a thing—this crazy man breaks in, threatens me—'

'Indeed?' said Mendoza, dexterously picking Hackett's pocket from behind of his police special and levelling it at Denny. 'How very ungrateful of him, turning on his employer. I *think* this is Angie, Art. It's awkward—I've only got one hand—maybe it'd be expedient to tap him lightly once, just to keep him quiet while you call up reinforcements. Who this is I don't know, but we'll sort it out later. Andreas Skyros, I have a warrant for your arrest on a charge of conspiracy to defraud . . .'

Mr. Skyros sat down in one of the dining room chairs and mopped his pink bald skull. 'Oh, dear me, it's some mistake, gentlemen,' he said mechanically. But if the truth were told, at the moment he was less alarmed at future danger than relieved to be rid of Angie.

*   *   *

Denny, as Goldberg had prophesied, talked. He tangled himself up in protestations of knowing nothing about any of it, ran out of lies, and then when they brought Jackie in—picked up in a Main Street bar without much trouble—he fell all over himself again to absolve Jackie from any connection. He was useful, filling in details for them.

Especially as Mr. Skyros, once he knew how deep in Lydia Bouvardier and Denny had put him, very wisely shut his mouth and requested a lawyer.

Jackie Donovan was unexpectedly amenable. Indeed, it almost seemed, as Goldberg said, that he was eager to tie himself into it, even before the museum director identified him. He drew the line, however, at taking the responsibility for Domokous—all he'd done to Domokous, he said, was knock him out. And got called a fool for it by Skyros. Domokous, walking in on them in Skyros' office that Monday night, after Donovan's first and only meeting with this Bouvardier dame—

'In,' said Mendoza, 'a hot car you'd picked up out in Exposition Park.'

Donovan shrugged and said sure, if he knew so much about it . . . He hadn't had anything to do with taking off Domokous. Thought Domokous'd found out about the deal, what he'd said then to Skyros—wanted to be bought off. Skyros acting soft with him starting to make up some tale, but Domokous had picked up that list off the desk, and well, my God, you could see—story'd been in all the papers, that stuff pinched, and if he didn't know he'd find out, seeing those papers—So Donovan had batted him one, that's all, and got the list away from him—and he'd sort of staggered back, and let go, and the second time Donovan belted him he passed out—

'A list,' said Mendoza. 'Of the collection?' That was stacked up neatly on his desk, twelve big boxes. He looked, and found the manila folder, and opened it and took out the list. A number of pages, a thick wad, once stapled at both top corners—now the right-hand staple missing, torn away with a sizable corner of the top page. 'Always so satisfying to see deductions proved,' he murmured, and took out of its envelope the little torn scrap of paper found in Domokous' pocket, and laid it on the top page, matching the corners delicately. 'Oh very pretty.' The edges blended exactly; and the first two top lines now read sensibly,

No. 1-A cl. F:
Messana, silver tetradrachm, approximately 400 B.C. Obverse, nymph driving cart drawn by pair of mules. Reverse, hare with small dolphin.

'Oh, yes, I see. How nice. You didn't notice that Domokous had torn this away when you grabbed the list from him, and put it in his pocket—probably quite automatically.'

'I didn't have nothing else to do with him, I didn't—Skyros says, fool, he didn't know nothing, but—'

And Skyros, of course, wasn't talking; and Denny hadn't been there, nor had Lydia Bouvardier. However, Denny had heard about it later, and—anxious to get Jackie clear, almost crying at the necessity to involve his old pal Angie in order to do that—he told them all about it. Which was nothing but hearsay evidence, but there were things to do about that too ...

Because after a fix, Angelo felt just fine,

and amiably answered all their questions. Sure, he'd done this little favour for Skyros, so long as Skyros gave him a rebate on the stuff he used. Skyros' idea it was, make it look like the guy was a user, just took too big a jolt one time, 's all ... it happens, and nobody pays much attention. Jackie, he had the guy in this car he'd hopped—Skyros, no, sir, he wasn't there—left it to Jackie—no, sir, why'd they go through his pockets? Skyros hadn't said to—no need—Skyros, he wanted him found, as who he was, and pretty soon. Planted an old hypo on him, sure, stuck him up a little, make it look good—open and shut ...

'*Terminar*,' said Mendoza. 'And don't tell me that any middling smart lawyer is going to claim self-condemnation, the confession for the fix. That I know. We'll just have to hope the judge has a little common sense and realizes it's a time and place to forget about the letter of the law. And what's the odds? If he gets off on the long count, he won't get off all the way—they'll send him for a cure—waste of the taxpayers' money—and I'll give you odds, if he does get off clear after that in six months he'll have killed himself the way he killed Domokous. What is it they say about the mills of the gods?'

★　　　★　　　★

293

And Callaghan said philosophically, 'Well, you can have Skyros. He's out of my hair, and when you've got enough on him to make it accessory to homicide, that'll put him away longer than a dope charge could. If the judge has got any sense at all—which I sometimes doubt any of 'em have.'

And Goldberg said, 'Well, I guess you've got the Donovans, a heavier charge than I could make, but I'd lay a bet that Denny anyway won't get as much of the book thrown at him as Jackie, and some day he'll be loose to make a little more trouble for me. All in the day's work . . .'

And Alison said thoughtfully, 'I really think I'll have to get a new car. The idea of them transporting that poor man's body in it—What a funny complicated business it's been.'

'Until we found out about it,' said Mendoza. 'Then, very ordinary. Just the way it came to light that made it look unusual at first.' He sighed. 'Now and then I wish something a little different would come along—one of those really interesting, bizarre, complicated cases out of a detective novel . . . But not in this weather. Say along in December or January. Which reminds me—'

Alison got up, tugged the curtains farther aside in the hope of slightly better air. 'It *should* begin to cool off a little now the sun's down. Would you like a drink?'

'Not that kind—rather have some iced coffee.'

'So would I, I'll get it.' . . . He followed her out to the kitchen, and there was a slight delay in filling the glasses. 'Here,' said Alison at last, 'the ice is melting, idiot, let me go. Very bad timing—between getting it out and putting it in the glasses—if you'd just think a little about these things—'

Mendoza swore as he hit his hand on the drainboard. 'Damn this thing. They're taking the stiches out tomorrow, did I tell you?'

'I don't know that I should leap for joy to hear it, you're bad enough with one hand.' She was struggling with the ice cubes, which hadn't melted enough to slide out easily.

'Stop fussing with that a minute and listen, I've got something important to ask you, *chica* . . . No, I can't talk to your back, damn it—turn around here—this is serious, now.'

'Yes,' said Alison. Her heart gave a little extra beat. She laid down the ice tray.

'I want you to think about it and be sure,' he said.

'Yes.' She turned around to face him. He *was* looking very serious and solemn. 'What—what is it?'

'Would you like a half-Abyssinian kitten for Christmas?'